COLD I

The Thrilling Sequel to Best Eaten

It was always too good to be true.

Finding her, arresting her, proving her guilt ... that should have been enough.

It should have been, but a small voice, deep inside him, refused to be silenced. The voice which whispered the same words over and over – how even a jail sentence wouldn't stop her.

And then Sam looked at Julie, standing tall in the dock waiting for the verdict. He watched her smile and knew the truth.

It would never be over. She would always find a way to reach out for him and the nightmares would become reality once more.

Tony Salter is the bestselling author of two previous novels – Best Eaten Cold and The Old Orchard. His fourth novel, Sixty Minutes, is due to be published in 2019.

He is also working on a series of illustrated children's books set in Norway.

He lives in Oxfordshire with his Norwegian wife.

ALSO BY TONY SALTER

Best Eaten Cold
The Old Orchard

COLD INTENT

Tony Salter

ETS Limited

Dawber House, Long Wittenham, OX14 4QQ

First published in Great Britain in 2018 by ETS Limited

ISBN: 978-0-9957977-4-1

For William, Evelyn, Anna, Jakob & Dylan

2011

Beginnings

It was still March. Dull grey clouds brushed an anaemic wash from horizon to heaven just like every other day. In the weak morning light, Fabiola watched as a chill draught caught the stream of smoke and tore it fluttering into pennant plumes. At some point, she'd need to get around to fixing the jammed window sash. At some point.

Also worth remembering to get a place with proper double-glazing next time. And south-facing would be a bit of a plan. Then again, she shouldn't complain; no-one else in the room owned their own flat and, if she'd had to bet on it, Fabiola would have put good money that none of them ever would.

As Jax handed her the joint, Fabiola felt the raw energy passing between their fingertips like static electricity. She shivered and leant back against the wall.

Why did they call it static electricity? It was about movement after all. Was lightning static? Hardly. Or when kids rubbed party balloons against the sofa and their hair stood up like the bristles on a paintbrush? Not even slightly. It seemed like a stupid name and, at that happily stoned moment, Fabiola felt a burning need to know where the expression came from.

Hash always calmed her and allowed her to focus on the random, mundane details which were easy to overlook in normal life. She didn't care that those fascinating nuggets were invariably not as interesting in the cold light of day. It was all about the moment – the flow of time slowed to a trickle and the here-and-now was everything.

Jax was different. When Jax smoked, she became even more

1

wired than usual and that morning she was on fire, her body alive with a pulsing energy which seemed to throb inside her. Even from inside her cosy contemplative bubble, Fabiola felt her stomach curling in on itself and the familiar thrill tingling through her body. Being with Jax was never, ever boring and never, ever predictable.

She reached over and touched her lover's cheek, stroking it with the back of her fingers. Her eyes and rational brain told her that the skin should be burning hot, but Fabiola knew it wouldn't be. Jax's face was as porcelain cold as always.

'You planning on smoking that?' Daz had arrived half an hour later than the rest of them and was carrying the nervous adrenalin of a night shift with him. He was smiling, but only just.

Fabiola was irritated by the interruption and considered ignoring him, but the moment had passed and anyway she always ended up feeling guilty when she teased Daz. It was too easy.

'Here you go,' she said, taking a last quick toke before leaning across to him. 'Sounds like you need it.'

Daz half-grunted a response and dragged hard and deep, the thin paper crackling, glowing red and spitting sparks as he sucked in more and more smoke, seemingly without end. At last he stopped and held his breath, the joint now hanging loosely between his thumb and forefinger. Fabiola counted the seconds … thirteen, fourteen, fifteen … until he sagged forward and blew out a mushroom cloud of smoke like a steam train, a genuine smile now spreading contentment across his face. There was a reason everyone called him "whale lungs".

'That … is … much … better,' he said, passing the remains of the joint to Linda. 'I needed that.'

'You still coming later?' said Fabiola. 'You look knackered.'

'Yeah,' said Daz. 'Course I am. I'll be sorted in a bit. Just needed something to take the edge off, didn't I?'

Linda threw the useless cardboard roach into the ashtray and reached for the Rizlas. 'You took more than the bloody edge off though, didn't you? Greedy bastard! Sharing is caring, my mum always said.'

'Sorry,' said Daz, mumbling into his beard. 'Long day. You know how it is …?'

'Were the nutters being naughty then?' said Jax.

'Don't call them that,' snapped Daz, his soft, brown eyes hardening as he looked past Fabiola at Jax.

'Why not?' said Jax, doing her best to play the innocent child, but not fooling anybody. Fabiola never understood why Jax put so much effort into winding Daz up. He was a good guy and didn't deserve it. She also couldn't imagine what it would be like to do his job.

'Cos it's people like you talking about nutters, headcases and loonies that are half the problem,' said Daz.

'So, if I hadn't called them nutters, they'd all be OK would they?' Jax had stopped bothering with the butter-wouldn't-melt-in-my-mouth look. 'They'd all be as sane as the rest of us? Like, by magic or something?'

'Most of them are a hell of a lot saner than you are, Jax,' said Daz, standing up and looming over everyone. 'Why can't you stay out of my face? Just for once.' Fabiola could see his shoulders tensing and his hands clench into fists before he turned and walked away mumbling, almost to himself. 'Whatever. I'm gonna to take a shower.'

Jax put her arm around Fabiola and whispered in her ear, lips just brushing the lobe. 'Why do you let him use our shower? I hate it. He always leaves it looking gross.'

'That's bollocks,' said Fabiola. 'For a big hairy lump, he's amazingly clean … And why do you give a monkey's? Aren't you supposed to be the Queen of Chill?'

The shutters flickered lizard-like at the back of Jax's eyes and Fabiola felt the warmth of her smile, but not before she'd caught the tiniest glimpse of something else, something darker. Jax was always – almost always – in complete control, but every now and then she would let her guard down and reveal what lay beneath her cool and effortless charm.

A tiny voice kept trying to tell Fabiola that the true Jax was wrapped up in that hidden darkness, but she couldn't – and wouldn't – listen to it. There was so much anger and hatred – a cold inhuman fury – which couldn't be the truth of the person she loved. It was only the odd glimpse here and there. She must have been imagining it.

Today was worse than usual. Tormenting Daz was par for the course, but something else was going on and Jax wouldn't tell her what. It had something to do with the protest march and the new crowd Jax had started hanging out with, but that was all Fabiola knew. One thing she did know was that she wasn't even slightly interested in spending time with Jax's new friends.

From everything she'd seen and heard, they were a bunch of smug, self-important idiots, always dressed in black and regurgitating revolutionary philosophy and politics quotes as though they'd written them themselves. And there was a dark edge to their narcissism which gave Fabiola the shivers. What did Jax see in them?

The little voice inside her was becoming more insistent every day and, for the first time, Fabiola wondered if it was time to move on. She had never imagined that she would end up living this kind of life and often felt like an imposter, anyway. She could argue politics with the best of them, and made a point of going on all the marches and protests, but did she really care that much?

Much as she might have wanted to escape her small town upbringing, that was who she was. She'd been a marginally rebellious teenager, not an urban warrior, fighting for injustice. This life, and everything about it, started and ended with Jax.

And their relationship was the biggest surprise of all. Falling in love with a woman was the last thing anyone would have expected her to do, especially Fabiola herself. This was Jax's world, not Fabiola's. It was as though she was living someone else's life, wearing a stranger's skin, and that skin was beginning to itch more and more every day.

Then Jax leant forward and kissed her, the fingers of her right hand sliding under Fabiola's hair and stroking the soft fuzz on the back of her neck.

Leave Jax? How could she ever consider that? Why would she ever consider that?

'Can I borrow this backpack?' Jax was standing in the corner of their small bedroom, holding up the small daypack which Fabiola had bought to carry text books when she was at Bristol.

'No problem,' said Fabiola, smiling as she went through the motions of giving her permission.

When Jax asked for a favour or to borrow something, she would phrase it as a request, but the question was always rhetorical. It was also important not to expect to see the borrowed item again, or to expect any gratitude or payback. It was just the way Jax was.

'What's with the hoodie?' said Fabiola. 'I've never seen you wearing that before.'

'Oh, this thing. I got it last week,' said Jax, who was squatting down and reaching under the bed. 'Keeps my ears warm.'

'It's not that cold today, and it looks stupid. You're not a bloody cat burglar.' Fabiola saw Jax pushing a plastic carrier bag into the backpack. 'What've you got there?'

'Nothing,' said Jax. She zipped up the pack and turned to Fabiola. 'And what's with the bloody third degree? Are you still pissed off about me giving Daz a hard time? Get over it, why don't you?'

'Give me a break,' said Fabiola. 'I'm in a strange place these days.'

'Well don't take it out on me,' said Jax. 'Save it for the Tories.' She turned to face Fabiola and smiled. 'We'll have a chat later if you want.'

'Yeah. Sure,' said Fabiola. 'Look, just ignore me. I'm being an idiot. Shall we get moving? We need to be at Embankment by half eleven.'

'OK,' said Jax. 'Let's do it.'

By twelve o'clock, the crowd stretched up and down from Charing Cross Bridge as far as Fabiola could see. The papers had been saying that over a hundred thousand protesters were expected and Fabiola decided that there must be at least that many – although she accepted that she wouldn't have been able to tell the difference between ten thousand and a million if it came down to it.

Anyway, there were a lot of people and they seemed to come from every walk of life. Young, old, some scruffy, some in city suits and loads of families with kids. A few were carrying placards, and she saw rolled up banners everywhere she looked. They would surely unfurl as the march got under way.

The three years since the banking crash had hurt everyone and now the government planned to turn the screws even tighter. It hadn't seemed possible that there might be even more injustice and inequality in a developed country like the UK, but apparently anything was possible. A few fat-cat banker heads had rolled as a token gesture, but not many, and those sacrificial lambs weren't exactly going to be wondering where their next hot meal was coming from.

It was no wonder that so many people had made the effort to come out and protest together. Fabiola may not have been as committed as the others – especially not Daz or Jax – but that didn't mean she couldn't feel the pain and anger on the streets. There had to be another, better way of doing things. It was billed as the March for the Alternative and Fabiola was convinced that a better alternative existed. People just had to want it enough.

On the dot of twelve, someone let rip with an air horn and the crowd came to life. She couldn't see much apart from the bodies surrounding her, but she imagined what they must look like from above. Not serpentine – although the massed bodies were snaking along the Victoria Embankment for mile after mile – the march would probably appear more like a ponderous primaeval crocodile, swaying from side to side as it lumbered inexorably forward.

Daz and Linda were walking together just ahead, pressed close together – was there something going on between them? – while Jax dipped in and out of the crowd, chivvying people along like a hyperactive sheepdog. What had got into her?

At times, Fabiola wondered if they were moving at all and it seemed almost as though they were standing in a crowd at a gig rather than walking on a march. But they were making progress and by two-thirty, they were inching their way along Piccadilly towards Hyde Park.

The noise and excitement had grown as the road widened and people were able to spread out. The electric tension of the mob reminded Fabiola of her first protest in Germany and she shivered as the first tingles of fear ran through her.

'Isn't it amazing,' shouted Jax, bouncing up and down in front of her. 'Such a buzz.' Her eyes were bright and her coal-black, fully dilated pupils darted back and forth like tadpoles. She must have taken something. Those eyes weren't normal.

'It's getting too hyper for me,' said Fabiola. 'D'you see that smoke over there? What's that all about?'

Jax put one hand on Fabiola's shoulder and jumped, pushing herself up to see over the heads in front of them.

'They're having a go at the Porsche showroom,' she said. 'A few Black Bloc there as well. Should be a laugh.'

'No, it won't,' said Fabiola, suddenly afraid. 'That's not why we're here.'

Jax wasn't listening and seemed transfixed by the smoke and the rhythmic hammering coming from just ahead of them.

She heard Daz calling. 'Fabiola! Fabiola!'

He was pointing towards the source of the noise and smoke and Fabiola pushed her way towards him.

'Look at those bloody morons,' he said, shouting over the swelling noise. 'It's no wonder no-one listens to us. That'll be tomorrow's front page, not the cuts. I don't know why we even bother.'

There was a massive cheer and Fabiola saw the cracks spidering across the huge window as the first shards of heavy plate glass smashed onto the pavement. Black-clad masked figures were already climbing through the gaping hole, hammers and ice axes in their hands.

Daz grabbed her shoulder. 'Come on, let's get out of here,' he said. 'This is gonna turn nasty.'

'OK.' She turned to look for Jax, but couldn't see her.

'Can you see Jax?' she said to Daz.

'Wasn't she right behind you?'

'Yeah. Just a few seconds ago.'

'Well she's gone now,' he said, standing on tiptoes and looking around. 'That might be her over there, but I can't tell what with the hoodie and the backpack. Looks like her though.'

'She all right?'

'Yeah. She looks fine. She's pushing through the crowd towards the action.'

'Maybe she needs the toilet,' Fabiola said.

'Yeah. Maybe,' said Daz. 'You believe what you want to believe, but it doesn't look that way to me.'

The bedroom was almost pitch-black – no stars, no moon, and the streetlights had gone off. Fabiola rolled over onto cold sheets and stretched out her arm. Jax still wasn't back. Where had she got to?

After Jax had disappeared into the crowd, Fabiola and Daz had cut down through Green Park to avoid the trouble and made their way to the rally without problems. The final event had been huge, but peaceful. Most of the speakers had been either union leaders or politicians and Fabiola couldn't help thinking most of them were focusing a little too much on their personal images and not enough on looking for practical solutions. People couldn't feed their kids with words.

She didn't want to be such a cynic, but idealism was turning out to be harder work than she'd expected.

Fabiola closed her eyes and rolled back to the warmth of her side of the bed. Jax had probably crashed at a friend's place and anyway there wasn't much she could do about it until the morning. As she felt her body sinking into the softness of the bed, the sound of a glass clattering in the sink caught her and snatched her back from the edge of sleep. Jax must be back. Why hadn't she come in to say hello?

'Jax?' she called out.

'Yeah. In here. Give us a minute,' came the reply.

Fabiola was fed up with being messed around and there was no way she was getting back to sleep. She pulled on a dressing gown and stumbled out into the living room, blinking in the bright light.

Jax was sitting on the edge of the sofa, leaning forwards with her head in her hands. If Fabiola hadn't known her better, she'd have guessed she'd been crying.

'Hiya,' she said.

'Hey,' said Jax, before lifting her head and glaring at Fabiola. 'What are you doing out here? I said to give me a minute.' Her voice was unusually harsh and raw. 'Go back to bed. I just need to be on my own for a bit.'

'Can't I do something to help?' said Fabiola. 'You don't look great. Let me get you a cup of tea?'

'No. Just go to bed. I'll be fine.'

Jax was wearing a dressing gown and had left her clothes in a pile by the bathroom door. Fabiola walked over and bent down to pick them up. 'At least I can throw these in the wash,' she said. 'I'm awake now, anyway.'

'Leave those!' Jax's voice cracked across the room like a whip.

Fabiola pulled her hands away as though she'd been stung. 'What the hell, Jax?' she said. 'What's wrong with you? You disappear without saying a thing, then roll in at four in the morning biting my bloody head off. Something's not right.'

'I'm fine. How many times do I have to tell you? Just leave me alone and go to bed.'

'Come on Jax,' said Fabiola. 'How can I do that? There's no way I'll get back to sleep now. What happened? Where have you been?'

'I don't want to talk about it. OK?'

'Why? What's wrong?'

'Nothing's wrong. I just don't feel great. Cut me some slack, will you?'

'That's rich,' said Fabiola. 'I've been worried sick about you.'

'Nothing to worry about,' said Jax. 'I'm fine … but one thing … I've been here with you all evening. Right?'

'But …'

'I was right here. With you!' Jax had pulled her knees into her chest, her chin was jutting forward and she was snarling like a rabid fox. 'It's not that complicated, is it?'

Fabiola flinched and shrunk backwards as Jax began to rock back and forth, fixing her with unblinking eyes. It was as though she'd become a different person and Fabiola shivered. The two young women stayed trapped in that gaze for long seconds until, with what appeared to be a conscious effort, Jax shook her head violently like a dog drying itself after a swim.

Fabiola took a deep breath and then, as if by magic, the stranger was gone and Jax was back in her place, smiling like a cheeky cherub. 'Sorry, Fabs,' she said in a gentle voice. 'It's not your fault. Just promise me … Please.'

'OK,' Fabiola said. 'No problem. Of course I will.'

'Whoever asks. Whatever they ask. Whenever they ask. You'll tell them I came home with you and we stayed in?'

'Sure.'

'You swear it? On your parent's grave?'

'Yes, Jax.' Fabiola didn't understand what was happening, and the memory of that other Jax still pulsed blood red behind her eyes. 'Yes, for Christ's sake. I promise. Now stop this. You're freaking me out.'

'OK. I'm done. Thanks,' said Jax. 'Now I have to sleep.' She rolled over onto her side, knees still pulled up like a small child and, before Fabiola had a chance to respond, she heard the sound of gentle snoring.

Fabiola went to the cupboard, took out a blanket and spread it over the sleeping Jax, leaning over to plant a delicate goodnight kiss on her cold cheek. The flat was freezing and she couldn't stop herself shivering as she walked back to the bedroom. By the time the bed had warmed up and Fabiola had stopped shaking, dawn's greyness was already creeping into the room.

Sleep wasn't an option; her mind span out of control, racing in spiralling circles. She didn't care what Jax had been doing, although it was unlikely to be good. That wasn't the problem. Other thoughts filled her head as she lay on her back staring at the ceiling. Unthinkable thoughts. Was she falling out of love with Jax? It seemed impossible, but it was the only conclusion which made sense.

Not a conclusion to jump to after a sleepless night and, in any case, it wasn't the most worrying of her thought spirals. There had been a few incidents over the previous weeks and months, but the way Jax had been when she was sitting on the couch earlier was by far the worst. That kind of behaviour wasn't right. As the first rays of weak sunlight crept up the wall, Fabiola realised that she was starting to be afraid of her lover?

The day of the anti-cuts march changed everything.

After a few days, everything between them had slipped back to normal. At least it had on the surface. But Fabiola couldn't shake off the image of Jax glowering at her from the sofa; it slipped into her thoughts all the time however hard she tried to push it away. She worried that Jax would notice something had changed and would say something. It was very difficult to lie to Jax.

They'd been together for almost four years. Fabiola would always remember their first kiss in that massive camp in Germany and the way her life had changed since. Rostock had been Fabiola's first anti-government protest, and she was now fairly certain that Hyde Park would be her last.

She'd sleepwalked through those years together, caught up in a multi-coloured dream which had been so bright, joyful and exciting that it had seemed unreal. Better than real life.

That night after Hyde Park when Jax turned up at four in the morning marked the beginning of reality's return. Not from one moment to the next, but following an inevitable path like one of those comets which returns to Earth after lonely decades rushing through the empty blackness, growing brighter and brighter and more obvious every day.

Something had happened that day, but Jax refused to discuss it. She'd been scratched and bruised all over and had thrown out everything she'd been wearing. Fabiola's backpack had disappeared and wasn't mentioned.

She couldn't be sure how much Jax had actually changed and how much it was only that she was now looking at her with different eyes. It didn't matter. Something in their relationship had broken and it couldn't be fixed. As the fun and joy faded, Fabiola's sadness was mixed with acceptance and relief.

A little perspective was allowing her to see she'd developed a range of bad habits, sacrificing her individuality to their identity as a couple and, Jax being Jax, becoming the acquiescent, slightly subservient partner. As Fabiola's vision cleared, she went out on her own more often. Sometimes with Daz, sometimes for a quick drink after work with colleagues. It was wonderfully refreshing and Fabiola felt her old self pushing up into the daylight and stretching out after years of hibernation.

Jax soon figured out that something was wrong, but passive acceptance wasn't her style. She threw energy, passion and charm – everything she had – into making Fabiola happy. It was clear she had no intention of giving up on the relationship and Fabiola knew that Jax would never accept it was something she couldn't fix.

Unfortunately, once Fabiola's eyes had been opened, she began to notice the artifice behind Jax's charm. Once she knew where to look, it was always there. Almost imperceptible – a smile which started or ended too abruptly, or a glimpse of the cold intelligence whirring behind her shining eyes, keeping ahead of everyone and everything, planning what to say and what to do. Even when and how they made love was organised and timed as if by a master choreographer.

She knew Jax really loved her. That wasn't a trick, but with her newfound awareness Fabiola realised that the way she was loved was wrong. For Jax, Fabiola was a prized possession. Prized above anything else, perhaps, but a possession nonetheless. Fabiola didn't regret their time together, but if she didn't find a way out soon, she knew that the regrets would creep in one by one.

Funny about things that appear to be too good to be true.

'Sorry I'm late,' said Daz, panting and coughing as he stopped running. 'Bloody Central Line.'

'That's OK,' said Fabiola. 'These two gentlemen gallantly offered to keep me company.' She laughed as she remembered the clumsy way the guys had approached her not fifteen minutes earlier. Still, standing alone outside the Lamb and Flag on a summer evening was a little sad, so she'd accepted the offered drink readily enough.

'Oh. That's great,' said Daz, the disappointment obvious as his shoulders slumped and he stared at his shoes. A total lack of guile was one of his most appealing sides. That, and his unswerving visceral loyalty.

'Don't worry,' she said, resting her fingers on his arm. 'We'll have a quick drink with them and move on.'

Daz smiled, a big, cheesy grin bursting out through his beard. 'Good,' he said. 'I'd hoped we'd have a chance for a proper chat.' He stretched out his hand towards one of the interlopers. 'Hi. I'm Daz.'

Both of her saviour knights were dressed in tan chinos and blue shirts – brown belts and brown brogues completing the uniform. One was about six foot and the other not much taller than Fabiola.

'James.' The shorter of the two shook Daz's hand vigorously. 'Very pleased to meet you.'

'And this is Rupert,' said Fabiola, laughing as she turned towards the tall one. 'He's very posh.'

The Path of True Love ...

Fabiola couldn't remember why she'd given Rupert her number, only that her stomach had rolled over with glee at the time – it had felt like a mini rebellion. Harmless enough and no-one would ever know, anyway.

But then the stupid idiot called.

She and Jax were sitting on the tiny roof terrace – accessed by climbing out of one of the leaky, sticky sash windows – enjoying an early evening beer and some spicy Mexican dips which Jax had brought home.

'Hello?' Even on the third floor, the street noise made it hard to hear anything.

'Who is this?'

As she recognised Rupert's voice saying his name in that confident, plummy accent, Fabiola felt another tickle of illicit excitement.

'Oh. Hi there.'

'Who is it?' said Jax.

Fabiola lifted her free hand, one finger raised, and turned to face away.

'Sorry. I can't hear a thing,' she shouted at the phone. 'Can you try again later?'

She waited for a confirmation before hanging up, putting the phone back into her pocket and picking up her beer.

'Who was that?' said Jax, never one to give up. What did it have to do with her?

'Oh. Just someone from work,' said Fabiola.

'On a Saturday?'

'Yeah. She's a friend. We might hook up tomorrow.'

'Oh,' said Jax, looking straight at her.

Fabiola knew Jax didn't believe her, but she didn't care. There wasn't enough ammunition for Jax to start a fight and Fabiola was fed up with being checked up on. Fed up, but not brave enough to tell the truth.

Fabiola hadn't kissed a man for years. No-one since Joe.

The way that had ended, everything that happened as a result of that teenage madness, had left her feeling empty and numb. She'd found herself embracing chastity wholeheartedly and, even if she hadn't, the strings of snuffling suitors at Bristol were no more than immature boys, all pointy elbows and Adam's apples. They paled in comparison to Joe; whatever the consequences of their affair, there was no doubt that he'd been a man – a gorgeous man.

She'd fended off her fellow students during the early months at uni with the help of an imaginary boyfriend back in Bedford. Everyone around her seemed to be at it like rabbits, but Fabiola couldn't have been less interested.

When Jax happened, she was caught unawares, and the rulebook was thrown out of the window. There were no comparisons to be made, no potential consequences to give her sleepless nights, and anyway Jax had been – still was – unique, a fairytale figure from another world. She defied comparison.

Their years together had been a perfect dream. Fabiola had lost track of the number of times she'd thought of Jax and felt her heart swell and ache, literally bursting with love. She didn't know when that had started to change – she still felt a kind of awe whenever she looked at Jax. But there were plenty of lessons to be drawn from the old fairy tales – evil apple-poisoning queens were often the most beautiful and charming, after all. Although Fabiola's star-sprinkled dream wasn't quite over, a happy-ever-after ending was looking more and more unlikely.

Fabiola wondered if she'd always known what would happen when she gave Rupert her phone number. At the time, she'd convinced herself that it was a harmless flirtation, but with everything else that was going on, maybe she'd seen how the story would unfold even then. There had definitely been a spark, and a part of her was looking for something, anything, to set fire to her enchanted world and bring it crashing down in a blazing inferno.

When they met again, Rupert surprised her with his gentleness and patience. She hadn't told him anything important, nothing about Joe or Jax, nothing to frighten him away. Even so, he seemed to understand intuitively that she was fragile and there was never a hint of pressure.

His sense of humour was ridiculously boyish, and he was less politically aware than the average five-year-old, which made a pleasant change from the hours of intense well-meaning debate that had filled her life for years. When he laughed, it was simply because he found something funny, and Rupert could find humour almost anywhere.

Adding to the freshness and contrast, Rupert had no filters between thought and emotion, action and reaction. It reminded her of being with her father and uncles before she left home. If spontaneity led to stupid or insensitive blunders – which it frequently did – laughter and a heartfelt apology would usually save the day.

When he kissed her goodnight after their first date, Fabiola felt all of him through the soft touch of his lips. She felt his uncertainty, his joy, his kindness and, underneath it all, the promise of a burning passion.

He was exactly the sort of man she'd spent five years learning to despise, but he made her feel happy and free. As she discovered how much she enjoyed being with him, her doubts about Jax were thrown into even sharper focus. Wasn't it important to be happy?

She turned away from that tender kiss and walked home alone through the shadows of Camden, seeing her life through fresh eyes. She threaded her way through staggering black-clad figures, some loud and boisterous, some shrunken into solitary silence. She avoided stepping on bodies, discarded curries or worse. She noticed the sirens and flashing lights as if for the first time.

Fabiola took a deep breath and turned up Jamestown Road towards the flat. Jax would be waiting up for her. What was she going to say about her evening? The truth still wasn't an option. Not yet.

Her hand was trembling as she took the keys out of her bag.

That was the other thing about Rupert – he made her feel safe.

Sex with Rupert, when it happened, was exactly as Fabiola had imagined it would be.

They'd been out for drinks three times since that first phone call and she'd had plenty of time to let her imagination wander. A nagging voice kept telling her that she wouldn't enjoy being with a man, but why should that have changed? She had enjoyed it before and she was still the same person with the same body. And, if she listened carefully, the nagging voice sounded like Jax, anyway.

As she opened her mind to the possibility, or the likelihood, that she would go to bed with Rupert, she thought back to those times with Joe – what had been different, what had been better and what, frankly, hadn't. Although she accepted it was unlikely that a man could ever understand her body as well as another woman, there was something about the feeling of strong arms holding her tight which she remembered feeling natural and right. As for the somewhat clumsy mechanics of the process, it was, after all, the way people had been designed in the first place.

She still hadn't told Rupert about Jax and he couldn't have had any inkling of the mischievous thoughts which doodled around in her head like tiny butterflies, occasionally sparking an involuntary smile. Those smiles had almost got her into trouble more than once.

'What's so funny?' said Jax, who was slicing tomatoes next to the sink.

Fabiola had looked at the huge knife gleaming in Jax's hand and reflected that telling the truth was often overrated. She was going to have to talk to Jax one day, but "one day" was still a fairly loose concept.

'Oh. Nothing,' she'd said. 'I was just thinking about something Daz said yesterday.'

Jax had sniffed and turned back to her tomatoes. Fabiola knew Jax couldn't understand why she bothered with Daz, and was uninterested in anything he might have to say.

Only a week after that incident, Fabiola was smiling at happy memories rather than imagined fantasies. She was running out of excuses and explanations; Jax knew something was up and there was going to be a reckoning sooner rather than later.

It would be worth it though. Making love with Rupert wasn't only like she'd imagined, it was much, much better. Partly because he was a kind and sensitive lover, partly because she could feel herself falling in love with him, and partly because she'd remembered how much she enjoyed being with a man.

They'd both taken the afternoon off work and sneaked back to his flat in Battersea. Afterwards, they'd collapsed next to each other, stretched out in the afternoon sunshine. Rupert had wrapped both arms around her as though afraid she might escape and Fabiola had lain still and secure in his embrace, bathed in his musky male scent. Then there was a magical moment, a gap in time when he slipped from waking to sleep and she felt his grip soften and his body sag.

Fabiola had no interest in sleeping; she was loving every moment of being with Rupert and imagining many more of them. She'd changed, as though a switch inside her had been thrown and, whatever happened next, she would never be the same again.

It was time to tell Jax.

'I've met someone …', said Fabiola. Jax and Fabiola had just finished eating and sat at the small dining table enjoying the last glass from a bottle of Chianti.

'You've what?'

'I've met someone … a guy.'

'You mean …?'

Fabiola could feel the heat of Jax's gaze, like an open flame.

'Yes,' she said. 'He's called Rupert and …'

'Do you think I give a flying fuck what he's called,' screamed Jax, jumping up from the table and sending her chair flying backwards. 'How could you do that to us? How dare you?'

'How dare I?' said Fabiola. 'How dare I? What the hell does that mean? It's like you think you own me.'

'That's not what I meant and you know it,' said Jax

'No. I don't know it. You're always trying to control me and tell me what I should think and do.'

'Oh, don't be so ridiculous. Of course I'm not. Don't you dare try and push this back on me.'

'There's that "dare" again,' said Fabiola. 'I'm not being ridiculous, Jax. Being with you isn't good for me. We've had an amazing time together, but I need to move on. I'm sorry.'

Fabiola saw Jax clench and unclench her fists, her eyes darting around the room like a cornered vixen. She took a step towards Fabiola snarling and spitting out her words.

'You … you …'

Fabiola looked around for somewhere to run to – she should have chose a public place for this – and then Jax stopped dead as though frozen in time. Fabiola held her breath and waited as the shutters came down one by one and Jax took herself back under control. She'd seen it happen before and recognised the signs. The maelstrom roiling inside Jax needed to be kept in check and luckily she had the raw willpower to do that. It didn't mean that her anger was gone, or the issue resolved. It only meant that Jax was back in command and was working out a more controlled, measured response so that she could get what she wanted.

Not this time. 'You can stay in the flat,' said Fabiola, once she was sure that the danger had passed. '… As long as you want. At least until I need to sell it.'

Jax looked at her and smiled. How could she manufacture such a beautiful, charming smile at a moment like that? Even knowing her so well, Fabiola couldn't see the cracks.

'It's not over between us,' Jax said, her voice as soft and seductive as her smile. 'I love you and you love me. I don't know what's going on with this guy, but we'll work it out. You know we will.'

Jax was irresistible when she turned on the charm, but Fabiola had built her walls well. 'It's not really because of him,' she said. 'I've been thinking about it for a while.' She could hear her voice cracking with emotion as she spoke. It was the right decision, but that didn't stop it from hurting. 'I can't really explain,' she continued. 'Yes, I still love you, but I can't be with you.' She looked into Jax's eyes until she made a connection. 'I'm not going to change my mind.'

The smile hardened. 'We'll see about that,' said Jax. 'Don't think you can just airbrush me out of your life … And besides, I know all of your dirty little secrets.'

Threats really weren't going to make a difference. And there was no point regretting idle moments of pillow talk. In any case, Fabiola suspected that the skeletons in Jax's cupboard were a lot more frightening. 'What about you, Jax?' she said. 'What about your dirty secrets?'

Jax looked genuinely shocked. 'You promised,' she said. 'You gave me your word.'

'And I'll keep my word.' Fabiola took the opportunity to stand up and walk to the door. 'I just need you to let me go. Please.'

The door slammed behind her and she ran down the stairs. It wasn't until she was outside on the street that she dared to breathe. She stood still, half expecting the door to burst open and Jax to come running out, but the door sat still, heavy and lumpen in its wooden frame.

She'd agreed to spend the night at Rupert's and, as Fabiola turned to start walking to the tube, she looked up and saw, at the third-floor window, a white face pressed against the dirty glass. Too far away for her to make out Jax's expression, but it wasn't difficult to join the dots. This was by no means over.

As she sat with Daz in the grubby van, Fabiola reflected that sometimes it wasn't great to be right.

It had been three weeks since she'd told Jax about Rupert and nothing was close to being over. She'd seen Jax four times and forgiveness had been off the agenda on every occasion. Fabiola could probably have lived without being forgiven, but the frightening aspect was that Jax seemed unable to accept the reality of the break-up at all.

It would have been easier if there'd been a series of escalating slanging matches leading to words being spoken, lines being crossed, and eventually to a defined moment that would mark the end. Instead Jax had been at her most charming, elegantly avoiding any discussion of the break-up and peppering each conversation with discomforting phrases – 'when you're back …' or 'what are we doing for Christmas?'.

Fabiola hadn't known how to respond and, on the last occasion, she'd caught herself trembling as she tried yet again to bring up the subject of moving out. If Jax was going to stay on in the flat they needed to agree on the rent and put contracts in place. Jax refused to discuss it, and her wry smile made it clear that there was no point. Fabiola would be back soon, anyway.

This trip with Daz and a rented van was his idea. They would make sure Jax was out, pack all of Fabiola's things and leave before Jax got back. Presenting Jax with a fait accompli would almost certainly send her into some sort of incandescent hissy fit, but they'd be well clear by then and the rage would burn itself out, eventually. And, while Fabiola would have asked Rupert to help, the idea of ever telling him about Jax was losing more and more appeal every day.

Fabiola had never known exactly what Jax did to make money. It was something to do with computer security and it paid well …

Jax had spent hour after long hour trying to explain how one day, she would build the Next Great Thing which would change the world. It wasn't that Fabiola didn't believe her – Jax was smart and determined enough. Fabiola just wasn't interested in dreams of global domination; it wasn't her fault that she found herself heavy-lidded and falling asleep as soon as the subject came up.

Whatever it was that she did, Jax wasn't standing still. She'd set up a small office on Gower Street and even had a pretty young assistant manning the phones and making tea. Fabiola knew there was no point in suggesting that those capitalist baby steps might be slightly in conflict with Jax's commitment to passionate (and violent?) anarchism. Jax had her own – somewhat fluid – set of principles.

Fabiola and Daz had been sitting in the van since half past ten –

she was almost certain that Jax never managed to drag herself out of the flat any earlier.

She looked at her watch. 'I make it nearly eleven-thirty,' she said, sinking back into her seat. 'What about you?'

Daz looked at her and nodded. 'Yup,' he said. 'Over an hour and no sign of her.'

'Sorry about this,' said Fabiola. 'It really is Sod's Law that we've picked a day when she's decided to finish reading War and Peace before going to work.'

Daz laughed. 'Never mind,' he said. 'We've got all day.' He poured a cup of tea into the lid of his thermos and handed it to Fabiola. 'Anyway,' he added. 'This is nice.'

It was after twelve when Jax finally appeared. She was hunched into her down jacket, cap pulled forwards over her eyes. Fabiola might have missed her if she hadn't recognised the jacket and the cap – they were both "borrowed" from Fabiola. As she strode away from them towards the tube, Fabiola was reminded of how different Jax could be when she thought she was unobserved. Even her walk was different.

They gave her five minutes before getting out of the van and crossing the road. Fabiola found herself looking up and down the street like some sort of Cold War spy. Her pulse was throbbing in her neck and she could feel how clammy her hands were as she fumbled for her keys. This was ridiculous. It was her bloody flat after all.

She almost jumped when Daz rested one hand on her shoulder. 'Calm down, Fabs,' he said. 'Everything's going to be fine.' He took the keys from her and opened the door. 'Come on. Let's get this over with.'

Fabiola had decided to leave most of the furniture, glasses, pots and pans and they packed all of her personal belongings into a motley assortment of suitcases, boxes and shopping bags. It didn't take them much more than an hour and, as she looked at the sad pile heaped up by the front door, she felt a pang of loneliness. Was this it? Was this her life? No family, and she'd have no friends to speak of by the time Jax had finished twisting them against her.

Daz would always be her friend, but she couldn't imagine him and Rupert getting along. The Tory public school boy estate agent and the anarchist mental health nurse. That was never going to happen. She smiled at the thought and picked up the first box. As she started down the narrow stairs, she realised what had been worrying away at the back of her mind like a dog scratching on the door to come in out of the rain. For a while at least, she would only have Rupert and that was a lot to ask of a guy in his twenties. Was he up for it?

Twenty minutes later and the van was packed. Fabiola went back up alone and stood in the middle of the living room, saying goodbye – to Jax, to her friends, to her parents once again and also, in some strange way, to her youth. There was one last thing to do but, as she reached into her pocket, she heard the slam of the outside door. She froze. Had Jax come back for some reason? Had she spotted them in the van somehow? How would she react when she saw Fabiola?

She stood motionless, holding her breath and silently praying as the sound of footsteps reached the top of the stairs. She waited for the sound of a key scratching its way into the lock, but it never came. She held her breath until she heard the sound of her neighbour's door slamming shut and then sagged forwards, gasping. It was definitely time to leave.

As Fabiola took the letter from her pocket and placed it on the table, she thought of the hours spent trying to find the right words. She wanted to tell Jax how much she'd meant to her, that she still loved her, but also to make it clear as glacial ice that their relationship was over. Jax needed to accept that and move on.

In her heart, she knew that it wouldn't help, but at least she'd tried.

When Rupert came back from work, Fabiola was sitting in the middle of the pile of bags and boxes, wearing a t-shirt and nothing else. It was one of Rupert's t-shirts – long, but not that long.

She grinned at him and stretched her arms wide. 'Is this what you wanted?' she said.

'Oh yes,' he said, stepping forward and reaching down to lift her from her cardboard throne. 'I thought you'd never do it.'

Fabiola felt the happiness and relief flood into her. This was where she was meant to be. A perfect future with this man and, yes, his children. She wanted to make the leap of commitment even if it left her exposed and vulnerable. He was the one.

In the midst of her euphoria, she felt a cold draught sneaking in through the open door and shivered.

'One thing though, Roop,' she whispered in his ear. 'One condition.'

He pulled back to look at her, worry lines crinkling his forehead. 'Of course. What?'

'Promise you'll always look after me.'

Rupert laughed and span her round, mindless of the boxes sent flying in the process. 'Too easy.'

Fabiola held his gaze and lifted one hand to touch his cheek. 'I'm serious,' she said. 'Promise me.'

'I promise.'

'Whatever happens.'

'Whatever happens.' He took her hand and placed it on his heart. 'I'll always look after you.'

And that was that. The chill breeze disappeared as though never there and Fabiola was ready to begin the rest of her life.

2015

A Time to Grieve

I stepped silently into the cool shade of the old wood-beamed porch, checked no-one had seen me, and slipped behind the blocky stone pillar into the same pew as before. Most of the people in the front rows had been at the christening, but the flowers and the clothes they were wearing couldn't have been more different. I could still remember the first time I'd been here, watching Fabiola and Rupert smiling and laughing as their son was welcomed into the God's family. Bloody hypocrites. The bitter taste of betrayal on the back of my tongue was the same.

One thing we all had in common; none of us could have imagined, just two years earlier, that we would now be gathered together, in this place, for this reason. The same vicar who'd christened Sam was droning on about what a wonderful wife and mother Fabiola had been, and I was filled with a fresh wave of fury. I sat like a statue, squeezing my eyes closed in a vain attempt to hold back the red waves which swept across my vision. At least the blood thundering in my head helped to drown out the vicar's feeble platitudes.

What did the smug God-fearing idiot know about Fabiola? He'd probably only met her once before – at the little brat's christening. He wouldn't know who she'd really been, what she was like – as a wife, mother, friend or lover – but was apparently qualified to share his thoughts, regardless. Why? Because he was a vicar.

It was ridiculous and, anyway, no-one else had known Fabiola like I had. We'd been granted a unique once-in-a-lifetime bond which had been destined to burn for eternity. Even after she'd allowed herself to get pregnant, I'd known that Fabiola would eventually come back to me, like a wild salmon – running free for a time, but destined by the laws of its deeper nature to return to its true home. If she'd only kept a little perspective.

No regrets. There was no point, and I couldn't allow myself to think that way. I returned my attention to the vicar. A few months earlier, the Church of England had agreed to allow full funerals for suicides, but the decision wasn't yet approved. By rights, Fabiola should still be buried half-in and half-out of the consecrated graveyard like some sort of criminal. I knew that wouldn't be happening; one way or another that cow of a mother-in-law would have pulled whatever strings were necessary to make sure everything was neat and conventional – her family's name was what mattered most of all. And the fact that Fabiola had been Catholic definitely shouldn't interfere with a dignified funeral in the local Protestant church and an elegant reception with just the right amount of restrained grief. The whole thing was bloody Victorian.

Looking at Rupert, who was standing hunched over the coffin holding his wriggling brat, I wondered if the reception might end up being a little less dignified than his mother was hoping for. He was a mess, his whole body shaking and his face corpse-white with rage and grief. If he hadn't been holding the baby, I imagined him throwing himself on top of the coffin, wailing and tearing his clothes like they do in the movies. And then there was Daz, misery tucked away behind his scruffy beard, wrapping a meaty arm around Rupert and the kid and leading them back to their pew.

What was that all about? One moment Daz is a creepy stalker, bringing Fabiola's unsavoury London past into her new squeaky-clean world. The next, he's the family friend, sitting on the front pew and comforting the grieving widower. It must have somehow been their fault that things had gone so badly wrong. Nothing I had done was enough to make Fabiola do what she did – I'd thought the plans through so carefully. It must have been the child, or the mother-in-law, or Rupert, or Daz, or all of them together. They were to blame.

I hadn't believed I had room for more anger. Every waking moment for the previous three weeks had been filled with visions of grabbing Fabiola by the shoulders and shaking her like a doll. Why had she been such an idiot? She had deserved to be punished for leaving, and she had been, but what had made her react like that? When I hadn't been shaking her, I'd been holding her close and mumbling silent apologies into her cold, unhearing ear.

There had only ever been Fabiola. Before her, after I finally escaped from my father, I had made a commitment to stay alone – apart from sex, of course – to keep my vow and to never cede control to anyone. Meeting Fabiola had blindsided me, and the fact that I still had the ability to really care about another person had been both a shock and a surprise. It was as though a gentle summer breeze had rekindled embers which I'd long assumed to be black, cold and lifeless. For a while that new flame had felt so wonderful that I hadn't cared how vulnerable I was becoming.

For a while…

I caught a movement at the edge of my vision. A man had moved out of the shadows and was now sliding along a pew on the opposite side of the church? Mirroring me, he was hiding from the other mourners, tucked behind the twin of my own stone pillar. I knew him from somewhere. He was older than Fabiola – maybe late forties – and good looking in a washed-out Hollywood matinee idol way. I'd seen his face before, but couldn't remember where. It would come to me.

The vicar had finished his pointless eulogy, and the pallbearers were standing on either side of the coffin. I heard the grunt and the collective gasp from the small congregation as the six men lifted the polished box with its precious contents onto their shoulders. Rupert and Daz stood at the front and, knees wobbling, they made their way past me and out of the door.

I shrank back against the pillar, but the mourners all had their heads bowed and no inclination to look around. As the last of them passed me, I saw the mystery man still copying me, pressing himself against the cold pillar and shamelessly allowing weak tears to flow down his cheeks.

That was it! He'd been much younger in the hundreds of black and white newspaper photos, but my secretive mirror double was

Joe Taylor, the teacher who'd seduced Fabiola when she was a schoolgirl. Fabiola had mentioned her fall from grace soon after I'd moved into her flat and I'd read everything I could find on the scandal. She'd walked away and his life had been destroyed but, almost fifteen years later, it was clear that his heart was still broken. No surprise there. Fabiola had been as modest as she was gorgeous; she'd been blind to the trail of emotional wreckage which followed her.

Joe might understand the black emptiness churning inside me. It was such a struggle to stay strong when everything that mattered was gone. Lifeless, rotting flesh in a wooden box; a wooden box that was slowly sinking into a gaping grave, washed down by meaningless tears and empty words.

As if any of that made a difference to anything. Fabiola was gone for ever.

She'd died alone, slumped forward under an ancient oak in Odell Wood, alone in the inky blackness. I remembered that night. Waking with a start, wide-eyed, shivering and doubled over with cold stomach cramps. I hadn't understood it at the time, but as soon as I learnt what had happened, I remembered that instant of pain and recognised it for what it was – the ripping asunder of the bond which had joined the two of us like an umbilical cord.

I would never again allow myself that weakness. The hard icy shell which was growing around my heart would protect me as I'd always intended it to. The world was out there for the taking; everyone and everything within it would be mine to use or discard as I chose. There would be bumps on the way, but that was fine. A few bumps and potholes wouldn't slow me down – I would move too fast for that.

With one exception. A single exception, but I had plenty of time to make sure she became who I wanted her to be – who I needed her to be.

As for that bumbling fool Rupert, his stuck-up mother and the bawling brat, they would get what was coming to them. And Daz too … He was the proverbial bad penny. Whatever I did, he just wouldn't go away.

If it hadn't been for their weakness and stupidity …

As I left the church, I saw them standing under a yew tree in the far corner of the graveyard. I'd been to the open grave earlier that morning. It was a nice spot with a view past the church into open fields. Fabi would be all right there.

It was time for me to leave. I'd been tempted not to bother coming, but I was glad I had. Our time together had been a sweet, sweet anomaly, and I was glad to indulge in a few last moments of sentimentality, but no more. I stood in the shadow of a grey limestone buttress, my lips mouthing a silent litany as I renewed the promises I'd made to myself ten years earlier when I walked away from my father's bleeding body. No weakness. Never depend on anyone or anything. Stay in control.

I looked one last time at the dark figures which circled her grave with bowed heads like so many hooded vultures. They would all be going next door to the vicarage. Cucumber sandwiches and Earl Grey most likely. I hoped that Rupert would be secretly tucking into the whisky and there would be a sloppy embarrassing scene, but I knew it probably wouldn't happen. He was too much of a toff and would somehow hold it together. Maybe Daz would surprise everyone by losing it and smashing the place up?

Nah! It wasn't a day for wishes to come true. If I wanted to get even with them, I'd need to do something about it myself. But not today. Those plans could wait and mature softly like an expensive wine.

I turned and started walking down the lane towards Oxford.

I was almost at the ring road when a car shot past, almost clipping my arm before pulling over with a screech of brakes. It was the old Ford Fiesta I'd seen lurking in the corner of the church car park, its pale-blue paint battle-scarred with scrapes and dents.

The door opened, and a man got out. It was Fabiola's teacher-lover and, at close quarters, he was a mess. He looked as though he hadn't eaten or slept for a week, his eyes were red and puffed and, even from a distance, I could smell the sweet stench of stale alcohol oozing from every pore.

He walked towards me with careful steps. 'I saw you at the back of the church,' he said. 'Not welcome at the reception, eh?'

'Not exactly,' I replied. 'You neither?'

'No. I doubt any of them even know I exist. And I'm sure they don't want to.'

'I know who you are though,' I said, waiting just a couple of seconds to get his full attention. 'You're Joe Taylor, aren't you?'

His ravaged face was still able to show surprise, and it amused me to imagine how confused he must have been.

'How the hell do you know who I am?' he said, at last.

'Fabiola told me about you. We were good friends for a few years.'

I was wearing black jeans, Doc Martins and a scruffy old Crombie coat; I imagined my face was a patchy mess of streaked and smudged mascara. So much for never crying again.

He looked me up and down and nodded his head. 'So, she left you behind as well, did she?' he said, pressing his lips together as his eyes lost focus and he stared out across the empty fields. 'Fabiola had a habit of moving on … And up, of course.'

I could easily have explained that it wasn't like that. That it was ridiculous to compare his sordid relationship – almost child abuse – with Fabiola and me. I could have explained that, but I found myself lost for words and lacking the energy to look for some.

And so we stood facing each other on the empty road, two unwelcome mourners from an unwelcome past, alone in our grief and confusion.

I don't quite know what came over me, but the pointlessness of everything was suddenly overwhelming and I felt a deep exhaustion sink into my bones. At least Joe looked worse than I felt and I realised that he might be the only person alive who understood some of what I was feeling. How pathetic was that?

'Fancy a drink?' I said and reached out my hand. 'I'm Julie.'

It didn't take me long to piece together the shards of Joe's dull and broken life. After the scandal and his divorce, he'd moved to

Glasgow to escape the media and had stayed there, finding work wherever he could and with limited success. Patches of road were visible through the rusted footwells of his knackered Fiesta, but it seemed determined to stutter onwards – a bit like its owner. He wasn't going back North until the following day, so we parked up at his hotel – the Premier Inn in Cowley – and started to walk towards town.

Cowley isn't the Oxford which most people imagine – too shabby even for the poorest students, it's a long way from the dreaming spires. A miserable drizzle added to the bleakness as we walked past dull pebble-dashed houses and sour-faced mothers dragging screaming brats behind them. If it weren't for the dark faces, I could have been back on the estate where I grew up.

We got as far as The Original Swan, one of the most unpleasant pubs I'd ever seen. It was a complete shit hole but, despite the sports TVs and pink neon behind the bar, it suited the two of us just fine. Less than half an hour after Joe had stopped and picked me up, we were sitting at a corner table with pints of Stella and chasers beside them – whisky for him and vodka for me.

'Cheers,' I said. It was the first thing I'd said since we'd left the car.

'To Fabiola,' he replied, lifting his glass. 'She totally fucked up my life, but I wouldn't have missed it for the world.'

We didn't talk much until after the third round of pints and shorts, by which time the church and all that went with it seemed far enough behind us.

'So you said you and Fabiola were good friends?' said Joe.

'Uh huh.' I kept my face buried in my beer.

'You seem pretty cut-up if she was just a mate?' It was obvious he had no intention of letting this go. 'Were you "good friends" if you get my drift?'

'You might say that,' I said. Our relationship was private and personal, but that didn't seem important just then.

He giggled like an idiot. 'Now that I wasn't expecting,' he said. 'How long were you together?'

'Over four years. Until that posh twat Rupert showed up and

stuck his oar in.'

'Shit,' he said, shaking his head from side to side like one of those stupid nodding bulldogs. 'That would have stung a bit.'

We did talk more, but not about anything memorable. We were both too focused on getting rat-arsed and banishing the ghost of Fabiola. By the time they kicked us out, we'd definitely managed one of the two.

The Morning After

I've never had to worry about hangovers – something genetic – and woke up clear-headed at seven-thirty. Clear-headed, but struggling to piece together the events of the previous evening. I was lying naked in an oversized bed in a purple room with a comatose Joe stretched out beside me. So, we'd gone back to his room, but had anything happened? I wasn't too fussed either way, but I'd like to have known.

Looking at Joe's sagging body I had no sense he would be joining the world of the living any time soon and decided I might as well get up. In any case, I needed to do some thinking.

Many people give Premier Inns a hard time, but they have good beds, the showers are spacious, warm and powerful and they do great breakfasts. Plus, Joe was paying.

Fabi's funeral marked a turning point for me in all sorts of ways. I would never forget her or what had happened to her and I certainly wasn't going to forget about Daz, the child and the rest of the Blackwell family. But now she was gone, my life would be simpler and I would have the time and focus to work on building my business.

Whether or not I'd slept with Joe and whether or not he'd been good in bed, there was a definite serendipity to our meeting and I could see exactly how he would fit into my plans. After all, even if he turned out to be a poor lover, most things could be improved with a little training.

It was after eleven by the time he came down to the restaurant and by then I had every detail worked out. Step by step, a new strategy was falling into place and my mind was on fire. Whatever name I might have to use with other people, Jax was back.

Joe didn't look so good … and had probably felt better. People should know their limits. We needed to have an important conversation, but not right then.

'Morning,' I said, smiling and pouring him a cup of coffee. 'I've ordered you a fry-up.' Even in his diminished state, I watched him melt as I turned on the charm. Men were so pathetic.

He made the effort to pull in his stomach, to sit straighter and to push the hangover demons back where they'd come from.

I guessed that he couldn't remember what had happened the night before either, which made things easier.

'I enjoyed last night,' I said, half closing my eyes and tilting my head in mock shyness. 'A lot, actually.'

That seemed to deal with any uncertainties he may have had and he puffed up visibly. 'Me too,' he said. 'And considering how pissed we both were …'

His breakfast arrived; three rashers of bacon; two fat sausages stretched to bursting; two fried eggs, hash browns, black pudding, toast and baked beans; all of it glistening greasily in the bright lights. He looked at the plate and I saw the determination in his eyes. All he needed to do was to fight off his queasiness long enough to finish the food and he would make it through to the other side. It wasn't the first time Joe had woken up with a monster hangover.

I waited until he was almost done. Beads of sweat glistened on his pallid face, but he was over the summit and on the downhill stretch. 'Do you have to go straight back to Glasgow,' I said. 'Like, have you got work tomorrow or something?'

He looked up at me. 'Not really,' he said. 'I'm between jobs at the moment. But I might as well get back. I've done what I needed to do here.'

'Why don't you come to London for a few days? I'll show you some of the places where me and Fabi used to hang out.'

Joe looked at me, trying to figure out what the catch was. He was mid-forties, a pasty-faced, flabby drunk, and knew I was light-years out of his league. He wasn't totally stupid and I could almost hear the cogs whirring in his head. What was I up to?

But, if there is anything that anyone ever needs to know about men, it's that, in a war of brain vs. dick, there can only ever be one winner. He wasn't able find an explanation for my proposition which made sense, but he was never going to dig any deeper. I was a gift horse materialising from the ether and he wasn't going to risk that opportunity by looking at my teeth.

'I could do that, I guess,' he said, eventually. 'Might be fun.'

I'd got my act together in the years after Fabiola moved out. Jax Daniels was no more and with my new identity, Julie Martin, I was becoming an increasingly influential security consultant. My first book was selling well, and I was a regular on the conference circuit. I had no plans to stay a consultant for ever, but phase one was looking good.

Major hacking scandals were becoming daily events, the personal online security market was on fire and I'd picked up a lot of demanding, high-end clients. But I'd made a point of clearing my diary for the week after Fabi's funeral and, despite a slew of messages and email alerts, I didn't bother to check any of them.

My original idea had been to spend that time clearing my head and researching my new business, but that could wait for a while. First, I had plans for Joe. Whether or not we'd had drunken sex in Oxford quickly became a moot point and by the Tuesday evening, I had him primed and ready.

I'd bought a two-bedroom flat on Randolph Avenue in Little Venice. It had cost an obscene amount of money, but was worth it. At the back, there was a small private garden which led straight onto the landscaped communal gardens. My tiny terrace caught the evening sun and Joe and I were sitting enjoying a glass of Sancerre (from the second bottle), before the last rays dipped below the white stucco terraces on the other side of the square.

'There's something I need to tell you,' I said.

'Sounds serious,' said Joe, laughing, but not smiling. 'Are we out of wine?'

'Don't be stupid. There's plenty of wine.'

'Good. Because I could always pop out to …'

'Shut up, Joe,' I said. 'This is important.'

He almost certainly thought I was going to tell him we were done, and I watched as his face began to sag like a warm waxwork.

'It's not a bad thing,' I carried on quickly, not needing to see more of his pathetic puppy dog expression. 'At least I don't think so. Just listen.'

'OK,' he said, properly engaged at last.

'It's about something Fabiola told me when we were together. Almost five years ago now. It came completely out of the blue – we were drunk, or stoned, or both – and then she turned to me, grabbed me by the wrist and blurted it out.'

'Blurted what out?' said Joe.

'She told me she'd had a baby. A little girl.'

'What?' he squeaked, leaning forward, almost out of his chair.

'She got herself pregnant and had a little girl, but she didn't want anyone to know and she was too young. So she abandoned her at a hospital and walked away.'

Abandon is a desolate word at the best of times and I watched Joe's eyes open wide and his jaw drop.

'Oh, my God. How awful.' said Joe, his hand moving up to cover his gaping mouth. 'When was this?' I heard the cogs whirring again.

'It was in 2004. I'm not sure when exactly.'

'Oh my God,' said Joe again, lost for any new words. 'But that means … that means …'

'Yes,' I said. 'You have a daughter with Fabiola.'

Joe's expression jumped through extreme emotions like a bad mime artist's. Disbelief turned to euphoria which quickly turned to pride and joy. Pride and joy didn't last long before his eyes dropped and his beaming smile faded.

'But she'll have been adopted as a baby,' he said. 'I'll never be able to find her. She must be … what? … ten or eleven by now?'

'She was eleven two weeks ago,' I said. 'She had a small party at home. Ten friends and a caterpillar cake. I think she had fun.'

Joe jumped to his feet. 'What? … But … '

I was finding the process of toying with Joe amusing, but there was a real risk that he might be about to have a coronary. It was definitely time to calm him down.

'Joe!' I said, in the voice I reserved for clients who weren't taking me seriously. 'Sit down and listen. I'll explain everything.'

'OK,' he said, holding himself still and sinking back into his chair, but unable to hide the hyperactive thoughts racing behind his eyes.

I held his hand and began to stroke his palm rhythmically and gently. He began to breathe again, but I waited another ten seconds before continuing. 'First, you need to promise me a few things,' I said, still using my consultant voice.

He nodded.

'The first one is that you promise never to tell anyone – including Nicki – that she is Fabiola's daughter.'

'But …'

I stared at him. Hard. 'I can see I need to be even clearer,' I said. 'This isn't a negotiation. I'm trying to do you a favour but, if you don't agree to my conditions, I promise you'll never find her.'

'But if you found her, then I could …'

This time a short stare was enough. He'd only known me for four days, but that was enough for him to understand that I didn't like wasting words.

'All right,' he said. 'Agreed. But I'll need to tell her something.'

'Don't worry. I'll come up with a story.' I smiled. 'A story that comes with bulletproof documentation just in case.'

Joe looked at me as though seeing me for the first time. 'I'm sure you will,' he said. Was that a note of fear creeping into his voice? 'What else?'

'Whether they give you visitation rights or full custody, I want you to live here. In this flat. I won't be around, but you can have the flat rent-free while she's growing up. I want her to be in London, not in Glasgow or some poxy little village full of idiot yokels.'

That surprised him. His brain appeared to be working overtime, but his comfort zone was already a tiny speck in the rear-view mirror. 'I'm hardly going to object to that,' he said, 'though I'll need to understand why you're doing all this. What else?'

'Actually, that's it,' I said, with a smile. 'Just the two conditions.

Easy to remember. But don't hold your breath if you're hoping I'm going to explain myself to you. Just think of me as a fairy godmother.' I reached forward and filled his wine glass. 'Now, I know you're impatient, but you need to let this settle before I tell you anything more. Get your mind around the fact you have a daughter and we'll go through the rest tomorrow.'

'Her name's Nicki. She was adopted when she was six months old. English stepfather and Japanese stepmother. The mother's been in the UK since she was seventeen. They live in a small village in Hampshire.'

We were sitting in the same spot a day later. Joe wasn't much calmer than before, but his initial shock seemed to have faded and been replaced with an anxious excitement.

'Nicki,' he said, in a soft voice. 'Nicki's a good name. Did Fabiola give her the name?'

'How the hell would I know?' I snapped. 'I'm a good hacker, but I'm not God.'

'But you tracked her down? That's impossible. They never give out that sort of information.'

'When I found out about the baby, I knew I needed to find out where she was. If nothing else, I could keep an eye out for her. Fabi said she didn't care, but I didn't believe her and wanted to be ready to help when the time came. As it turned out, the time never came. We didn't talk about it again. Not once.'

My mind filled with images of Fabiola, laughing, smiling or winking as she laid down the law about something or other. I normally got my way about everything, with everyone, but Fabi was nobody's pushover. Her determination was reinforced by a hardened steel core, but she never seemed to need to create conflict to get her own way. No-one was ever left feeling like a loser.

Maybe my plans hadn't allowed enough for that inner core. She'd found the strength to take her own life, after all.

Joe was still staring at me with the same confused, questioning expression. It made him look old and weak. One way or the other, he would need to go sooner rather than later. 'I get that you wanted to find her,' he said, 'but that doesn't make it any less impossible.'

'I'm getting there,' I said. 'You need to understand that there's always a way. Nothing's impossible.' I sipped my wine and leant back in my chair. I still got too much pleasure from showing off. That was a weakness and would need to change. 'So, anyway. I knew they wouldn't give out that information, but it had to be somewhere. The NHS data systems have more holes than a string vest, but the adoption stuff is on a separate, more secure database which meant I needed to get a physical connection to the server. Still not a major challenge. I picked up a social worker in a pub in Hampstead, borrowed her ID while she was sleeping and used it to clone one of my own. After that it was easy to get into their admin department and leave a keystroke tracker on one of the PCs. That gave me every system password I needed, and I was away.'

Joe was looking at me as though I'd grown an extra head. 'Am I understanding this right?' he said. 'You hacked into Social Services, stole the information and then what? You've been spying on my daughter ever since?'

'That's about it, but I wouldn't call it spying. I've just been keeping an eye on her to make sure she's OK.'

'But … but …' Joe's brain had gone into meltdown again.

I flicked my fingers in front of his nose. 'Would you rather I hadn't?' I said. 'Would you prefer it if I'd just let you know that you and Fabiola had a daughter, but you'd never find her?'

'No … but …'

'Yes or no, Joe. It's a pretty simple question.'

'No. Of course not,' he said. 'It's just that …'

These unfinished sentences were beginning to get right up my nose. Why were people so pathetic?

'Anyway,' I said. 'You should be grateful I've been watching out for Nicki.'

'Why?'

'Something's wrong. I'm worried about her.'

'Worried? Why?'

'It's the father, Damian. I always knew something wasn't right and a couple of years ago I started checking him out.'

'That sounds even more like spying.'

'Whatever, Joe. Call it what you want. You know what I do for a living and I'm very good at it. It's hardly my fault if people leave their front doors wide open, is it?'

'But ...'

'... There are no buts. If you're planning on getting on some moral high horse, none of this will work. That's OK with me. She's your daughter though, and I'd have thought you'd want to look out for her. Especially now.'

As I watched Joe crumbling in front of me, I almost felt sorry for him. 'So, what did you find?' he said.

'Mr Bloody Perfect Damian Randall isn't as squeaky clean as all that. It seems he's got a thing for young girls.'

'Oh shit,' said Joe. 'How young?'

'Difficult to tell from the photos, but young ... very young.'

If truth be told, there was nothing wrong with Damian and Akiko as parents and Nicki looked like a happy child. But they were too perfect for my liking. They lived in a tiny village and were small minded and safe; they were thoroughly nice people – the word "nice" was probably invented to describe them – and I wanted more for Nicki. If she went to live with Joe, full or part time, I would be able to control things in ways that I couldn't while she was with Damian and Akiko.

I didn't actually want to meet the girl. I couldn't deal with children. They didn't respond to manipulation like adults and tended to just make me frustrated and angry.

But I did want to know the woman she would become, and I needed to make sure she didn't turn out to be some smug do-gooder with no ambition apart from to marry the boy next door and breed. That wouldn't do at all. Joe wasn't ideal – and there was a limit to the number of times I was prepared to let him fumble all over me – but I could manage him, and the role he would play as Nicki's birth father was key. There was plenty of documented evidence about Joe and Fabiola's relationship and, with a tweak here and there, everything could be made to fit.

I had big plans and Nicki was going be part of them.

Governments around the globe were being so blind about the exponential impact of personal security vulnerability. For the first time since the days of Empire, they'd handed over control of the world's information to a few mega-monopolies which were bigger and more influential than most countries.

The piece of the puzzle that politicians and civil servants had missed was that the Googles and Facebooks of this new landscape didn't care about any individual's online security. In their brief corporate existences, these businesses had relied almost entirely on finding new ways to use and abuse personal data. They were hardly prime candidates to take on the role of global data policemen.

Yes, I had big plans and the blindness of governments and society would play right into my hands. Once I had built Pulsar into the giant I hoped it would be, I would need a successor and that successor would need to be sharp, ambitious and above-all ruthless. Nicki was only eleven; she still had the virgin potential of a fresh yew sapling; with the right nurturing and pruning, why shouldn't she become the person I wanted her to be?

If the social services took Nicki away from Damian and Akiko, settling her with her birth father would be an ideal option – especially as there was no indication that Joe had been involved in the decision to give her up in the first place. He hadn't even known she existed.

Joe was slouching slack-mouthed and blank-eyed, staring into space; he was well out of his depth and would require delicate handling for a while. 'Are you sure?' he said at last. 'Are there a lot of photos? Are they bad?'

'I've found almost five thousand images on his PC, but I expect there are more that I've missed. And yes, they're very bad. Do you want to see some?'

Joe shook his head. In fact there were over eleven thousand images stashed in a hidden encrypted folder on Damian's laptop. The files had been downloaded from a range of sites on the Dark Web over the previous three years.

Unfortunately for Damian, the forensic record leading back to him was clear, traceable and very incriminating. I'd even added attempts to wipe his tracks which were good, but not quite good enough. Even more unfortunately, the fool didn't know that the files existed; it had been the work of minutes for me to hack into his home WiFi and hijack his machine. Since then, poor Damian – or rather poor Damian's computer – had logged on to download new files every Tuesday night between three and four in the morning.

All that was needed now was for him to make a "mistake" when he downloaded the next batch. That would expose his real IP address and the police would have a warrant within hours. He would, of course, claim to have been asleep at the time, but that would be impossible to prove and the damage would already have been done.

'But that means Nicki might be in danger?' said Joe. 'She's only eleven.'

I clenched my fists and squeezed my eyes tightly shut. Really? D'ya think so Joe? It was like herding a particularly stupid sheep through a very wide gate.

'I know,' I said, trying to appear as amazed as him. 'I've been worrying about this for the past two months. Ever since I found out.'

The whole business with Joe came at an unfortunate time. I was in the middle of negotiations to license the key software which would eventually underpin Pulsar and I was bouncing back and forth between London and LA almost every week. At that time, no-one had understood how quickly fragile online security would threaten the entire global infrastructure, but I intended to be ready for when they did; Pulsar needed to be fully operational by the time existing systems started to unravel.

The enforced delays turned out to be a good thing as it took me a few weeks to straighten Joe out. He'd got himself tangled up in the way I'd hacked my way into Social Services and then kept tabs on Nicki and her adopted Dad. After his illegal affair with his student, Fabiola, I was unimpressed by his selective morality.

Other people see the world differently from me. They put up these pointless ethical barriers between their existing lives and where they want to go. I had no intention of ever doing that, but needed to try harder to take that into account where Joe was concerned.

At least for a while longer. If Pulsar achieved its destiny, I wouldn't need to worry about other people's doubts or opinions. It would be my way or the highway.

But that was a few years away and so I waited more or less patiently while Joe dithered. Eventually his desire to find out more about Nicki (and his growing fear of Damian) overcame those pointless ethical concerns, and we were able to move on.

We were sitting drinking coffee in Raoul's cafe when his shoulders slumped and he turned to me. 'So, what happens next?' he said, resignation colouring his voice.

I pulled my chair next to his and leant closer. 'I've spoken to a lawyer,' I said. 'The first thing we need to do is to establish that you're the natural father. After that, I'll arrange it so that the police find out about Damian. Then we wait. The lawyer says the eventual outcome depends a lot on how Damian's wife behaves. If she stands by her husband, you stand a good chance of getting full custody. If she's smart and dumps him quickly, it'll be less clear. In any case, all of her family's in Japan and she won't be allowed to take Nicki out of the country. Worst case, you should get visitation rights.'

'But that means we'll destroy their lives?' said Joe, still clinging on to a few vestigial scruples.

'But look at what he's been doing,' I said. 'He's brought it on himself … and it's only a matter of time until he gets caught, anyway.'

'I suppose so. But …'

'… And we have no idea what his wife actually knows. Maybe she's involved in some way? At the very least, she married a pervert. Are you still having second thoughts?'

'No,' Joe said with conviction. 'I've made up my mind. I hate your sneaky world of hacking and deceit, but I'd never forgive myself if I did nothing. Let's do it.' He looked at me with clear, sober eyes. 'And the first step is a DNA test?'

'Yes,' I said. 'It's critical that we're one hundred per cent sure before doing anything or telling anybody. I can arrange that for you.

And you should get a DNA sample from one of your other daughters to help them to cross check the results.'

'How can I manage that?' he said, slipping effortlessly into his default hangdog expression. 'My ex-wife turned them both against me years ago, and I hardly see them any more. The youngest one is Fabiola's age now – the age Fabiola was when I knew her – and she won't even talk to me. I'll have to tell them why I need it.'

I took him by the shoulders and stared at him, forcing his skittish eyes to hold my gaze.

'But you're not going to do that, are you?' I said, receiving a nervous head shake in return. I patted his cheek. 'Don't worry. We'll find a way. I'll get the sample kits and we can take it from there.'

2026

First Contact

'You must be very proud.'

I struggled to control my amusement as I rested one hand gently on Joe's shoulder. His reaction was exactly as expected, flinching like a startled deer as soon as he heard my voice. He recognised me in a nanosecond even though we hadn't spoken for years.

'Julie!' Joe turned to face me. 'What the fuck are you doing here?'

'Hello Joe,' I said, leaning forward to plant a chaste kiss on his cheek. 'Nice to see you too.'

I had always known Joe wouldn't age well. Maybe if he'd lived in California, surfing, cycling and drinking wheat-germ smoothies every day? Maybe then he would have held on to some of those cheeky, pretty boy looks. But living alone in London, drinking too much and not being burdened with an excess of willpower or self-respect? It was never going to turn out well. He must have been almost sixty and looked every day of it.

'Sorry. You just made me jump. How are you?' His eyes widened. 'You look … you look amazing.'

Unlike Joe, I had plenty of willpower and self-respect and he was stating the obvious. Even so, a little coy self-deprecation was probably called for.

'Oh. You know. I try to keep in shape.' I smiled and looked down at the floor.

Despite all the research, it still wasn't possible to know what really went on in other people's heads, but from the way Joe was looking me up and down, I'd have put money that his thoughts were fluttering between 'Did I really sleep with her?', distant memories of our nights together, and answering his own question. 'Bloody hell. I did. But how?' That was certainly the reaction I was hoping for.

'But ... but ... you look just like one of Nicki's friends. It's crazy.'

'Good cheekbones,' I said, already bored with the adulation. Luckily, we were distracted by a low murmuring from the crowd and the scrape of chair legs on the wooden floor as everyone shifted around to get a better look at the front of the hall. I pointed over the crowd and towards the stage where a row of black-gowned figures stretched out like crows on a telephone line. 'Hang on, Joe,' I said. 'I think she's going up.'

He span round to look and I felt my own heart fill my chest as I watched the tall, strong, clever girl walk up the two wooden steps onto the stage and stride confidently towards the row of crows. She was my exception. The single exception where feelings and emotions were allowed. She dipped her head as she took the beribboned roll of white paper and shook the outstretched hands one by one. Then, as she reached the end of the row, she turned to face us, lifting the paper high in jubilation, her white teeth flashing triumph in the footlights.

I ducked behind Joe who had his arms raised to shoulder height, clapping and whooping like a child. I loved it when a plan came together with clockwork precision and this day was like a Swiss watchmaker's wet dream. Perfect.

I reached forward and pressed the folded note into Joe's hand. 'I need to go,' I said, watching the girl pushing through the crowded room towards us. 'Don't be late.'

I turned and slid backwards into the crowded room before he had a chance to speak. It wasn't time for Nicki and I to meet. Not like this. Not quite yet.

Joe wasn't late.

I walked into the crowded pub and saw him, propping up the bar and chatting to the young mini-skirted barmaid. He'd always been a sleazeball – Fabiola had been proof enough of that – but it was surely time for him to hang up his spurs and try to hold on to a few scraps of dignity?

'Nicki looked happy,' I said, pulling up a stool next to his, pointing at his half-empty pint glass and raising two fingers – the polite way around – to the barmaid. The Warrington had been an institution for over a century and the place was humming.

'And so she should,' he said. 'If you'd told me four or five years ago that she'd be picking up a First from Imperial, I'd have laughed in your face.' He'd had time to gather his thoughts and his body language was furtive and defensive. 'Probably not such a huge surprise for you, I guess. But then again, nothing ever is, is it?'

'Choices and actions are rarely written in stone where people are concerned,' I said. 'Especially young people. There are so many wrong paths to take.'

'Cheers to that,' he said, lifting his glass to me in a toast. 'Life would be dull as hell if we didn't have free will. She made her own choices, worked bloody hard and, let's face it, she must have got her brains from Fabiola after all.'

I smiled and raised my glass in reply. Free will? That hadn't been what I'd meant at all. 'Is she out with her friends tonight?' I said.

'Yeah,' said Joe, in a sad little boy's voice. 'She managed a quick glass of bubbly with her old man and then she was off. The truth is we don't have so much in common any more. She's all grown up and I haven't understood anything she's been studying for years.'

'That's how it should be,' I said. 'You've not done a bad job, though. In the circumstances.'

'I suppose not,' he said. 'But you've been watching over us, haven't you? All this time?'

I just looked at him. Did he really need to ask that question?

'The thing I really don't get,' he continued. 'The thing that bugs me more than anything, is that you don't want to meet her. You've spent shed loads of cash – hundreds of thousands – helping her, but she's never seen you and doesn't even know you exist. It's all a bit too weird for me. What's in it for you?'

'Whatever made you think that?' I was genuinely surprised by his stupidity. Did he think it was all just some random act of charity? 'Of course I want to meet Nicki. And soon.'

'So why run away at the ceremony? I could have introduced you then. You could have talked AI and quantum computing.'

'It wasn't the right time or the right context,' I said. 'That's why I wanted to have this drink, Joe. I needed to go though a few things with you first. I need to make sure that we understand each other and that you haven't forgotten what you promised.'

'I'm not that stupid,' he said. 'I've always been able to figure out when I'm on to a good number. Nicki doesn't know anything about Fabiola or you. I've stuck to the story you gave me and she's given up trying to find out more.'

'Good. You understand it would be a mistake to cross me, don't you?'

'I understood that a long time ago,' he said. 'I've seen what happens to people who do.' He drank the first half of his pint in a single mouthful. 'Which reminds me of something you'll want to know. You remember her adopted father, Damian?'

I didn't bother to reply. I'd forgotten how tedious he could be.

'Well, he's tracked her down somehow.'

'What?' How had I missed that? He must have been very careful. I took a deep breath. 'How do you know?'

'He wrote her a letter,' said Joe. 'A couple of months ago. Nicki showed it to me.'

'What did it say? Did you get a copy?'

'She just showed it to me one time, but I remember it pretty well. He basically said that he missed her, he was innocent, and he'd like to meet up. If she didn't want to, he'd understand, and he wished her well. That was pretty much it. Oh, and he told her Akiko left him and went back to Japan.'

'I knew about that,' I said. 'Stupid of her to stand by him all through the investigation and then finally leave after she'd lost custody. And Nicki? What did she do about the letter?'

'As far as I know, she's not done anything yet.' He swirled around the last inch of beer in his glass and gulped it down. 'She said she wanted to finish her finals first and would figure out what to do about Damian afterwards. I think she'll meet him though. She never forgot them. I did my best, but I've always wondered if taking her away was the right thing to do, or if I was just being selfish. It took years for her to stop missing them and she's ended up becoming a bit of a loner.'

I didn't see a problem with that; in fact it was exactly what I'd been hoping for. Inner strength and self-sufficiency were vital ingredients of real success and Nicki was destined for great things. But seeing Damian wouldn't be helpful at all.

'It wouldn't be good for them to meet,' I said. 'I'll need to think about that.'

I then endured another hour of Joe's slimy company, dividing my energies equally between explanation, charm and intimidation, making sure he understood what would happen next, that he wanted to please me and that he was afraid of the consequences if he didn't. As soon as I was sure his mind was where I needed it to be, I left him, went home and took a long shower.

'So, Nicki. You have your degree and I'm guessing you already know you've done well in the interview process so far.' I took the thick stack of papers in front of me and made a point of turning it over face down onto the table. 'But you're applying for the most prestigious programme in your field and we have several other candidates with equally strong backgrounds.'

We were sitting in my new office at the top of Shard Two, looking across the river to the original Shard. I'd only moved in a month earlier and I was still getting used to the jaw-dropping views. The penthouse floors of Shard Two were now the most coveted offices in London; fortunately I'd put in an option seven years earlier – before the ink on the architect's drawings was dry, and while the ruins of Old Billingsgate were still stinking of cordite and wet ash. Pulsar had been less than three years old at the time and the agreed rent had been more than our total turnover, but I'd been confident. Things were going to be very different by the time the building was finally completed.

Nicki was dressed in a smart black trouser suit, no jewellery and her only nod to frivolity was the ruffled, dipping neckline of her cream silk blouse. If she was nervous, she hid it well. I felt my toes clenching with excitement. I had been watching her from a distance for almost twenty years, but this was the first time we'd been so close, the first time we'd looked into each other's eyes. Nothing about that moment was disappointing – it was like the long-awaited sip of a cold beer after a day trekking in the summer sun – everything imagined and a little bit more.

Of course, I still couldn't be sure that she was as tough and ambitious as I needed her to be. I'd done everything in my power to guide her and mould her, but would it work? It was much too early to say, but we were entering a new phase and that was thrilling enough.

I wasn't a patient person by nature and the pleasure I took in waiting and nurturing my projects wasn't the calm, peaceful acceptance of the forester or landscape gardener. Most people would describe me as calm and controlled, but they had no idea what went on inside. It had taken an exceptional effort to force the lid down on my bubbling, seething passions, to bite my tongue and to continue to wait. The denial was unbearable although it did give me a kind of masochistic sexual thrill. More the guilty, conflicted self-flagellation of the Opus Dei than the Buddhist monk, but we all had our crosses to bear.

Sam was only thirteen. I'd need to stay patient a while longer, but if he turned out as well as Nicki appeared to have done, my projects would have been worth the wait. In any case, he was quite different – although he'd only been a snivelling brat at the time, he was partly responsible for his mother's death and I couldn't forgive him for taking Fabiola away from me. Nicki was the lucky one – she had no price to pay.

'I know how competitive it is, Ms Martin,' said Nicki. 'No-one in the AI department talks about much else these days.'

With a cash bursary of at least double the nearest alternative, I wasn't surprised. Even so, I enjoyed seeing her eyes light up at the thought of winning and, as her perfect teeth pressed against her bottom lip, she looked hungry enough.

'Please. Call me Julie,' I said. 'We're at the final stage and you should be very proud to have made it this far. Not many people get an hour of my time these days.' I leant back in my chair and crossed my arms. 'Ultimately it's for me to decide which of the remaining candidates will be the Pulsar Scholar for 2026 and it's up to you to convince me to choose you.' The sun was angling through the floor-to-ceiling windows and lighting Nicki's face with the glow of a renaissance painting. She was beautiful, and I felt my throat tighten – I had waited so long for this. 'I don't want to talk about AI,' I continued after a few moments. 'I don't want to hear about your final thesis or your plans for your Masters. I want to hear about you. Who are you? How has your life led you to this point and what do you want from the future?'

She laughed. 'No pressure then,' she said. 'Do you mind if I start with the future part?'

'You have until five o'clock,' I said.

'OK.' She leant forward and I could almost see the neurones sparking in her head. 'My assumption is that you've created the scholarship because you're looking for talent to work for Pulsar long term?'

I shrugged. Stating the obvious wasn't moving us forward.

'The future work I'd like to be involved with revolves around whether Pulsar even exists in the long term. Or at least whether it exists as a global leader.'

'Explain,' I said. 'Are you talking about new product development, competition, new technology? What exactly?'

'All of those and more,' she said. 'I want to be involved in looking forward, in strategic innovation, in change and growth. If you're looking for a manager who's just after a big salary, power and a job title, I might not be the right fit.'

My God! I'd forgotten how young people could be so ballsy. And stupid; if she'd not already been a shoe-in for the scholarship, I'd have probably have kicked her arrogant little arse out of the door on the spot. But she had no idea that she was the only candidate with a chance, no idea that I'd created the scholarship just for her, nor how much work had been involved in bringing us together in this room. She had no need to know, but she would need to tone that attitude down a few notches.

'Fine,' I said, keeping my face deadpan. 'I admire your passion.

And I have no intention of spending all of this money just to pick up another wannabe Vice-President of something-or-other. But … and you should listen carefully … I don't have room for prima donnas at Pulsar. I look after my people, but I expect them to get on with their jobs without questioning everything they're asked to do. Is that clear?'

'Of course.' She pulled back, her perfect composure spider-webbed with tiny cracks. She was only a kid after all. 'I didn't mean …'

'Don't worry about it,' I said. 'There's nothing wrong with passion and confidence. Now tell me about you. Where did you grow up? What about your family? Brothers or sisters?'

'No,' she said. 'No brothers and sisters. Just me and my dad.'

'… and your mother?'

'I never knew her,' she said. 'She died in a car crash when I was a baby.'

'So your father brought you up as a single parent?'

'Yes.'

Now, that was interesting. She'd decided not to mention Damian and Akiko. To wipe them from her past. Was it because she was ashamed of them, or was it was just easier to airbrush history? Maybe she'd decided it was none of my business.

If she only knew.

It was fascinating to watch Nicki think. She flicked so easily between personal life and professional goals. However much I tried to divert and distract her, she managed to hold on to each and every thread and made sure that she covered everything she'd planned to say. She reminded me of a younger me before my mind started to slow down. I was still more on-the-ball than most, but Nicki was better.

It was almost five o'clock, but I didn't want the moment to end.

'What are you doing after this?' I said, almost without thinking. 'Do you have time for a drink?'

I suspected that Nicki had been about to launch into her summing up … this is why I'm the best candidate … you should employ me because … I believe I could make an invaluable contribution … and she sat with her mouth half open for several seconds before replying.

'Yes, of course,' she said, eventually. 'Thank you, Julie. I'd love to. I just need to make a quick call.'

I took her to somewhere a little classier than the pub where I'd met Joe just a week earlier. Nicki's eyes opened just a little wider as my car appeared outside the office and she sat primly on the edge of her seat as we set off to the Connaught. I couldn't stop myself wanting to show off to her even though she was barely twenty-two and only a few weeks out of a student flat. At some point, I needed to start acting my own age.

'Can I ask you an awkward question, Julie?' she said, as we crawled through the London rush hour.

'Of course,' I said. 'Fire away.'

'OK. You're obviously super intelligent and you have this reputation for knowing exactly what's going to happen before it actually does.'

'Do I?' I said.

'Absolutely,' said Nicki. 'But what I want to know is … how did you know?'

'How did I know what?' I replied, genuinely confused.

'How did you know that global personal security systems were going to implode like they did? You must have set up Pulsar at least two years before there was any real indication.'

I laughed. For a moment, I'd been worried that Joe had been shooting his mouth off. 'It was almost four years before, in fact,' I said. 'And the answer is very simple. I didn't know. I took a punt and got lucky.'

We had pulled over in front of the Connaught, but I took a moment to enjoy the expression of naïve wonderment on her face. 'Are you serious?' she said, eventually.

'Of course,' I said, getting out of the car. 'But I should probably add that it was an educated guess.'

Nicki relaxed after that and I could tell she got a buzz from the way the hotel staff treated us as they whisked us through into the bar.

'What was it like growing up without a mother?' I said, after we'd settled down at a corner table and been served drinks. 'If you don't mind me asking.'

'Well I actually did have a mum until I was almost twelve,' she said, stirring her mojito and watching the ice spin and tumble. 'She was a good mum.'

'I'm sorry,' I said. 'Did she pass away?'

'No. No,' Nicki said. 'Nothing like that. She wasn't my real mother. She was Japanese, not that it matters.'

'So, she was your father's girlfriend? Or wife?'

'No. My dad didn't even know I existed at the time. My mother died when I was a baby and I was adopted. I had a different mum and dad until just before I went to secondary school.'

I rested my hand on top of hers. 'That sounds tough,' I said. 'Maybe we should drop this?'

'No. It's fine,' she said. 'I might as well tell you the whole story now.' She finished her drink in a single gulp. 'I thought my adopted dad was great … and he was great … until he was arrested for child pornography.'

'Oh God. How awful! You must have felt so betrayed.'

She put her empty glass on the table and looked up at me. 'I don't know why I'm telling you all of this. I've never really spoken about it with anybody, and now I'm pouring my heart out – to Julie Martin of all people.

I held her gaze and smiled. 'Funny how life pans out, isn't it? Don't worry. We're off the clock. I've had a long week, and it's remarkably pleasant to talk to someone normal for once.'

'You mean someone poor?' Nicki said, laughing.

'I guess that's exactly what I mean,' I said. 'But I didn't mean it to be patronising. Go on. Finish your story. You're here now, so at least it must have a happy ending.'

'Yes,' she said. 'I suppose it does, although things were touch and go for a while. If my real dad hadn't found me, I don't know what would have happened. I was a mess. I was only eleven when they dragged me away from my parents for reasons which weren't properly explained and didn't make sense to an eleven-year-old, anyway. Then they dumped me into the care system. It was the worst time of my life; I don't think anyone who hasn't experienced it can understand what it's like.'

I nodded and put my hand gently on her shoulder. 'Sounds terrible.'

She didn't seem to notice me and continued, blank eyes staring at the marble table top. 'You can't trust anybody in those places. Everyone says they're there to help you, or to be your friend, but they've all got some sort of agenda. A few of the other kids weren't too bad, but most were ... and the staff ...' She squeezed her eyes tightly closed and sat quietly for a moment.

I could remember that time vividly. After Damian's arrest, Nicki had been in care for over a year and she hadn't dealt with the upheaval well. I'd employed a private investigator to keep an eye on her – Pulsar was keeping me on the road all the time – and the weekly reports weren't pretty reading. She'd been hanging around with much older kids and apparently there'd been one cocky pretty boy – there's always one – who'd had the rest of them trailing after him like little acolytes in a mini cult.

The investigator had clear instructions, and he'd been forced to step in when matters got out of hand. Nothing anyone could ever have linked to Nicki, but the pretty boy hadn't been so pretty, or cocky, after that. I hadn't known about any issues with the staff though. It would have to look into that.

There had been moments back then when I'd wondered whether I should have left her with boring Damian and Akiko, but there was no going back and Joe's paternity test was already registered with the court. It was going to be over soon enough.

I looked at the pretty young girl sitting in front of me and watched as she dismissed her demons, opened her eyes and smiled. 'I really don't believe I'm telling you all this,' she said.

'That's OK,' I said. 'I wanted to get to know you and we all have secrets in our past. It's what makes us who we are. At least the story seems to have a happy ending. I assume that, once your dad found you, things improved?'

'After a while,' she said. 'I think it took me a couple of years to learn to stop being so defensive. Luckily, Dad's always been amazingly kind and patient and I calmed down eventually. In a weird kind of way, I think he's always felt guilty for not having known about me before.'

'You've been through a lot in a short life,' I said. 'At least that's all over now.'

'Not quite,' she said, shifting in her chair. 'My adopted father, Damian, got in touch with me last week. He wants to meet.'

'Really? And you've not seen him since ...?'

'No. I think he went to prison and my mum went back to Japan. I'm pretty sure he's not supposed to contact me, though.'

'Will you see him?'

'I think so. I'm in a good place now and I've always wanted to hear his side of things. I googled his trial transcripts a few years ago and saw that he denied everything right to the end. There was such a lot of evidence against him, but he never changed his story.'

'Hmmm,' I said. 'That's probably not so unusual, but you have to do what you feel is right. I'm sure you'll be OK as long as you take care to meet in a public place.'

We spent over two more hours in the bar, drank too many cocktails and got to know each other. Or rather, she learnt as much about me as I wanted her to and, let's face it, I probably knew more about her than she did herself.

Even so, taking my puppet-master hat off for a moment or two, there's no substitute for direct interaction and Nicki had turned out to be everything I'd hoped she would be, and more. Nature or nurture, it didn't matter – it had been worth the wait. If I could manage the next ten years as well as the last, I would have my perfect successor.

The whole business with Damian was a wrinkle I didn't need and would have to be dealt with. People should know when to stay away.

2037

Plans, Plans, Plans

'Jane?'

'Yes, Ms Martin.'

'I left some details for a company called Odell Services on your desk last night.'

'I saw. I was about to ask you what you wanted me to do with them.'

'Send them to Nicki Taylor and ask her to carry out an acquisition target analysis, please.'

'Of course.'

'I'll need it by Monday close of play … And Jane?'

'Yes.'

'Book in a follow-up meeting with Nicki on Tuesday afternoon. Block off half an hour.'

It had been ten years since Nicki won the Pulsar scholarship – no surprise there – and it had equally been no surprise that we'd then offered her a full-time job. She wasn't perfect by a long way, but she was smart and learned quickly. I still felt confident that we were on track.

Pulsar was a big company, and I'd worked hard to develop my reputation as a reclusive, semi-mythical founder. It allowed me to minimise the time I spent with ambitious idiots trying to further their careers. They weren't idiots, of course – over three hundred of our employees had one or more PhDs – but that didn't stop them behaving as though they were.

My stand-offish reputation meant it would have been highly

unusual for me to have much contact with a junior employee – even a high-flyer like Nicki – and, for a long time, I'd only been able to justify seeing her a few times a year. And when we did meet, it was always in a larger corporate context – conferences, product launches or strategy meetings.

She'd needed to make her own way through the Pulsar organisation until she was ready for the next big step. Or at the very least, she'd needed to believe she was making her own way.

During those years, I'd devoted my time to building the company from big to huge and, by the time Nicki was closing in on a senior management position, Pulsar was closing in on the world number one spot. Global population figures had stabilised at just under ten billion and by March 2037, over four billion of them were using a Pulsar product to manage their online security.

They were marvellous years – I loved the feeling of being in control of everything around me – and most of the time, I managed to discipline myself to only think about Nicki and Sam once per month. On the appointed day, I would take a day trip to my place in Provence, catch up on everything going on in their lives and initiate any necessary tweaks and nudges. I would then have dinner delivered to the villa and would sit on the balcony with a glass of wine. As the sun sank slowly into the sea, I built the future in my mind, layer by layer.

Finally, the long wait was coming to an end; six months earlier, Nicki had been promoted to Vice-President of our small acquisitions department, elevating her to the senior management team for the first time. It had given me more opportunities to have one-to-one meetings with her and I was finally ready to move on to the next stage in my strategy.

As for Sam, my plans were just about to begin …

Nicki sat across from me, sitting bolt upright and occasionally straightening the document in front of her while I made a show of leafing through my own copy.

'Interesting report,' I said, once I felt she'd suffered enough. 'But I was unsure quite what your recommendations were?'

I'd not left my office until almost midnight the previous evening. The eight-page report in my hands was exactly what I'd been hoping for. The analysis was precise and the research impressive, considering the time available. The conclusions were weak, but I had a sense there was more to come.

I didn't have to wait long to find out. 'I'm sorry about the weak summary,' said Nicki. 'There is a reason. Some of my conclusions are controversial and I wanted to explain them face-to-face.' She was still sitting upright, a picture of corporate confidence. She had come a long way, but I could see her right thumbnail digging hard into the soft pad of her forefinger. It was all right to be nervous, but she would need to learn to hide it better.

'Odell is an interesting business,' she continued. 'Very secretive, but I'd expect that for a political consultancy. They appear to have attracted some impressive clients over the past few years, although I should stress that it was hard to find any solid data.' Nicki opened her copy of the report and turned it towards me. 'You can see the provisional client list in the appendix here. I've marked the ones I'm confident about in red, the others are mostly hearsay and rumour.'

'As, you say an impressive list,' I said. 'If you're right, this company has been involved in every major election campaign for the past three years.'

'Indeed. And working for the winning side every time.' She closed the report and put it on the desk. 'Especially impressive for a company that materialised from nowhere less than five years ago. They seem to have left the competition in the dust. And I can't trace the actual ownership. Lots of holding companies, but drill too far and there are brick walls everywhere. I might be able to dig deeper, but not without flagging our interest.'

'There are ways,' I said. 'I can explain how, but another time.'

'I'd love that,' said Nicki, 'and I won't forget to remind you. Anyway, I want to run through a bit of historical context before I get to my real point. It's going over familiar ground, but please bear with me. It won't take long.' She seemed to take my lack of response as agreement and continued.

'As you know, there's been a huge amount of money and research spent on social media influencing ever since the infamous Facebook experiment in 2012 and the scandals of election-rigging which followed for years afterwards. Brexit, both Trump elections and dozens more – the Russians and the Chinese had their fingers everywhere. By 2020, there was a huge amount of hard evidence proving that massive focussed use of bot and troll armies could leverage social media to influence people's views, opinions and, in a significant percentage of cases, their actual decisions. Cognitive linguistics was the hottest skill in tech and, in a world where most elections balance on a knife edge anyway, democracy was up for sale.'

'It was a fascinating time,' I said, nodding. 'I enjoyed watching the liberal media thrashing around like dying catfish in a half-drained swamp. They'd been wallowing in smug complacency for too long and couldn't understand why their influence had evaporated. As a result, election-rigging scandals were much more newsworthy than personal security and identity protection ... fortunately for me.'

Nicki gave me a sideways look before continuing. 'As you also know, the end of democracy turned out to be yet another storm in a teacup. I wanted to understand why and have been working on a detailed meta-analysis of all related investments. According to my numbers, between 2020 and 2040 at least twice as much money and resource was devoted to blocking social media manipulation as was applied to actually doing it.'

'That is interesting,' I said. 'I've never seen it quantified. The numbers make sense though.'

'And if you combine that with the collapse of Facebook and the fragmentation of social media channels, it's not that surprising that the rumours and scandals around social media influencing have faded rather than grown.'

'Indeed,' I said. 'These things often tend to balance themselves out, don't they? Laws of Nature.'

'Yes.' Nicki leant forward. She was excited about something. 'Until Odell Services came along. They seem to be playing by different rules ...' She paused and sat back in her chair. 'Can I ask why you asked me to prepare this analysis?' she said. 'Are you thinking of acquiring them?'

'Do you think we should?'

'Well, on paper they're a long way from our core business, so it's not an obvious call.' She drew a deep breath before continuing. 'But it might just be a very smart move.'

'Really? Why?'

'That's the part of my report I didn't want to write down,' said Nicki, her thumbnail pressing even harder into her soft skin. 'I don't want to speak out of turn. And I think Pulsar is an amazing company, but in my opinion we're nothing like as strong as we think we are. We're vulnerable in a fundamental way – even great people, innovation and exceptional new product development can't be relied on to protect us. There are fundamental threats which are out of our control and, perversely, they become stronger at the same time as we do.'

She looked up at me with puppy-dog-pleading eyes, unsure whether she was about to get a pat on the back or a sharp rap on the nose.

'Go on,' I said, not willing to indulge her with either response. Not straight away, at least.

'OK,' she said, a slight tremor creeping into her voice. 'My thinking needs a bit of context. We've seen a new pattern over the past thirty-odd years. From the turn of the twentieth century, technology created a platform for global monopolies to exist in a way that they hadn't for a long time, if ever. The big monsters like Google, Facebook and Amazon came from nowhere and took over everything. With their hyper-dominant scale and market share, there was a moment when it seemed that they were invulnerable. They had moved beyond governments, stepped outside the normal rules.'

'Particularly the rules about paying taxes,' I said, trying to stay with the subject and stop my thoughts running backwards against my will.

I couldn't separate those rollercoaster years from the shock of Fabiola's death. If only I could have brushed over those memories, redacted them with a fat, black marker pen … I'd done my best, but the harder I tried, the sharper the memories became.

Nicki continued, oblivious. 'But look at what happened. Facebook lasted barely twenty-five years, Amazon not much longer. Google is still around, but a shadow of what it was.' She leant forward again, face alight with the passionate certainty of youth. 'None of that could have happened without government and media interference. There is a well-developed theory that the writing was on the wall for them when the US government started referring to them as Standard Social, Standard Search and Standard Commerce. Just like Standard Oil a century earlier. Too big to fail, but too big to be allowed to continue.'

'I'm sure you're planning to tell me something I don't know at some point, Nicki.'

'Sorry,' she said, apparently unfazed by my tone. 'My point is that we're in a different era, but the old rules still apply, whether in politics, media or in finance. There have always been rich and powerful people and they've always done whatever it took to stay rich and powerful. What they can't allow is brash new kids on the block threatening that power and control.'

I raised my eyebrows and struggled to restrain myself from drumming my fingers on the table. When would she get to the point?

'Bear with me,' she said. 'The campaigns which undermine the usurpers are often framed in terms of populist memes – tax avoidance, labour exploitation, privacy breaches – but these public outcries are always orchestrated from behind the scenes. Orchestrated by the vested interests who feel threatened. I'm not saying it's some sort of co-ordinated global conspiracy. It's instinctive. Like cornered animals, self-protection is in their blood.'

'And you're saying that they're going to come after Pulsar in the same way? Because we're too successful?' Nicki needed to work through this process for herself, and I needed to allow her to. Her conclusions were, however, not exactly news. A global company as powerful as Pulsar might as well have had a big archery target as a logo.

'Maybe not this year, maybe not for a few more, but at some point soon,' she said. 'We're too big, too influential. We're Standard

Personal Security. They'll have to clip our wings.'

'OK,' I said. 'Whether or not that's true, it's a coherent argument.' Of course it was true; I knew of at least ten major government bodies which were investigating ways to either force us to share our technology or to tax us into oblivion. 'Let's say you're right,' I continued. 'How would owning a political consultancy like Odell Services help us to protect ourselves?'

'Odell has become an important tool for a lot of influential players. Incumbents will want Odell to help them in the future and they certainly won't want them helping their rivals. Governments, businesses, it's all the same. They rely on the goodwill of their customers or voters. It's an existential necessity for them. But goodwill is fragile and a company like Odell can help them to keep it for longer.'

'That sounds like you're proposing a very expensive lobbying strategy.'

'I think it's more than that,' she said. 'I know you already have close relationships with the great and the good, but I'm not sure that's enough. If we could add Odell to the mix with its kingmaker reputation, it might be possible for Pulsar to stay on top of the wave for longer.'

'Hmmm,' I said. 'But how does that fit with your earlier examples? Cambridge Analytica wasn't able to help Facebook. Let's face it, they couldn't even protect themselves.'

'I know,' said Nicki. 'But that was very different. There was no co-ordinated strategy involved, and Facebook had no control over Cambridge Analytica. They both got caught with their pants down.'

Nicki sat back in her chair. Having said her piece, she was looking at me for clues. Did I agree? Was I impressed? Or had she just committed professional suicide?

Unfortunately for Nicki, looking at me wasn't going to help; I was impressed by her analysis and delighted by her conclusions, but I'd learnt my poker face from the Sphinx herself and wasn't planning on giving anything away. Surprisingly few people understood the power of silence in discussions and negotiations. Quiet nothingness is often more powerful than words, and when you allow it to grow

… and grow …

Nicki crumbled quickly enough. She needed to fill the void. 'In any case, I'm not saying that it would be easy, or even possible, it's just something that is worth considering …'

I left Nicki hanging after the meeting. Told her that I would re-read her report and think it over. She'd done everything I'd hoped for, but it wouldn't be good to move too quickly – and besides I needed to spend a little time on my other project. Luckily, I'd made sure I had a good team in place to run my businesses on a daily basis. That stuff was becoming boring while my personal projects were turning out to be anything but.

I imagined it must be similar for those people who lay down a wine for twenty years. All the anticipation building as the ideal drink date approached. Personally, I preferred to order the twenty-year-old wine whenever I wanted. Then, if it turned out to be no good, I could always send it back.

I didn't have that luxury where Nicki and Sam were concerned. If either of them turned out to be corked or simply *vin ordinaire*, there were no alternatives. I'd been forced to be patient, which had been painful but, as I started to taste the first bottles, I could see the upsides. Every sip had the potential to be a little sweeter after such a long wait.

Nicki was developing well, and it was finally time for Sam and I to meet. He'd been two years old when Fabiola died. Not able to be guilty of anything, or at least not consciously. My feelings were inextricably tangled; Sam was both her final gift and the catalyst which had led to her death. I didn't know whether to love him or to hate him. The future would have to decide.

Sam had grown up with his dad, Rupert, and I'd only been able to monitor and manage his life with a very soft touch. Rupert had become quite paranoid about technology after what happened to Fabiola and he still saw a lot of Daz who'd always had an uncanny ability to smell my presence. "Uncle Daz" was one of the few people I'd ever met who was totally immune to my charms. He'd always hated me when I was Jax, and I knew he wanted to believe she was involved in the events which led to Fabiola's death.

Fortunately, there was no evidence of that whatsoever, and he and Rupert had been forced to accept that Fabiola must have imagined all of those strange emails and cancelled appointments. The unravelling of her life had all been driven by her unstable mental state. In any case, they had no idea whether Jax was alive or dead and certainly not that Jax Daniels had become Julie Martin. I intended to keep it that way.

That soft touch meant that, rather than fitting Sam into a strategy of my creation, I'd been obliged to fit a strategy around him. A different challenge, and I had impressed even myself with the elegance of my solution.

I took another look at the CV on my desk. I shouldn't have been surprised, but Sam Blackwell had turned out to be a very good-looking young man. In fact he was gorgeous. There was something of Fabiola in his eyes and mouth and I was sure he would have her smile – charming, slightly mischievous and filled with laughter.

Time to find out. I touched my vis screen and Jane's face appeared.

'Is Mr Blackwell here?' I said, knowing perfectly well he'd been sitting in the lobby for twenty minutes.

'Yes, Ms Martin,' said Jane. 'Should I bring him in?'

'Yes please,' I said. 'And hold all my calls.'

Nothing about Sam in the flesh was a disappointment. He was tall, loose-limbed and physically confident in the way that public school boys tended to be. Rowing, rugby and cold showers hadn't done him any harm.

I remembered tapping in to one of Fabiola's conversations with her counsellor; she'd been going on and on about the snobbishness of Rupert's mother, Virginia, and how there was no way she was going to be strong-armed into sending her little boy to boarding school. If she'd really cared so much, she should have stayed around to make sure of it. Rupert on his own hadn't stood a chance.

Fit and handsome maybe, the poor boy was only twenty-four, and as he walked into my office and caught his first glimpse of the view, and of me, his mouth was hanging open like a baleen whale.

Sam took the offered seat at the low glass table and, by the time Jane had established how he liked his coffee, he'd managed to bring his lower jaw back under control. Although I was a minimalist by nature, the sparse furniture and art I had chosen was as spectacular as the view. He looked around, taking in the full splendour of the surroundings.

'Wow,' he said, at last. 'This is … well, it's amazing.'

'Thank you,' I said, lowering my eyes modestly. 'That's very kind.'

What was I doing? Shamelessly flirting with a boy just out of short trousers. It was ridiculous.

Jane brought in the coffees while I made a pretence of flicking through Sam's CV.

'You've been at the FT for two years now?' I said.

Yes,' said Sam. 'I'm in charge of collating and sorting through all of the third-party article proposals we receive. Everyone wants to have something published in the FT.'

'And what exactly does that mean day-to-day?' I asked.

'Well …' He looked up at me and that's when I saw it – the hint of steel behind the boyish charm and gentle politeness, just like Fabiola. 'I'm sorry, Ms Martin,' he said, 'but I really don't know what I'm doing here. Even though the headhunter tried her best to explain what you're looking for, I can't see how I'm a potential candidate. I haven't got any relevant experience. Let's face it, I've hardly got any real experience at all.'

'Good,' I said. 'The fact that you've got enough balls to get to the point is a plus point. I can't stand waffle.'

I thought it best not to mention that I'd been known to fire people on the spot for the sin of burbling on. The last time I'd done it had cost us almost a hundred thousand euros in compensation, but it had been worth it.

I could see that Sam was relieved to have shared his confusion, and I continued. 'Of course you don't have a CV packed with years of relevant experience, but that's not what I'm looking for. I want a fresh voice, not some jaded hack who's eventually accepted that no-one wants to read their ditchwater-dull novels and turns to ghostwriting to pay the bills. And, as an aside, the fact that you were the editor of the Cherwell newspaper for an exceptional two terms could be considered a slightly relevant qualification.'

The jaw was beginning to drop again, so I ploughed on.

'There's another factor, which couldn't be in the formal brief for good reason. You've signed our NDA?'

'Yes.'

'And I would hope you've researched me well enough to know that crossing me is inadvisable? Especially where my private life is concerned?'

'You do have quite a reputation …,' he said.

'Good. I think we understand each other,' I said. 'Then let me clarify a couple of things.' I put the CV face down on the table. 'I'm seeing this as a two-year project. It will involve the writer building a deep understanding of Pulsar today and tomorrow as well as telling the story of how the company began.'

'OK.'

'Well. Pulsar is, to all intents and purposes, me. I founded the company and still control it very tightly. If someone is going to write the story of Pulsar, they'll need to shadow me – in daily life, at meetings, at conferences and at media events. That will involve strange hours as well as a lot of time spent waiting around. I will need someone I can trust. I wouldn't pressure you to write lies, but I would expect you to write the book I want to be written – about the company and not about my private life. It will be a difficult balance.'

'I can see that,' he said. 'And it sounds fascinating, but I still don't …'

'Let me finish,' I said, raising my hand and sharpening my tone. 'I'm not a great one for making compromises. I like to have my cake and to eat it. If I'm going to spend that much time with anyone, I don't intend it to be with some fat old smartarse. I want someone young, charming and handsome.'

I looked at Sam and smiled. He didn't appear to be breathing.

'The fact that you're a presentable young man is a major factor,' I continued. 'Does that offend you?'

Don't Kid Yourself

Julie Martin's penthouse office was on the ninety-seventh floor and, when I came out of my interview, I couldn't resist running up the three flights of stairs to take a look from the top. I'd be late back to work, but work suddenly seemed a world away.

Even ten years after the opening ceremony, Shard Two was still the tallest building in Europe – not exactly dwarfing its older sister, but definitely head and shoulders taller and scooping out wider at the base. There was a great spot on Southwark Bridge to have a good view of the pair of them, straddling the Thames like the legs of the Colussus with Tower Bridge sitting toylike in between. The contrast made Tower Bridge appear somehow unreal – like an elaborately decorated birthday cake.

I'd been up to the hundredth floor observation deck once before; Dad had brought me here for my eighteenth birthday. He'd decided to take me on a boy's night out in London, which had still been the exotic "big city" to me. For reasons known only to himself, Dad had decided to mark my coming of age with a dry martini at the hottest venue in town, the Shard Two cocktail bar. I think he'd made the reservation months earlier.

Before we got to the top, I'd been giving him a hard time about his antiquated James Bond fantasies, although he didn't seem even slightly interested in my opinion. Apart from anything else, he'd insisted that I dress up. Jacket, no jeans, smart shoes – I felt like a complete prat.

One of the curious – and bloody annoying – things about my father was his habit of being right more often than not. As we'd stepped out onto the open balcony, the white light of a late May evening had transformed the grubby Thames into a ribbon of mercury and London was unfurled around me as though I was standing Gulliver-like in the centre of a huge map. I'd been up tall buildings before, but this was something else.

The breath-stealing impact wasn't only a result of the hundred floors. A lot of clever architecture and engineering was making its contribution as well. I didn't know how they did it, but there was no sensation of acceleration or weightlessness in the express lift and the absence of flashing floor numbers meant that nothing much seemed to change during the ten uneventful seconds between Ground Floor and Observation Deck. A normal lift journey, a smart, steel-panelled corridor, the hiss of opening doors, and then ... then ...

Dad had definitely enjoyed the look on my face and he'd still been chuckling to himself by the time we'd made it down to the cocktail bar and were watching our martinis being made. It was important to let him have his fun; indulging him in his little pleasures had always been a key element of our relationship and I couldn't see it changing.

My second visit to the viewing gallery was very, very different. Although the view was as impressive as before, my mind was somewhere else. What had just happened?

My confused thoughts flitted about like butterflies, moving from one impossible scenario to another, each one of them threatening my sense of reality. Was I seriously a contender for this project? Had I really just spent an hour with Julie Martin in her penthouse office at the top of Shard Two? Did that amazing woman actually want me to accompany her around the world? I hadn't even had the presence of mind to ask what the job paid.

I tried to avoid thinking about how stunning she was. I'd never had a thing for older women and Julie was forty-seven according to my research. I'd put money that nine out of ten people would have placed her at less than thirty-five but, let's face it, fancying anyone much over thirty was straying into cougar country.

The interview had encompassed the most amazing sixty minutes of my life from start to finish. Admittedly that made me sound like someone being interviewed just after they'd been kicked out of a reality TV show, but that was what I felt. I'd not seen or done anything much in my life, and certainly nothing that came close to the sublime experience of spending an hour with Julie Martin.

Adding surreal to sublime, she seemed to be seriously considering me as a candidate to write the official history of Pulsar. How insane was that?

There would be a catch, of course. A team with hidden cameras waiting to jump out and explain the joke. But why? It wouldn't be particularly funny, just sad, pathetic and cruel. And why would someone so rich and powerful get involved in something like that? None of it made any sense.

I looked down through the light mist to where the FT offices squatted next door to Shakespeare's Globe Theatre – almost spitting distance if the wind was right – and tried to imagine the look on my boss's face if I told her I was quitting. Marie had stuck her neck out to get me the job; she was a loyal company soldier, and I doubted she'd understand why I would ever consider walking away from such a gold-plated, blue-chip opportunity.

Unfortunately, it was the whole blue-chip, respectable job business which got under my skin – the thought of working my way up a corporate career ladder filled me with deep despondency and gloom. I knew it was irresponsible, but there was a whole world to see and experience.

My dad was amazingly supportive of my unconventional point of view. He'd grown up middle class and, before the Brexit vote, most kids with his background had believed they could have it all. There was a general sense of entitlement and a pushback against the money-oriented, career-focused attitude of their parents' generations – the Millenials wanted multiple interesting jobs, one or more gap years and to be part of a borderless community of global citizens.

My dad hadn't embraced that world – he'd been a little too straight, a little too conservative and, by the time he started thinking that there must be more to life than selling houses, he found himself with a young wife and a baby. When he'd had a drink or two, he would often say how much he regretted not travelling more before he got married, and I supposed a part of him wanted to live that dream vicariously through me.

Unfortunately, the Millenial dream hadn't lasted long, and the world had changed more than anybody could have imagined. By the time I entered the job market, very few people were foolish enough to walk away from good jobs, which left me nursing an impractical dream.

I checked my phone for messages. There were three missed calls from Louise DuPont at Hanson Parker, the headhunters who'd approached me about the Pulsar project in the first place. Hanson Parker were real enough; they were probably the biggest media industry search firm in London.

'Hi, Louise. It's Sam.'

'Oh, Sam. Thanks for calling back. How was it?'

'OK. I guess. I still don't understand what I was doing there.'

'Ms Martin explained the elements of the brief that weren't in the written document?'

'Yes. But …'

'… And you don't have any issues with her requirements?'

'No. I don't care about that sort of thing. But …'

Louise probably didn't have to deal with candidates talking themselves out of jobs that often. And I was sure she wasn't used to dealing with candidates as young and inexperienced as me.

'Sam!' She didn't sound angry or annoyed, although I did feel as though I'd been dragged by one ear into the headmistress's office. 'Please stop worrying about why you're on the list. It's an unusual assignment, but not the strangest I've seen. I just got off a call with Ms Martin's assistant who told me that it was a positive meeting, which is great news.'

'That's good to hear.' I didn't know what else to say.

'Apparently she's given you an assignment?'

'Yes. She asked me to draft an opening chapter for the book.'

'Will that be a problem?'

'No. Of course not. We agreed a week, but I'll have it done well before then.'

'Good. Let me know if you need anything from us.'

After she hung up, I sat down on one of the polished aluminium benches and stared at the blank screen of my phone. Louise was a senior partner at Hanson Parker and had chased me in person ten minutes after the interview. She wouldn't be doing that if there weren't some hefty fees involved. I'd probably have to start taking this seriously.

But not straight away. First, I needed to get back to work. I could come up with some excuses as I walked.

Marie was out at meetings all afternoon, and no-one else cared where I was. I was disappointed as I'd come up with an excellent story to explain my three hour lunch break; that would have to sit on ice until the next opportunity.

A few of the others on my floor were mates and four or five of us would go for an after-work drink once or twice a week, often meeting up with other friends. That was the only way to manage social life in London; everyone I knew lived out of the centre and perversely in different directions. The last thing anyone wanted was to schlep home for an hour or more on a hot, sweaty tube train and then turn around and go straight back into town.

My social group from the FT were friends, but also colleagues and I wouldn't have dared to talk to them about Pulsar. I sat at my desk until almost six o'clock pretending to work, watching blurred text dance around on the screen. I couldn't get the whole crazy idea out of my mind and was desperate to tell someone about it. My heart was pumping as a result of five or six coffees – not drunk because I wanted or needed them, but because our small cafeteria had a floor-to-ceiling glass wall with a fabulous view of Shard Two.

I'd figured out which windows belonged to Julie's office, the tiny rectangles of soft yellow light glowed in clear contrast to the harsh whiteness of the other floors. I imagined myself sitting on the designer chairs at the end of a long day, looking thoughtful, asking questions and taking notes. Maybe she'd decide that I needed a flat closer to where she lived for ease of access?

That took my mind off into taboo territory and I tried hard to close down those avenues. Easier said than done when the imagination is in full flight. My fantasies were out of the cage and soaring free – there wasn't much I could do to control them.

Karl was my Swedish flatmate. A junior solicitor for one of the big City firms, he was the most outrageously self-confident person I'd ever met – most people would probably say that self-confident was a generous way to describe him. There was no obvious reason for his cockiness; he wasn't particularly good looking, with his watery blue eyes staring out of a red-blotched pale and puffy face and lank chalk-blonde hair hanging down in an affected forelock.

He wasn't even charming or witty, but details like that weren't an issue for Karl who remained evangelically certain that he was God's gift to women – and everyone else for that matter. Anyone who dared to contradict that conviction was simply *spraying water on the goose's back* as the Swedes would apparently say. He didn't care.

And it worked. I was amazed at the string of beautiful women who gravitated to him like moths to a lamp. They must have been drawn to some kind of arrogance pheromone oozing out of him.

He was exactly the person to talk to about Julie. Although he wasn't even slightly discreet, his self-obsessed narcissism would ensure that the whole conversation would drop off his radar within an hour or two. He was delighted to share some gossip – even more so if it involved rich and beautiful women – but, if the gossip wasn't about him, it wasn't worth actually remembering.

'… You wouldn't believe how gorgeous she is.'

'I would. And I do,' said Karl in his slow, precise Swedish English. 'I've seen photos.'

Unlike me, Karl had a thing for rich, older women; his salary didn't leave him as much spending money as he needed for smart clothes and expensive restaurants. His parents were some sort of Swedish aristocracy and sent him extra cash, but any opportunity for more treats wasn't to be missed.

'She's more than gorgeous,' he said. 'What could she possibly see in you?' He raised his hands palm upwards and shrugged. 'Me? I could understand … But you?'

The fact that he wasn't joking when he said stuff like this didn't make it any less entertaining. I think it was a Scandinavian thing. The total absence of a politeness/thoughtfulness filter between brain and mouth.

'Beats me,' I said, grinning. 'I really think I've got a chance to win this contract, though. God knows why.'

'I doubt it very much,' said Karl. 'Although I do agree that it's most unusual for someone like Julie Martin to waste any time with someone like you. Are you sure it was really her?'

'Of course I'm bloody sure,' I said. 'I was sitting in her office at the top of Shard Two.'

'Hmmm,' said Karl. 'It is strange …' His eyes focused into the distance and he appeared to be thinking deeply. After a year of living together, I knew him well enough to realise he was just bored.

'Did I tell you about my new pitching wedge?' he said after a few seconds. Karl was a very good golfer. 'It's only forty-two degrees, carbon shaft …'

There was a great place for breakfast around the corner from our flat, and my favourite Saturday treat was a couple of hours settled in with the papers, sometimes with Karl, sometimes with friends and sometimes – the best times – on my own. The name, Salvador Deli, was stretching bad puns to the absolute limit, but otherwise it was perfect.

Whenever I took my dad there, he would burble on about not being able to find proper cafes any more, not like the "greasy spoons" he knew growing up. I could never figure out why I was supposed to lust after slimy gelatinous eggs, paper bacon and cardboard sausages. Soft poached eggs and sourdough toast worked for me. And what was so wrong with avocado, anyway?

Luckily for me, Karl was taking his new carbon-shafted pitching wedge out on the golf course with his Swedish friends, leaving me to enjoy a peaceful morning at Sal's. Peaceful, but not lazy; I'd taken my laptop and, after a macchiato and a plate of smashed avocado on sourdough, I was planning on finishing the first draft of my Pulsar opening chapter.

The research process had been eye-opening and eye-watering in equal measure. There was a huge amount of publicly available information about Pulsar which included details and context which surprised and shocked me more than I'd expected.

It's easy to take familiar things for granted; like everyone I knew, I'd trotted off to be fitted with Pulsar Trust inserts on my sixteenth birthday. It was no different from going to the dentist or optician – a fifteen minute painless procedure – and I'd never wasted time considering what life would be like without them.

As I read through the newspaper reports and articles from the mid-twenties, I began to understand how the world could have been a very different place if it hadn't been for Pulsar. The things we take for granted aren't carved as deeply in stone as we imagine.

I opened the pad in front of me. I began by trying to list all the instances when my Pulsar Trust implants had been used to identify me in the previous twenty-four hours: getting on the tube, getting off the tube, going in and out of the office three times, buying two coffees, buying a sandwich, activating and reactivating my computer at least ten times, using my phone maybe twice as often … On each occasion, an electronic authorisation request had been sent to the tiny devices in both my arms, they had independently verified the unique pattern of my heartbeat, compared notes and confirmed that I was indeed Sam Blackwell.

When my tally reached forty, I threw down the pencil and leant back in my chair, subconsciously rubbing the small scar on my left bicep where the first implant had been inserted. No wonder Pulsar was so successful.

As the truth about those days started to come into focus, it was easy to imagine a very different present day to the one I knew; authors and film directors had been imagining dystopian futures for a century or more, but the reasons they chose for society's collapse were never as mundane as the inability to protect identity.

I'd found a mass of information about Pulsar, but almost nothing about Julie Martin. After drawing a total blank, I'd asked one of the senior research analysts at work to help me. He was easily flattered and looked at me with smug superiority as he started digging; it wasn't going to take him long to show me how a real researcher could get results. Fifteen minutes later, the wide-eyed look on his face had spoken volumes. He was renowned for knowing every backdoor and search trick around, but the data simply wasn't there.

My second-year degree thesis had been on George Orwell and part of my research had been to examine the way Stalin's Russia had dealt with truth and history; the routine way facts and real people had been airbrushed away. A century later that sort of revisionism was almost impossible; the tentacles of the information age had worked their way into every tiny crevice of the datasphere and everyone had a digital history of some kind. These histories usually included a mass of tagged photos of youthful indiscretions which were much too dispersed to be tracked down and deleted.

Julie was an exception. Her digital life started at the same time as Pulsar and, even that life was a bland PR-drafted imitation of a real life. There were very few photographs for someone so influential and almost none of those were taken outside the professional environment.

We did find some High Court records which helped to explain the black hole which was Julie's publicly visible life. In 2032, she'd won ten million euros in compensation from the Sun newspaper. Although the details of the case were sealed, there were plenty of other references indicating that she'd sued the Sun for privacy violations. She'd taken on the best lawyers and thrown millions at the case, as well as diverting Pulsar's advertising budget away from all News Corp companies. By the time the dust had settled, two journalists, and the editor were out of work and a lesson had been learned.

Julie had made it very clear to me that she didn't want her personal life to be the star of the book and I could see that she'd gone to extraordinary lengths to protect her privacy. Although the secrecy and mystery had found their way under my skin, I wasn't intending to push any harder. That would result in a short sharp end to any chances I had of winning the dream contract.

A quiet Saturday evening and an early night had seemed like a good plan at the time. My first draft was finished; it wasn't perfect, but not shabby at all. I was off to my Granny's for lunch on the Sunday and was excited to hear what my dad and Uncle Daz would have to say.

Karl was going out to a new Scandi bar in Little Venice with his golf buddies. Although I could have tagged along, they'd all have been doing the doobie-do, doobie-da Swedish bit, congratulating themselves on being amazing chaps, and singing silly drinking songs. Fun for an hour or two, but I couldn't face a whole evening of it and the consequences of lunch in Oxford after necking gallons of rough akevit didn't bear thinking about.

Karl was also on a promise with a new girl in town – Ella or Elsa or something like that – and I would probably have ended up staggering home alone. All in all, a night in with a takeaway and a film was a much better plan.

I was going through a phase of watching classic Sci-Fi movies from the turn of the century and settled in with a Pad Thai to watch The Matrix with Keanu Reeves. In spite of the laughable special effects and the obscure plot, the vision wasn't as out there as it must have seemed back then; the newest VR gaming platforms were already able to deliver immersive full world simulations which were almost indistinguishable from the real thing.

The film had been a welcome distraction from my circular thoughts about Julie and Pulsar. Unfortunately, the diversion didn't last and I lay in bed for hours before finally getting to sleep. I couldn't have been asleep for more than half an hour when the door of the neighbouring flat slammed with enough force to knock my phone off the bedside table.

My neighbours were a nice couple from Andalucia, always smiling on the stairs if I was up early enough to catch them on their way to work. Not that night. Both their voices were loud and slurring and, after a while, I could only hear her screaming and shouting, punctuated occasionally by the flamenco-trained stomping of feet and more slamming of doors. Although, I knew a little Spanish from school, I couldn't make out a word.

Her tirade lasted for almost half an hour – I imagined him curled up in the corner of the sofa, trying to apologise for whatever it was he'd done and looking up at her with pleading eyes. And then, a final door slamming, the clattering of shoes on the stairs and … silence.

I picked up my book – a real paperback – and switched on the light. Going back to sleep was not an option; there were no more sheep in the field.

Sheep

I felt a childish urge to start skipping as I weaved a path though the Knightsbridge crowds. How could people cope with walking so slowly? It was as though their brains had been switched off and they were shuffling along on some sort of autopilot. No wonder most of them never achieved anything.

It was what the Irish called a "soft day"; a fine rain filled the air, almost a mist, but with droplets just large enough to dampen everything. No point in using an umbrella although the shuffling masses hadn't quite grasped that. Idiots. Besides, my hair was naturally straight, and I loved the feeling of fresh water on my face.

I looked at my watch – ten past. I was due to meet Dave at eleven and it wouldn't do to be early. I wasn't in a skipping mood because of him though. Dave was just business.

Pulsar had been involved with Imperial College for more than ten years. I hated the stuffy arrogance of most of the academics, but having research links with such a prestigious institution was worth the pain. Although we also had programmes running with Stamford, MIT and Tsinghua in Beijing, our link with Imperial was the most important by far and gobbled up 95% of the funding – over fifty million euros were earmarked for 2037 alone.

Professor Dave Bukowski made a pleasant change from the crusty old farts. He was only in his early thirties, but already the recognised world leader in nano-genetic research. Most importantly, he hadn't picked up the arrogance of his colleagues (yet) and still had something approaching a sense of humour.

We'd arranged to have a coffee in his favourite local haunt, Zak's

Cafe. I'd met him there a few times before and it was patently obvious why he liked the place. Apart from the best cakes for miles around and half-decent coffee, the women who frequented Zak's were South Kensington's finest. Yummy-mummies or yummy-mummies-to-be who had all of the time, all of the money and all of the motivation to look like a million dollars, day and night. For a farm-boy nerd from the Midwest like Dave, it must have been the equivalent of taking a trip to Charlie's Chocolate Factory.

I was still pleased to notice that Dave's eyes stopped wandering as soon as I walked in. I couldn't imagine what I'd do when I stopped getting that kind of reaction from men like Dave. It didn't bear thinking about.

Dave's research, which was exclusively sponsored by Pulsar, was critical to our future. Our current flagship product, Pulsar Trust, was already four years old and it wouldn't stay secure for ever. The two titanium implants – one in each arm – worked as a pair to authenticate identity based on an individual's biorhythms. They were virtually tamper-proof, but "virtually" wasn't good enough and we'd recently manage to hack them ourselves under controlled lab conditions.

Dave was the key to our next generation of products, which would combine on-the-fly DNA sampling and biorhythm matching using nano-genetic carriers. It was a few years away from being a functional solution, and we had a number of parallel projects, but this was by far the most promising. Dave was our golden boy – and didn't he know it!

Our meetings involved a lot of dull technical conversation, combined with the occasional lewd proposal from Dave. The way his mind could seamlessly bounce between genius/savant and lecher/moron was breathtaking. Fortunately, I was almost certain that I would never need to do any more than tolerate his inappropriate banter. That being said, if he'd ever realised quite how important the project was to me, I would have been in trouble. One of many reasons to develop a good poker face.

I'd arranged to meet Nicki at Zak's once Dave and I were done. It would be useful for her to meet him, even in passing, and to understand what we were working on.

My urge to skip was because I was seeing Nicki. I suspected that everyone who knew me thought I was cold and calculating, always one step ahead, never switching off. That was true to an extent, but mostly because people have a tendency to become who they pretend to be. We put on a conscious act, a carnival disguise, to achieve our goals and gradually – in thousands of changing breaths of wind – the disguise bonds with our skin, transforming us forever.

I'd played a role for so many years that I could no longer tell where the act ended and I began. Even so, there was always a place deep inside of me where nerves and excitement and uncertainty lived on and this was a hugely important day. If I had miscalculated, I might find that I had lost Nicki for ever. If my calculations were right, however …

I hadn't seen Nicki since she'd left Pulsar almost a month earlier. The look on her face when I'd told her Odell was actually my company had been exquisite. Only bettered when I explained that I'd set up the firm for almost exactly the same reasons she'd laid out to me. A small part of her might have been disappointed that I was one (or several) steps ahead of her, but what did she expect?

Almost exactly the same reasons, but not quite. Nicki had been wrong when she'd suggested that the world was still controlled by the same old elites. Most people believed that, but it wasn't entirely true.

The true locus of influence and control really had shifted forever during the data revolution. The early pioneers like Facebook and Google hadn't understood what they had, or how to exploit it. They'd started from the wrong place; a fluffy dream of empowering ordinary people, or inanities like Google's corporate mission, "Don't be Evil". Neither was a great starting point for effective global domination.

Even though the data pioneers had failed, managing elections, public reputations or any other form of power broking was no longer about murmured conversations taking place in dark wood-panelled rooms. Influence wasn't the exclusive domain of privileged men sharing golf and sailing anecdotes whilst slowly marinating themselves in a fug of whisky fumes and cigar smoke. Amazingly enough, those men, and a token few alpha females, still believed they had a firm grip on the reins of power, even though they were barely holding on by their fingertips.

Their world had started to fade into sepia-tinged nostalgia even as the millennium clock was ticking away the final seconds of the twentieth century. Nothing happens overnight, but by the time Nicki learned about Odell, those rich and powerful establishment figures were well on their way to becoming mere puppets.

The future of true power really did lie in the ability to access and manipulate huge amounts of personal data. With enough access and the right skills, entire populations were no more than herds of sheep moving from pen to pen as one or two sheepdogs flashed yapping at their heels. And, whatever they imagined, the old guard had always been beholden to the masses.

It wasn't easy. People, like sheep, had the ability to be stubborn and contrary, but with the right sheepdogs and a good whistle, it wasn't that difficult either.

Nicki had taken longer than expected to become convinced, but I had a lot of hard data to back me up. I could tell she was disappointed that I was turning her primary thesis upside down. Once she was on board with the logic, however, she'd started to get excited by the implications.

Managing that much data effectively would require massively complex algorithms which could operate independently and evolve. I understood the basics, but Nicki had been living in that world since she was sixteen.

Any remaining disappointment she might have had evaporated the instant I told her that I wanted her to become CEO of Odell. She didn't have the political, espionage or relationship skills, but those were ten-a-penny. What Odell needed now – and what Nicki brought to the party – was her expertise in AI and quantum computing.

And, of course, she was the Chosen One.

We'd agreed that Nicki would have a month at Odell before we met again. She needed to get to grips with the details and develop her ideas before we could have a meaningful strategic discussion. As she walked into Zak's, she was almost bouncing with excitement. I knew that feeling so well – the sensation of a mind on fire, fizzing with so many ideas and visions that it feels as though they're leaking out of your mouth and nose and eyes and ears in streams of glistening, golden genius-dust.

She would need to control her impatience for a little longer. I wanted her to meet Dave. And I wanted him to meet her.

'Nicki. This is Professor Dave Bukowski.'

I watched carefully as the two of them shook hands and sized each other up. Dave might have had a brain the size of the planet, but he didn't have the good manners to stand up for a lady. Not such a big thing where he came from, apparently.

Seeing them together reminded me that Dave was fast becoming my third "project". Not like Nicki or Sam for obvious reasons, but they were all lead actors.

'Nicki used to work for us at Pulsar,' I said. 'Until a month ago. But she's an ambitious lady, and she's moved on.'

'I'm surprised you're still talking to her,' said Dave. 'Not really your style.'

'Nicki's an exception,' I said, smiling. 'Life would be dull without exceptions, wouldn't it?' I pushed my chair backwards and started to stand. 'Are we done, Dave? If not, I'm sure Nicki can give us another ten minutes.'

'No. We're good,' he said, his brow furrowing as though he was trying to remember something. 'I'll see you in a few weeks at the dinner.'

Home Comforts

Despite the lack of countable farm animals, I did fall asleep eventually and woke up at ten o'clock with the book spreadeagled over my nose and slobber all over the cover. After all my sensible plans, I was late for the train and had to skip breakfast and run for the tube.

I didn't run fast enough and ended up on the slow train which stopped at every station between Paddington and Oxford, and which was going to make me very late for lunch. At least I had plenty of time to catch my breath while pottering through the urban sprawl of West London and mile after mile of green fields with the odd glimpse of boats on the Thames.

It had been good to tell someone about Pulsar. Karl might have been less than a listening audience, but the act of actually describing the situation had helped me to stand back and look at it objectively. Whatever angle I took, I kept coming back to the conclusion that I had a realistic chance of getting the job.

If I did, it was also reasonable to assume that the salary would be decent and there would be a lot of expenses-paid travel. The experience would be exceptional, and would look good on my CV – probably better than another two years plugging away at the FT.

I was lining up my arguments like ducks in a row – mentally preparing for the grilling I was about to get from my grandmother. Granny was a firm believer in traditional post-war values – a job is for life, look after the bird in the hand, keep your head down, don't rock the boat.

Post-war values? It was incredible that so many references were still being made to the Second World War even though we were close to the centenary of the first shots being fired. A hundred years of relative peace was a reason to drag out the bunting; there'd been a few close calls since then and there were still lots of local conflicts, but humankind must be doing something right.

My conversation with Karl had also helped me to pour a bucket of icy water over my childish fantasies about Julie Martin. She wanted me to ghostwrite a book about her business and she had some unorthodox ideas about the candidate qualifications. That was it. No reason or room for imagined innuendo.

Dad was waiting in the car park, standing next to his new, red Mini Cooper. He looked good for his age, still wearing his trademark chinos, blue shirt and yellow jumper draped over his shoulders. He even had enough hair left to stop his Raybans falling down.

'Big night?' he asked as he gave me a hug. He stepped back and looked at my face. A single father of an only son could answer that question easily without waiting for – or caring about – whatever answer the son might come up with.

'You wouldn't believe it,' I said, grinning. 'For once, I'm totally innocent.'

He laughed as we got in the car. 'I might even believe you,' he said, 'but you're still late and you know what your Granny's like.'

We pulled away silently, and I heard him tut-tutting next to me.

'Drives well. Doesn't it?' I said, knowing full well why he was irritated.

'It doesn't feel right,' he said. 'It's not only the absence of noise. It makes my stomach feel as though it's falling backwards. There's something not natural about it.'

'Let's face it, Dad,' I said. 'Cars have never been that natural, have they?'

Although petrol cars had been banned for over a year, Dad was an old-school petrol head and had no plans to become an electric convert. Him grumbling about the imminent – and now recent – death of the internal combustion engine was part of the soundtrack of my life.

He laughed. 'Good to see you, boy. Granny says she hasn't

cooked you lunch for ages and Daz should be along later.'

'Excellent,' I said. 'Belly pork?'

'In the oven,' he said. 'She's been at it all morning.'

Granny's Sunday roasts were legendary, and I was suddenly very hungry.

'How's Gramps?' I said.

'I've not seen him since last week,' said Dad, 'but he'll be the same. This isn't something which gets better. He probably won't recognise you.'

My Gramps had been the glue which held our family together in the years after my Mum died. I'd been too small to understand anything, and the true story of her death had revealed itself bit by bit as I grew up. Dad had been a great father, but there'd always been a cloud hanging over him and I'd learned to spot the times when he was putting on a cheerful act for my benefit.

It wasn't until I was in my teens and learned that Mum had taken her own life that I began to understand what lay behind his sadness. I must have been unbearable – angry and resentful – and I hadn't been able to see past my own misery until Gramps sat me down and explained.

He made me understand how both my dad and Granny thought they should have done more to help Mum and how they each blamed themselves for what happened. Over a couple of years, and many quiet conversations in his small fishing boat, he helped me to realise how much courage it had taken for Dad to push back his feelings of grief and guilt so that he could look after me.

Gramps had always been strong; his confidence and sense of humour had been exactly what we'd all needed to support us through those hard times. When I'd needed to escape, I would always run to him for refuge and he'd always known exactly what to say, or when to say nothing at all.

As I sat next to my father, driving silently up the gravel drive of The Old Vicarage, I realised that I'd been avoiding coming here since Gramps started to decline. I hated seeing him with the light gone from his eyes and still childishly hoped that he'd miraculously turn a corner and come back to us.

We almost managed to get out of the car before Granny came out of the house. She moved quickly for someone who must have been almost eighty and her beaming face was solid evidence that she was very pleased to see us. I felt my own twinges of guilt and made a quick mental note to come and visit more frequently.

'Hello you two,' she said. 'Just in time.' She gave me a hug; her grip was still strong, but her body seemed light and insubstantial – almost bird-like – as though her muscles and bones were preparing for flight.

'Hi Granny,' I said. 'Sorry it's been so long.'

'Oh, don't you worry about that,' she said, scurrying round the car to give Dad his welcome hug. 'You're here now. That's what matters.'

As we walked into the hall, I peered through the living room door, expecting to see Gramps in his usual place. His chair was empty, cushions plumped up and untouched.

'Granny,' I called over my shoulder. 'Where's …'

'Come on through,' she said, striding down the hall towards the kitchen. 'Daz said he'd be late and that we should start. The crackling will be ruined if we don't eat straight away.'

I looked at my dad who shrugged his shoulders before following his mother into the kitchen. 'Better do what we're told,' he said.

Eventually we were all sitting down with full plates in front of us and Granny couldn't find reasons to avoid my question.

'Where's Gramps,' I asked her. 'How is he?'

Granny seemed old and frail as she looked first at me and then at my father. Her eyes were watery, the piercing blue gaze diluted to the washed-out aquamarine of a bullfinch egg.

'He's upstairs in bed,' she said. 'He's been there for a couple of days now. He's not well enough to come down.'

'Has the doctor been?' said Dad.

'Of course he has,' she snapped. 'He thinks that John would be better off in a hospice.'

'Well, maybe he's right,' said Dad. 'It must be very difficult for you to …'

'No!' she said. 'You know how much he'd hate that, Rupert.'

'Yup,' he said, looking down at the table. 'I know that …' He looked up at his mother. '… But I'm going to organise someone to come and help you, Mum. You can't manage all by yourself.'

As I watched the two of them, I realised what a selfish child I still was. All I'd been thinking about was the way I felt about Gramps. This was so much more difficult for them – a wife and a son – and I still expected them to be available to comfort me. It was time to grow up.

'Can we see him?' I asked, after the two of them had been glaring at each other for what seemed like an age.

'Not now,' said Granny. 'He'll be sleeping. We'll go up before you leave.'

'Anyway,' said Granny, serving second helpings to me and Dad without asking. 'Enough talk about John. He'd hate it. He's eighty-one, and he's had a wonderful life. What about you, Sam? Is there anyone special in your life?'

Nothing if not predictable. 'Not at the moment, Granny,' I said. 'Lou and I broke up a couple of months ago.'

'Lou?' she said, tilting her head to one side. 'Oh, Louisa. Shame. She was nice.' If I'd had to guess, her look was intended to express pity and disappointment. 'Pretty little thing, too.'

'Yes. She was lovely,' I said. 'But she moved to Munich, and it all got a bit complicated.'

'Hmmm,' she said. 'Relationships are always complicated, Sam. They always take a bit of effort and you don't want to leave it too late.'

'Of course not, Granny,' I said. 'Anyway, changing the subject. I might have a very exciting new job opportunity …'

The next half hour unfolded in an even more predictable fashion. Me trying to explain about the Pulsar opportunity, Granny not understanding and mostly disapproving, my dad interested and excited and waiting for an opportunity to ask me more. The ringing of the doorbell brought merciful relief.

Uncle Daz made any situation easier. He had a rhythmic calm which seemed to ripple steadily out from his core in slow-motion waves. A committed anarchist all his life, he was the last person anyone would have expected to become close friends with my Granny. I don't think he fitted a single one of her ridiculous social criteria.

He enveloped us in hairy-bearded bear hugs, each in turn, before wrapping an arm around Granny's shoulders and steering her out into the hall.

'We'll catch up in a minute,' he said to me and my dad. 'I want ten minutes with Virginia first.'

As he walked out, my father turned to me and spoke quietly. 'Daz has been calling your granny once or twice a day for the past few weeks. He's been amazing.'

Daz was a mental health nurse with a lifetime of experience and probably understood what was happening to Gramps better than most GPs. He would be able to give Granny the right advice on what was best for him and, just as importantly, for her.

They were out for a very long ten minutes which gave me and Dad time to clear up the kitchen. We expected to be in trouble for our unasked-for interference later on, but Granny had looked really tired.

By the time the unlikely couple returned, we were sitting back at the table, feeling pleased with ourselves and finishing off the delicious bottle of Burgundy we'd liberated from Gramps's cellar.

As Granny bustled past me to put the kettle on, I couldn't help noticing that her eyes were red; Daz didn't believe in white lies.

'So, young man. I hear you're about to sell out to the biggest, tax-avoiding, exploitative corporate devil of all time?' said Daz as he eased himself into the bench seat next to the Aga.

'It's not like I've been made an offer,' I said. 'Let's not get carried away.'

'But if they offer you the job?' he said. 'You'll take it? Despite everything I've tried to teach you?'

'Like a shot,' I said. 'I've thought it through and can't see any downsides.'

Daz shook his head from side to side slowly before grinning

through his beard. 'I suppose it's no worse than real estate,' he said, looking at my dad. 'You're a pair of lost causes. I give up.'

Granny had made it back to the table with a pot of tea and a heaped plate of home-made brownies. 'Don't be so mean to him, Daz,' she said. 'He's very excited.'

Would wonders never cease? I'd been terrified that she'd disapprove and there she was fighting my corner.

'Now, Sam,' she continued. 'You said you'd written some sort of introduction as part of the interview. Aren't you going to read it to us?'

All Coming Together

Dave took his time leaving Zaks; there were so many distractions on the way. Eventually he pushed reluctantly through the door and out onto the street. I turned back to Nicki.

'So, who's Professor Dave then,' she said. 'He looks young to be an academic.'

I gave her the potted history of Dave and our plans, but could see that she wasn't fully engaged. She wanted to talk about Odell and I had to admit that I was equally excited to hear what she had to say. The professor's nano-technology could wait.

She didn't need much of a nudge and seconds later was bent forward over the table, eyes wide and shining, preaching at me in a stage whisper.

'It's amazing. There's so much more potential than I imagined. The user database is unique. We can link social media and demographic data directly to over four billion people. Between seventy and eighty per cent of the voting population in the G10 markets. Even with the AI systems we already have, we can tailor personal messaging and adverts to every one of those four billion. Every individual will react differently to that kind of manipulation but, when we're looking at thousands and tens of thousands, the herd response can be predicted with statistical certainty.'

I smiled at her and shrugged my shoulders.

'I know. I know,' she went on. 'I should stop telling you things that you obviously already know.' She took a deep breath. 'It's still amazing, though. No-one else has anything close – not even the NSA. No wonder Odell is always on the winning side.'

'No wonder, indeed,' I said. 'Let's face it, the entire universe operates on the basis of random quantum movements. Why should tens of millions of people be any less predictable?'

Nicky nodded vigorously and, having released the head of steam that had been building inside her, she seemed to calm down and become more serious. 'Obviously, there are issues,' she continued. 'I can guess where the user profiles must have come from. Aren't we exposed?'

What Nicki didn't understand about me was the way my mind worked. At times, I almost wondered if I could actually see the future, but it wasn't that; I had the capacity to see multiple futures, each one laid out in infinitely dividing decision trees spreading far into the distance. I'd seen, and planned for, this particular scenario from the first days of Pulsar. And I'd covered all my bases.

I was hoping to glimpse similar abilities in Nicki, but sadly she appeared to have a more pedestrian form of intelligence; she was extremely sharp and analytical, but I couldn't see any real evidence of the clarity and certainty I was looking for.

'We can always get caught out,' I said. 'There's nothing more foolish than blind hubris. But Pulsar's user terms have always included a right to collect and use data for marketing purposes. The company might, and probably will, be obliged to delete or ring fence the profile data eventually, but the data we currently have is legitimate.'

'But Odell has nothing to do with Pulsar and we don't exactly use the data for marketing purposes do we?' said Nicki. 'Did Pulsar have the right to hand over four billion user profiles?'

'Ah,' I said. 'There's the thing.' I shrugged and grinned at her. 'It might be that Odell "obtained" that data without any actual permission as such.'

She looked at me with eyebrows arched. 'And the traceability?'

'Until they figure out how to reconstruct the journey of a physical hard drive in a handbag, I don't think that'll be a problem.'

'Good,' she said, moving on without a pause. 'Then we can park that. According to my initial estimates, we already have enough profiles to last at least twenty years even if we can't access updates going forwards. Probably longer. This gives Odell a massive competitive advantage.'

She kept stating the blindingly obvious, but I didn't care. My biggest worry had been that she would struggle to accept the questionable origins of Odell's massive database. Many of my plans for her would have been seriously compromised if she'd developed a sudden attack of morality.

By the time she'd finished her summary, I was even more certain we were on the same page. There was one more piece of the jigsaw to find and slot into place, but we were almost there.

Nicki wanted to talk me through the detailed numbers and assumptions she'd prepared for me, but I had a treat waiting for me at the office and was impatient to get back.

'Leave it with me,' I said to her. 'I'll spend some more time going through your report and we'll meet back here in a week or so when I'm back from the States.'

Her face sank as I picked up the folder, stood and turned to leave. Why were people always so needy?

'This is good work,' I said, stopping and spinning around to face her again. 'Really good work. Well done, Nicki.'

I waited long enough to acknowledge her grateful smile before leaving.

Although I didn't intend to start the book project until the New Year, I'd asked Sam to write a draft opening chapter as part of the final stage of the interview process. He'd been told there were three other short-listed candidates and the draft chapter would be an important factor in my final decision. Amusingly, he hadn't been even slightly put off by my admission that a key competency requirement was to be young and good looking.

What was it about men? Was it simply a hang over from millennia of unchallenged dominance? In a parallel scenario, a female candidate would almost certainly have been outraged and might well have sued me. Sam appeared to have simply taken it as a compliment and not felt even slightly patronised or demeaned. If I wanted eye candy, he would be happy to oblige.

One way or the other, he'd clearly moved from wondering why he was a candidate, to being very keen to be offered the job. I'd given him a week, but I had my draft chapter in three days. A single sheet of A4, close typed and crisp between my fingers.

That was my treat, and I felt a warm glow spreading through me as I sank into my chair and started to read.

PULSAR: BEHIND THE FIREWALL (Draft Opening Chapter)
When the world's banks decided to disable all online banking software in the autumn of 2025, a fundamental pillar of society started to crumble. Advances in crack-hack technology were making all existing forms of identity protection highly vulnerable and concerns about personal online security soared. Passwords, fingerprints, facial recognition; none of them could be trusted.

Punchy title, punchy first sentence. Sam might even end up writing a decent book as well … As well as what?

Global infrastructures had become almost completely reliant on internet-based interconnectivity. Without the ability to protect identity and to control online transactions, forecasters were predicting that the world's existing networks – in particular banking and online retail – would collapse within less than five years.
The economic and social consequences of this implosion were predicted to cost the global economy over 25 trillion dollars per year for the foreseeable future.
Luckily for us, those forecasters didn't take into account Julie Martin and Pulsar.

I was uncomfortable seeing my name in print for all sorts of reasons, but the myth of Julie Martin was inextricably bound up with the Pulsar story and couldn't be completely ignored. As long as the book didn't stray into my personal life or background, it would be all right.

Julie Martin was already an internationally recognised personal security expert when the systems started to break apart. She was a regular on the conference circuit and her 2015 book, 'How much is your Life Worth? Protecting your Identity in a Digital World.' had already become a key text. But when, in early 2023, she started to publish articles predicting a global security meltdown within two years, most people thought she had lost her touch.

Her predictions would prove eerily precise and almost all the world's foremost experts – including government agencies – were left with egg on their face. Demands for her consultancy services soared and she could have charged astronomical fees. But Julie had other plans.

Pulsar Plc was already eighteen months old by then and, as yesterday's dog's dinner started to hit the fan, both Julie and Pulsar were ready.

Was there a place for that kind of tongue-in-cheek language in a corporate book? It didn't quite cross the line, though. And it might not be such a bad idea to lighten things up a little.

By 2025, most major technology companies and banks were committed to fingerprint recognition as a means of secure identification. When a Russian hackers' co-operative launched a kit which allowed even amateurs to lift fingerprints and create latex simulations, there was widespread panic.

A number of researchers had already recognised that the unique shape of our cardio-rhythms might be a more foolproof option. They struggled, however, to find a way to match the rhythms quickly and accurately.

Julie Martin's 'moment of truth' was to recognise that the technology was already in place to solve this issue. She only needed to acquire the necessary copyrights and patents and to build the right commercial structure.

Matching cardio-rhythms quickly using small and noisy samples had always been a stumbling block. Julie Martin's most significant insight in those early days was to recognise that the problem had already been solved.

Almost twenty years earlier a team of academics from MIT had developed a unique waveform-matching technology to power a music-recognition business. When Julie Martin approached them, they were in financial difficulties and she was able to acquire an exclusive global licence for matching cardio-rhythms – fully protected by their patents – for a minimal upfront payment and a small ongoing licence fee.

By the time the dust had settled, they were making much more from this licence than from their entire music business. It was, however, only a tiny fraction of the billions being made by Julie Martin and Pulsar.

Not bad. Not bad at all. I found myself wanting to read on, to know how the story continued. Young Sam was actually going to make a decent fist of the book.

I threw the sheet of paper onto the table and leant back in my chair with my eyes closed. He really was a very attractive young man.

And that smile – Fabiola's smile – I looked forward to seeing that again.

Pinch Me I'm Dreaming

'Hello?'

'Good morning. Is that Mr Blackwell?'

'Yes.'

'It's Hannah, Louise DuPont's assistant. From Hanson Parker.'

'Oh, yes. I emailed the draft chapter to you.'

'That's right.'

'Did you get it OK?'

'Yes. No problem. That's why I'm calling.'

I'd known in my gut that I wouldn't be offered the Pulsar job, but had hoped to hold on to the fantasy a while longer. It was only a couple of days since I'd sent in the draft.

'Louise is in meetings, but she asked me to call.'

'OK ...?'

'She wanted you to know that Pulsar would like to make you an offer.'

'I see. I understand completely ... What?'

'You're their preferred candidate.'

That wasn't possible. My heart was pounding, and I felt the blood rushing to my cheeks.

'Could you hold on a minute,' I said, walking as quickly as I could to the door. An open plan office wasn't the place to be having this conversation. 'I'm at work.'

'Of course.'

I half ran, half skipped down the corridor and pushed out of the main doors onto the South Bank.

'OK. I'm out now. Could you repeat that, please?'

'Pulsar would like you to write the official history of the company as per the brief. They want you to start as soon as possible.'

I felt my lips flopping up and down fishlike, pumping silent air. Long seconds passed as I tried to understand what was happening. 'But ... that's amazing ... I'm sorry, but this must be a joke. I'm waiting for the punch line.'

'Not a joke, Mr Blackwell. Are you available to meet with Louise at our offices? Tomorrow morning at ten?'

'Yes. Yes, of course. I'll be there.'

I stood on the South Bank leaning against the blue cast-iron railings, picking at the flaking paint with the edge of my thumb and staring out across the water. I spotted Daz before he'd made it half way across the Millenium Bridge.

As always, the bridge was packed with tourists shuttling between St Pauls and the Tate Modern, all stopping in the middle for photos and getting in each other's way. The cloud of personal selfie drones competing for free space above them must have made the chances of taking a decent photo almost zero. Technology didn't always make things better.

Uncle Daz stood out; taller and bigger than most, he was also wearing his trademark black donkey jacket while most of the tourists were in T-shirts or strappy tops.

I watched him thread a path through the erratic and unpredictable crowd, moving to his own unique rhythm. He was one of those big guys with dancer's feet whose bulk seemed to defy the laws of gravity – light and unexpectedly graceful.

There was something deeply reassuring about Daz. It wasn't only with me, he had the same effect on most people. If life started to take over and to get the upper hand, a short time spent in his company was enough to slice through the Gordian knot of most personal tangles.

He rarely gave advice or explained how to fix things. He didn't need to. When Daz was around, the right way forward soon presented itself as something obvious and simple. I'd been watching him perform that magic for years and was still no closer to figuring out how it worked.

'Thanks for coming, Daz,' I said. 'I couldn't get through to Dad. I've been trying since last night.'

'Well, he's got that thing, hasn't he?'

'What thing?'

'The thing he goes to every year … In the South of France. You know?'

'Oh that thing,' I said, laughing. 'The property conference.'

'That's the one,' said Daz. 'Can't think of anything worse.' He shook his head slowly. 'He'll have his phone off. Probably sleeping off a massive hangover.'

'I doubt it,' I said. 'But that explains why he's not picking up. I sort of knew he was going and then forgot.'

'Anyway. What's so bloody urgent?' said Daz. 'I had to call in a favour to get off my shift early. It's gonna cost me down the line.'

'Sorry,' I said. 'I had to talk to someone.' The glee which bubbled inside me was desperate to burst out, but I held it together somehow. 'They've offered me the job.'

Big bushy eyebrows arched skyward and for a moment even Daz was lost for words. 'What? The Pulsar book? No way.'

'Yes way,' I said, suddenly feeling like a small boy. 'I spent the morning at the headhunters. Two-year contract, a basic of a hundred grand a year, all expenses paid and a bonus of another hundred grand on publication.'

Daz stared at me. 'That must be double what you're earning at the moment? Even leaving out the bonus.'

'More than double,' I said.

Daz grinned and wrapped me in a hug. 'Well done, boy,' he said. 'You may be selling your soul, but at least you got a good price.' He let me go and stood back, hands still resting on my shoulders. 'Your dad's gonna be so proud. When do you start?'

'That's why I wanted to speak to Dad,' I said. 'I start tomorrow. I'm flying out tonight to meet Julie in LA … First-Class.'

Although I'd grown up in a comfortable and solid middle class world, I'd only ever flown at the back of the plane and I'm sure the same applied to my dad. It wouldn't have surprised me to learn that

Daz had never been on a plane, let alone turned left into a world of fine dining, fold-out beds and champagne on tap.

When I'd told Karl, he'd glared at me and mumbled something unintelligible in Swedish before turning around and disappearing into his bedroom. The outrageous cheek of me hijacking his fantasies was apparently too much to bear.

I'd never spared a thought for the stupid trappings of wealth, but when they suddenly started to be rolled out in front of me, I couldn't help being desperately, childishly excited; in a few hours I would walk up to the First-Class counter, to be greeted by beautiful stewardesses who would then usher me through priority queues to the First-Class lounge.

I could tell that Daz was beginning to think I was winding him up. 'So. No notice period?' he said. 'No orderly handover? You just walked in and told your boss you were leaving immediately, did you?'

'No,' I said. 'By the time I got in to see Marie, her boss had already told her what was happening. It appears that Julie Martin has a habit of getting what she wants, and when she wants it.'

'You're serious, aren't you?' said Daz.

I couldn't stop myself giggling. 'A hundred per cent,' I said. 'She wants me to take her to the 2037 Grammys tomorrow night. Pulsar are the main sponsor.'

A few hours into my new role and I could already see how going back to real life was going to be a shock. My only experience of the kind of life Julie led was through Reality TV shows and documentaries. They made the whole "Lifestyles of the Rich and Famous" thing seem tawdry and tacky, something to laugh at and despise. It was the only reason I would ever watch shows like that in the first place.

A-List life wasn't quite like that in practice.

The First-Class flight experience was everything I'd imagined and more, as demonstrated by one of the standout moments which came a few minutes after my first meal. I was leaning back in my chair, single malt in hand, browsing through the movie selection when the stewardess – not a disappointment – came up to me smiling and carrying a telephone handset.

'I have your father on the phone,' she said. 'May I tell him you're available?'

How many twenty-four-year-olds have that happen to them? I took the phone and laid it on as thickly as I could for twenty minutes, showing off like a puffed up Bird of Paradise while my dad indulged me with a string of appreciative grunts and exclamations. Apparently he wasn't as surprised as Daz had been, which did nothing to diminish my swollen-headed rambling. He also waited to add some fatherly advice until just before he hung up.

'Try and remember that there's another world out there, Sam,' he said. 'The one where you belong. Have your fun, but don't lose touch with reality and who you really are.'

Even though they were probably wise words, spoken from the heart, they were fading even as I handed the phone back to the stewardess and picked up my drink. I swirled the amber-gold liquid round and round, watching the hypnotic reflections glint and glisten as I felt an unbidden smile stretch my cheeks.

Wise words were all well and good, but my plan was to swan dive into the sapphire-blue waters of my new world with arms stretched out and eyes wide open. Real life was overrated.

After a polite welcome from American customs, I was stuffed in a black limo and whisked from LA airport to the Beverly Wilshire. No mundane check-in procedures for me – I was immediately ushered up to my room by the assistant manager, flanked by two fawning white-gloved bellboys.

Room was the wrong word; they'd given me an entire apartment. I'd never seen anything remotely like it, even in films. My welcome team led me like a half-sleeping child through the two bedrooms, the massive lounge, the dining room and the humongous wetroom with sauna. The assistant manager was talking continuously, almost certainly explaining how everything worked, but I didn't hear a word – I was needing all of my energy to stop my mouth from hanging open.

It wasn't until they showed me the small maid's apartment that I began to lose control of the giggling reflex which had been bubbling up inside of me since I'd left London. It was all too ridiculous; I wanted to scream and shout with glee, but suspected that wasn't the "done thing".

It took several more painful minutes to usher them out of the room and to sprint back to the sauna. As the door slid closed with a soft hiss of hermetic seals, I exploded, screaming cowboy "yeehahs" until my throat hurt, before collapsing in a heap on the wooden slatted floor.

I must have lain flat out for ten minutes, cycling between controlled deep breathing and uncontrollable fits of snorting giggles. Eventually I calmed down. Although it wouldn't be the last time that I was overwhelmed by the surreal transformation of my life, at least the initial hysteria was out of my system.

The sauna was minimalist to say the least – a perfect cube of unbroken frosted glass, back-lit on all sides in a diffused crimson glow. There was nothing as crass as a heater with stones; the cube was empty apart from two simple benches, seemingly folded from single pieces of wood. I couldn't see any indication of how the heat and steam would appear and even the door had slid into place with no visible joins.

I examined the touch panel on the wall which glowed with dials for lighting, temperature and humidity. There didn't appear to be a button to open the door. Surely it would be obvious? Why hadn't I listened to the assistant manager's explanations?

As I stared at the unhelpful display, fingers of panic grabbed my throat and squeezed – memories of suffocating blackness flooding in. It had only been a stupid childhood game – nothing unusual for a nine-year-old, but I'd never forgotten the moment when I pulled the car boot closed. I could still remember the crisp solid finality of the lock clicking into place and the realisation that my plan wasn't so clever after all. Even though my father had rescued me after a few minutes, I'd hated confined spaces ever since.

There was nothing helpful on the stupid screen and I jabbed randomly at the dials, only succeeding in turning on the heat. How ridiculous! A massive triumph of design over practicality. At least there was an alarm symbol in the corner of the screen – a bright red, flashing bell. If I pressed that, I would look like a complete idiot …

The door slid open to reveal the smug smile of one of the bell boys – had he been standing outside?

'Is everything all right, sir,' he said. 'The sauna alarm button was triggered.'

I took a deep breath and stepped out into the bathroom. 'Thanks. I'm fine,' I said. 'I couldn't figure out how to open the door.'

'Ah,' he said. 'It's actually very easy. Just touch anywhere on the door …' He reached out and the door slipped open obediently. '… And it opens.'

'Thank you,' I said, feeling like a village idiot let loose in the big city. 'I should have guessed.'

'Not at all, sir,' he said. 'We should have explained more clearly. I do apologise. Will that be all?'

As he closed the door behind him, I wondered if I'd have preferred him to laugh in my face rather than as soon as he was out of sight.

I'd slept well on the plane and, although I wasn't sure what day it was, I felt great. The adrenaline from my sauna debacle had settled down to a manageable level and, as I'd never been too worried by making a prat of myself, I forgot about the shame almost immediately.

The phone rang as I walked back into the lounge:

'Mr Blackwell?'

'Yes.'

'I have a message from Ms Martin.'

'Yes?'

'She would like you to meet her in the lobby at six o'clock this evening.'

'OK. Thank you.'

'… And she suggests the blue Armani. You'll find it in the closet.'

'That's fine. Thank you.'

What Armani? What closet? The place was full of cupboards and closets.

As it turned out, it wasn't difficult to solve that puzzle. There were two huge wardrobes in the main bedroom and each of them was filled with designer clothes – maybe twenty jackets and trousers, shirts and shoes to match. There were even drawers full of boxer shorts and socks.

I found the blue Armani and tried it on. It was no surprise that it turned out to be a perfect fit. I stood in front of the full-length mirror and turned sideways, brushing my fingers across the smooth silk and trying to look rugged and handsome.

A room full of designer clothes and a suite at the Beverly Wilshire; I might as well have been playing the happy hooker in Pretty Woman. The parallels were uncanny, and I thought back to watching the film with my dad – he always said that the Julia Roberts character looked just like my mum.

What would she have thought if she could see me now?

I hadn't seen Julie since the interview and my heart was in my mouth when I saw her walk across the lobby towards me. It must take a lot to turn heads in the lobby of the Beverly Wilshire, but Julie managed it. She was wearing some sort of body-hugging, red, backless dress and the narrowest, tallest, pointiest shoes I'd ever seen. She was stunning.

'You clean up well enough,' she said, looking me up and down. 'Were the clothes OK?'

I guessed that it wouldn't be smart to tell her that she cleaned up pretty well herself. I needed to remember that I was at work.

'They were amazing,' I said. 'All of them were a perfect fit. And you've been so generous with the First-Class flight ... and the room ...'

'... Nothing to do with generosity,' she said, cutting me off. 'I need you to look the part ... And you'll learn soon enough that I can be extremely demanding. I don't need much sleep and I'll expect you to fit in with my schedule, day or night. We'll travel a lot and I want you to be as well rested as possible. We'll also spend time working in your room and I don't intend to sit in some cupboard.'

She definitely had a way about her. A way of making people feel like her property. It wasn't quite as demeaning as that, not a master-slave attitude. More that she thought it was natural for everyone around her to prioritise her wishes and needs above their own. I figured I could live with that for a couple of years.

The red carpet was a let down. On television, it always appeared that it was reserved for the A-list celebrities. The reality was that everyone made their way through the gauntlet of screaming fans – ordinary invitees and superstars mixed together. The TV cameras just knew how to keep the rabble out of the picture.

It was only after we'd made our way through to the main arena entrance that the selection process began. Julie's bodyguard whispered in the ear of an attendant and we were funnelled into a narrow grey corridor which ran down the length of the building.

I'd always been puzzled by the small blocks of empty seats at major events. The Wimbledon Men's Final, Henley Regatta, a stadium gig or a Twickenham international, it didn't matter. Look carefully at the shoulder-to-shoulder crowd and two or three little islands would stand out in the sea of fans.

Five minutes after we arrived at the Grammys I had my answer. Those were the VIP seats, and the VIPs had more important things to do. Actually going into the stadium to watch the match, show or concert was for the normal, ticket-buying plebs.

We reached the end of the corridor, a fire door opened and we walked into the noise and hubbub of a posh cocktail bar, filled with gorgeous people and familiar faces. Images of the awards stage and the arena flickered on a big screen in the corner, but no-one in the room seemed even slightly interested. A select few had a role to play on stage and they would disappear for ten or twenty minutes to retouch their make-up and present an award. Beyond that, the real action was backstage in the Green Room.

The 79th Grammys had already been under way for five hours by the time we arrived and the major awards were coming up. As main sponsor, Julie was presenting the Lifetime Achievement Award to Ed Sheeran who, at less than fifty, was the youngest recipient ever.

Ed had been making hit records since before I was born and had been a key part of the soundtrack of my life – it was difficult to imagine a year without a new Ed Sheeran album. Other artists lost the plot, became self-indulgent or ran out of things to say. Ed kept on churning out new material, fresh and relevant and ... and ... there he was, walking towards me and Julie with a massive grin on his face.

Donkeys

Nicki was waiting for me at Zak's. The café was around the corner from my flat and meeting at either one of our offices would be a bad idea. At eight-thirty in the morning, Zak's was almost empty; the yummy-mummies-to-be weren't up yet and the yummy-mummies were still on their way back from the school run.

I'd already read though the detailed financial plans, and we spent half an hour talking through her assumptions. I was impatient to hear her explain why her sales forecasts assumed so many unsuccessful sales pitches.

It was only by challenging those conservative sales forecasts that I managed to nudge her towards the core issue – large groups could be managed consistently and predictably, but individuals – especially rich, arrogant ones – didn't always behave rationally. The fact that the world's elites had lost most of their real authority didn't take away their potential to screw things up.

'… It's a delicate balance,' Nicki said, bringing her explanation to a close. 'You know what these people are like. We're coming into six major election cycles and five of the favourite candidates are still sitting on the fence. We'll sign up two or three of them, but not all. Even with guarantees of results and the threat that we'll support their opposition, some will go elsewhere out of sheer stubbornness.'

'Your plans assume that you can't control the individual factor one hundred per cent?'

'Exactly. However good we are, some people will always shoot themselves in the foot. It's a fundamental weakness which we've had to factor into all of our growth plans.' She shrugged and sat back in

113

her chair.

I thought back to all the possible people Nicki might have become, the number of paths she could have taken over the past twenty years, and the likely results of each deviation. I'd done whatever I could to keep her on track, but there'd been so many ways to lose control. Apart from the uncertainties of emotions and hormones, I couldn't preclude the thousands of scenarios which ended sharply and suddenly – a drunken kid with a knife or a stolen car, a random virus or an icy slip into a frozen river.

I looked at her as she sat facing me. We'd come so far and she couldn't have turned out better. Was I proud of her, or proud of myself for bringing her to this point?

Did it matter?

But my task wasn't over. Nicki was still a work in progress. She had one final step to take.

'I disagree,' I said, having left her to stew for long enough. 'We don't have to sit back and accept that those decisions are out of our control.' I could see the "but" forming as she leant forward, and I raised my hand to make sure she gave me time to finish. 'We just need to understand that some people have a tendency to shoot themselves in the foot. It's our responsibility to persuade them that it would be a mistake.'

'Easier said than done. You know the kind of people we're talking about. They're fickle and unpredictable. They can always be tempted to change direction by bigger bribes, blackmail or sudden attacks of moral conscience. There's often no method.'

'Indeed,' I said, pleased that Nicki had understood her clients so well, and so quickly. 'So let's continue with the farmyard metaphor. The masses are sheep and we know we can manage them. Our clients are donkeys and in order to keep a donkey on the right path, you need a stick as well as a carrot.'

'You're suggesting we should threaten them in some way?' Nicki shook her head. 'That kind of strong-arming never works. At least not consistently. Look at Italy.'

'Nothing so clumsy,' I said. 'My kind of threat has never existed before. I think our problem clients will take it very seriously.'

I was no longer smiling and a thin sheen of moisture was glinting on Nicki's forehead. 'Go on,' she said.

'What would these clients do if you told them you had the power to destroy their lives at the flick of a switch? Set something in motion which couldn't be stopped, couldn't be traced or tracked and which would take away their wealth, their reputation, their family and their freedom. If they believed you could do that, might they be persuaded to see the light?'

Nicki stared at me for a few seconds. 'It might work if it were that credible, I suppose,' she said. 'After all, we're only asking them to make the smart choice. I don't know what you're imagining though. A team of black-suited assassins hiding in a fortress at the top of a mountain?'

'Nothing so dramatic,' I said. 'Although much more frightening.'

'OK. Let me explain what I have in mind,' I said. 'First, I need you to imagine an independent AI agent which resides within the cloud, within all of the clouds, fully dispersed through the world's IT networks, clever enough to find its way through, or round, every firewall as soon as it is put in place, but so fragmented that it can't be traced, identified or eradicated. A true super-virus with a single goal and which is capable of evolving in order to achieve that goal.'

'I can see how that could be designed,' she said. 'But I'm not quite with you. What goal?'

'Each virus would be given a single individual as a target, and its mission would be to destroy that person's life piece by piece.'

'I don't understand,' said Nicki, but the tremor in her voice told me she was beginning to.

'The agent virus would be pre-programmed to start by addressing a set of obvious pressure points – financial, reputational, legal, family etc., and would monitor the effectiveness of each action through public media, correspondence analysis, satellite data, surveillance systems, whatever is available. It would then refine its attacks as it learns what works best.

'So it might, for example, block funds, create fake media scandals or implicate the target in criminal acts?'

115

'Exactly.'

'That's pretty extreme, Julie.'

'Let me finish,' I said. 'Firstly, we're not talking about nice people here; secondly, we're not pressuring them to do anything terrible and, most importantly, this is a stick which is designed to be rarely used. If it did become necessary, we would use it sparingly and as a last resort.'

'But from what you're saying, this super-virus would persecute someone for ever. It would go on and on like something out of Dante's Inferno.'

'Which is why you needed to let me finish. We would give it a fixed lifetime, a pre-arranged and inevitable time of "death" built into its genes. It could be a day or a week or a month. That depends on the situation. After all, we don't want to kill our donkeys – just to keep them on the path.'

'OK,' said Nicki in a soft voice. 'I think I see what you're driving at. A software version of the nuclear deterrent?'

'A good analogy,' I said. 'And we would hope to never need it … although I suspect we will need our own Hiroshima to prove the concept.'

Nicki sat silently, presumably thinking. 'It might actually work,' she said. 'These people are all afraid of something, and by dehumanising and automating the threat, it would frighten them even more.'

'That's my thinking,' I said. 'Is something like this technically possible?'

'In theory, yes. It wouldn't have been a few years ago, but some of the research coming out of MIT has opened a lot of new doors and it's now possible to remotely access enough quantum hardware for it to grow and adapt fast enough. It won't be easy though.'

'I didn't expect it to be. Could you design something like this?'

'With the right help. I think so.'

'How long before you could have something viable?'

'I couldn't possibly say right away. It would take months just to get an idea of the scope of the project. But I'm certain it'll take years of development.'

'We'd better get started then,' I said. 'I know you need time to think through the implications – I've already been living with this idea for a while – but there's no reason why you shouldn't do that while you're scoping it out.'

'I suppose not,' she said. 'It's definitely going to cost a hell of a lot. I won't need a huge team, but they'll need to be the best. I'm guessing that the individual developers will need to be unaware of the actual purpose of the programme?'

'I knew you were the right person for the job,' I said, smiling. 'And you know that you'll have whatever funds you need.'

The next hour passed in a blur. We chatted about this and that – relationships, favourite restaurants, anything to keep the conversation light and to distract Nicki from dwelling on the true implications of the project we'd initiated. All the while, my mind was picturing a thousand bright threads converging like maypole ribbons on a single point.

I'd been waiting for such a long time and there had been so much uncertainty along the way. As I sat there, half-listening to Nicki blathering on about some amazing new TV series, I realised that my plans for Nicki and Sam were truly coming together at last. For the first time since I could remember, I could just sit back, relax and enjoy the show.

2042

Julie Martin – An Icarus for our times.

Barely two years ago, Julie Martin was flying high in the stratosphere. Her company, Pulsar, was already the world's third largest company and the number one spot was close enough for her to touch. The book chronicling her success, "Pulsar. Behind the Firewall" (written by her handsome young boyfriend, Sam Blackwell), was topping best-seller lists around the world.

Beautiful, famous, successful and richer than Croesus. What could go wrong?

The answer, as we now know, is absolutely everything.

Next week a jury is expected to reach their verdict in what has become the trial of the century. Julie Martin stands accused of deliberately blinding a policeman with ammonia during the TUC riots of 2011. We have also learned that she has had at least two other identities and a chequered past full of dark rumour and scandal.

To add insult to injury, she was brought down to earth by none other than her former lover, Sam, and Dave Bukowski, a genius professor who has benefited from millions in Pulsar grants. As the police closed in and Julie went on the run, Bukowski engineered an aggressive takeover of Pulsar.

The theories about why the pair turned on her are the stuff of Greek tragedy. Did Julie murder her father with a kitchen knife? Did she deliberately drive Sam's mother, Fabiola, to suicide? Did she "groom" Sam as part of some warped Oedipal obsession?

We'll probably never know the truth, as the evidence is slim and Julie Martin's lawyers still have sharp teeth. It won't matter; people will believe what they want to believe and juicy scandals tend to stick.

We are coming to the end of an era. Julie Martin has lost her company and her reputation. Will she lose her freedom next week? The Sun believes she will.

The story is as old as time; Julie Martin's life seems destined to end, like many others who flew too close to the sun, in a pile of burnt feathers.

Change of Plans

The glass screen in front of me was grey and blurred, streaks of smudged fingers smearing the spots of spittle into tiny tadpoles. It wouldn't have hurt them to give it a wipe from time to time. As soon as I found out where I was going to end up, I'd need to get a few things organised.

It had been three weeks since Sam's visit with his unwelcome news about the new DNA evidence. He'd enjoyed himself too much, and too transparently, as he drove in the final nail – a spiteful boy after all. I could understand why he hated me so much – he had a point – but I didn't feel the same way. I wanted to punish him, that was as it should be, but I didn't hate him.

I pictured his beautiful face and felt my thoughts floating away as I focussed on the centre of the screen where the spit spray had concentrated in a pink-brown cloud. I hadn't hated anybody since my father. Hate and love were such foolish emotions, equally blind, equally dangerous.

I'd hated my father, and I'd loved Fabiola; neither of those stories had ended well. Sam had only been a toy, but even with him, Fabiola's long shadow had blurred my vision and tempted me to let my guard down. I needed to be more disciplined. It was the only way.

What about Nicki? Did I love her? Not like Fabiola, obviously. But was it love?

I looked up at the clock above the gunmetal-grey door. The round perspex face sparkled in the fluorescent lights, a curious anomaly against the dismal concrete wall. Five past. She should have been here by now.

My lawyers had asked for an adjournment as soon as the new evidence was officially submitted, but two weeks was the best they'd been able to manage and we were due back in court after the weekend.

Although I was over my initial shock, it was hard to keep the snarling black wolves at bay. I was tired and the list of names in my little black book was growing out of control.

It would be good to see Nicki, but where was she?

A buzzer broke the silence and the pink cloud faded out of focus as I saw the door open and a slim figure walk in. She was looking a lot better than I felt, although her trademark sharp, black trouser suit with a white blouse and shoulder pads left a lot to be desired – it must have been the fourth time shoulder pads had been back since I'd watched Dallas as a child and they'd never been much of a look.

She was breathing heavily as she slumped onto the metal chair. 'Sorry I'm late, Julie. Swiss Cottage was a nightmare.'

'Don't worry. It's not as if I'm going anywhere.' I managed a decent attempt at a smile. 'Take a second. Catch your breath. We've got half an hour.'

Nicki opened her bag, took out a leather notebook and pen, straightened her jacket and leant forward. 'OK. I'm with you.'

'Good,' I said. 'I'll get straight to it. Things have changed, and I needed to speak to you before the trial ends.'

'It isn't going as planned?'

'Unfortunately not.'

'What's happened?' I could hear the squeak of anxiety in her voice. The last year must have been tough on Nicki. She'd only ever known me as a figure of power and control and, although I'd tried, it wasn't easy to maintain that image from behind bars. Losing Pulsar had been tough enough, but having Odell had helped. Being in prison was worse.

'Don't worry,' I said. 'Everything will be fine in the end but, for now, it appears that Dave Bukowski, with a bit of help from Sam Blackwell, has stuck his big nose into my life one more time.'

'What do you mean?' I loved the angry snarl on her face. 'What's wrong with them? Why can't they leave you alone?'

I shrugged. 'I guess hell has no fury like a lover scorned,' I said. 'Anyway, Bukowski has used a side effect of his nano-genetic fingerprinting to help the police link the shards of glass found in that policeman's face with me. They're saying that it places me at the scene of the crime. It's bullshit, of course, but the media have been against me from the start and my lawyers are saying I'll be found guilty next week.'

'But that's ridiculous,' said Nicki. 'It's not fair.'

As she spoke, I felt my body sag into my chair and unfamiliar wetness blinking at the corner of my eyes. For once, it would be wonderful to embrace the unfairness of life and to wallow in a cotton-wool bed of self pity. Why not stop fighting and let the future be what it chose to be? Would that be so bad?

My moment of self-indulgence couldn't have lasted more than two or three seconds. Of course that would be bad. I'd travelled a long way down that road almost a year earlier, after watching helplessly from Rome as Pulsar was taken from me. I could still remember the feeling of slowly breaking apart and becoming insubstantial. They weren't good memories and besides, I had my little black book to consider.

'Come on, Nicki,' I said. 'You must've learned at least one thing from me. The concept of fairness is pointless and redundant. I may not be guilty of this, but I am guilty of letting my guard down, and I'm paying a price for that. It won't be for long though. We'll win on appeal.'

'I'm sure you will. And then you'll make those bastards pay.'

'And some …' I said, leaning forward closer to the grubby glass. 'The thing is, Nicki. I don't want to wait. I need you to drive the first phase forward while I'm away. It would be too obvious to start as soon as I'm out. Where are you with our pet project? Last time we spoke, you'd made some breakthroughs.'

'Yes,' she said. 'It's going well. We've now called it Damocles and we're making great progress on the updated version. The self-learning algorithms are completely new, so we don't quite know how it'll develop once it's out in the real world, but the initial results are very promising. The bit we're struggling with is the fixed lifetime and abort sequences. Once the current versions are unleashed into the test environment, they develop an uncanny sense of self-preservation. They disable their own control systems, become self sufficient and totally focused on their goal – like the killer robots from those old President Schwarzenegger movies.'

'It sounds as though it's working too well if anything,' I said. 'I don't think that will be a problem for the first phase, although you do need to figure out how to control it.'

'Don't worry. We will.'

'Good,' I said. 'When will it be ready for release?'

'It's going to be six months at best.'

'I need it in two weeks. Can you do that?'

Nicki almost jumped out of her chair. 'Not a hope,' she said. 'Even with a massive increase in resources, and accepting that there might be some unexpected side effects, we couldn't get a working beta version operational in less than eight or nine weeks.'

'You have all the resources you need, I assume?'

'Yes. Odell is twenty per cent up on budget for the year and that's showing no sign of slowing down.'

'Good. So we're agreed. Assuming I'm found guilty next week, you'll activate against the two primary targets in two weeks?'

'But I just told you. It won't be ready.'

'I heard you loud and clear,' I said. 'But that's when it has to happen. You'll have to go with whatever you can get done by then and hope it works. Spend whatever you need.'

I could see the fight in Nicki's eyes. She wanted to be professional, and I was pushing her into a corner. I held her gaze and waited until the resolve faded. 'OK,' she said, eventually. 'I'll do what I can. And the others?'

'The others can wait,' I said, my mind filled only with images of Dave and Sam's smug faces, toasting my upcoming conviction, smiling and clinking champagne glasses. I took a deep calming breath. 'I want to see Sam and Bukowski squirm first of all.'

Nicki must have seen something in my eyes and pulled back from the glass. 'Remind me never to become your enemy, Julie,' she said. 'I don't think I'd like that.'

I smiled. 'Don't worry. That could never happen,' I said. 'And one more thing. We shouldn't see each other again until after the trial. If you need anything, speak to Simon Jacobs.'

Time to Pay

I couldn't just sit down and wait. It was impossible.

My father and Daz were perched on one of the long pine benches, seemingly relaxed and chatting away. I knew they weren't really calm, but how were they able to lounge around and pretend to be? I didn't have it in me.

The lawyers had told us the jury might take hours, or even days, to reach a verdict. I needed to settle in for the long haul, but all I could do was pace up and down, walking along to the looming Tudor-arched windows at the end of the corridor, peering out through the dirt-stained glass, then turning and striding back towards the stairwell. I kept my hands stuffed into my trouser pockets to stop my arms from waving around like an animated scarecrow.

The case had already taken three weeks, and I hadn't missed a moment. I'd eventually accepted that Julie would never be prosecuted for what she did to my mother, but if the evil bitch saw me in court every day, it would remind her of the real reason why she was there.

There was no concrete proof that it was Julie who'd deliberately driven my mother to question her sanity. Maybe she hadn't expected Mum to actually kill herself? Maybe her cold heart wasn't able to understand how far a mother might go to protect her child? It didn't matter either way; her cold-hearted obsession and jealousy was responsible and she needed to pay.

She would be convicted of a different offence, but I wanted her to understand that it was because of Fabiola that she'd been caught and it would be because of Fabiola that she would go to prison for the rest of her life. I needed her to know that.

Sadly, she'd recovered a lot of her poise since I'd seen her that one time in prison. When I'd told her about the new evidence, she'd looked broken – as though she'd given up fighting. But, as Daz had told me more times than I could count, Jax Daniels – to me she would always be Julie Martin – was an elemental force of nature and should never, never be underestimated. My mother had made that mistake and had paid for it with her life.

The cold fires which burned inside Julie seemed able to rekindle themselves again and again, however many times they were quenched. There was something inhuman about the way she managed to restructure herself and rebuild her ego whatever happened to her. Almost as though she was an android which could be rebooted after a system crash.

I'd watched her standing in the dock, day after day, with a quiet smile on her face, looking as young and beautiful as ever. Anyone who'd wondered how I could ever have been attracted to a fifty-year-old woman would only need to see her to understand. I'd been surprised when she'd refused to be a witness – she would have been able to use that opportunity to impose her charisma on the jury members – but her lawyer must have insisted.

It was agonising to see her looking so happy, healthy and relaxed but I kept reminding myself that, as long as she was found guilty, it didn't matter so much. The years in prison would wear on her eventually.

As long as the jury found her guilty.

The evidence was compelling; they might not be able to prosecute her for my mother's death, but they'd linked her DNA directly to the attack on that poor policeman. Even her lawyer had been lukewarm in his summing up. Surely no jury would see anything differently? She must be found guilty.

Unless – and there could always be an "unless" where that woman was concerned – unless she had somehow got to the jury. Threats or bribes, she'd proven that she was capable of both. I took a deep breath. There was no point in going round and round in circles – we would find out soon enough.

'Come on, Sam. The jury are on their way back.' I saw the familiar figure of Rishi Patel walking towards me, high heels clacking on the tiled floor. Rishi was the Crown's lead barrister, but she wasn't much older than me and, apart from the wig, she didn't look like any barrister I'd ever seen.

'What?' I said. 'But they can't be finished already. They only went out ten minutes ago.'

'It's actually been more like an hour,' she said. 'But they've been much quicker than I expected.'

She wasn't smiling, and I felt my shoulder blades spasm together. 'It must be a good thing, though,' I said. 'Right?'

She squeezed my forearm and forced a half-smile. 'I'm sure it is. Only, with Julie Martin, it seems as though anything is possible.' She pointed towards Rupert and Daz, her crimson nails flashing under the fluorescent lights. 'Anyway. Let's grab the others and go face the music.'

Quick had to be good. It had to be.

The courtroom was packed. Julie couldn't avoid publicity any more, and the world's press had gathered to gloat in her downfall. There weren't many human constants which spread across race, culture and geography, but the guilty pleasure of watching rich or powerful people take a nosedive was high on the list. Just twelve months earlier, Julie Martin had been owner and CEO of the fifth largest company in the world. She'd fallen a long way.

This last act in the story of her humiliating crash was attracting billions of rubberneckers and the trial had dominated water cooler gossip for weeks. What was good – in most ways – was how the media was picking up on my mother's story even though it hadn't been part of the evidence.

They understood how the story would resonate with their audiences. A beautiful young woman, a spurned lover and the evil methodical cyberstalking which had left everyone questioning their own lives and online security. And, even in 2042, the fluid sexuality still had the power to titillate.

Although I was happy to see the world judging Julie for what she'd done to my family, the downside was that the journalists were behaving like vultures and wouldn't leave us alone. There was also talk of a book, or even a film. I had my own ideas about that, but what I was really hoping was that, after the verdict, they would move on to something else so our life could start again.

As long as it was the right verdict.

The court clerk was struggling to keep discipline and hundreds of overexcited voices filled the room with wave after wave of babbling chatter. It wasn't until the judge came in that the atmosphere calmed and, even then, it was five minutes until something approaching silence returned.

The jury filed in and sat down, ordinary people facing an extraordinary task. They were a mixed bunch, although their faces were uniform, each mouth set into a grim expressionless line. I'd been watching them all week, trying to get a hint of something out of the ordinary, something to indicate that Julie might have got to them. But how would I be able to tell?

The clerk walked over to the jury foreman who handed him a folded scrap of paper. He passed it to the judge who then read it carefully before refolding it and placing it down in front of him. Time seemed to be moving so slowly. Were they deliberately trying to build tension?

The court clerk looked at the judge who nodded. 'Ladies and gentlemen of the jury,' he said. 'In the case of the Crown and Janice Cargill.' Just for a second I thought I saw Julie wince at the mention of her birth name. 'Have you reached a verdict?'

The jury foreman stood, arms by his sides. 'We have,' he said, his voice booming across the sudden silence. Everyone in the crowded room was holding their breath.

'And you all agree on this verdict?'

'Yes.'

The clerk continued. 'On the charge of administering a destructive or noxious thing thereby endangering life or inflicting grievous bodily harm, contrary to Section 23 of the Offences against the Person Act 1861. How do you find the defendant?'

'Guilty as charged,' said the foreman, looking down at the floor.

I squeezed my eyes tight with relief, but this wasn't the main charge. It carried a maximum sentence of ten years. Intent was the thing. That was what would make the difference.

'On the charge of throwing a corrosive substance with intent to do grievous bodily harm, contrary to section 29 of the Offences against the Person Act 1861. How do you find the defendant?'

The foreman looked up, turned towards Julie and thrust out his chin like a posturing cockerel. 'Guilty as charged,' he said.

The sound of a hundred people all gasping in unison filled the room before the clamour of a hundred chattering voices flooded back, rising and falling and swamping any attempts to quieten them. The cries of the clerk were now soundless and impotent against the lynch mob fervour.

It took a moment for me to realise that I was crying – I didn't know whether it was with relief, sadness or joy, although they were probably all mixed together. When I felt my dad's arm wrap around me and squeeze me tight, I turned to face him and saw he was equally overwhelmed.

'Well done, boy,' he said. 'None of this would have happened without you and no-one would ever have known the truth. I'm proud of you … and right now your mother must be looking down on us with a massive smile on her face.'

I hugged him and buried my face into his shoulder. There were plenty of reporters watching us and I needed a few moments to get myself under control.

'Thank you,' said the judge, finally regaining control of his courtroom. 'And, ladies and gentlemen of the jury, thank you for your diligence in following what has been a difficult and most unsettling case. Considering the various complexities involved, I will defer sentencing until tomorrow.'

The full impact of the verdict still hadn't sunk in and we didn't know the final sentence, but guilty on both counts should mean at least twenty years, which would be enough.

It really was over.

I looked across at Julie, who was facing straight ahead, standing tall and looking at the judge with that familiar half-smile. I saw nothing in her expression to show that anything was troubling her, let alone that she'd been found guilty and was facing a possible life sentence. If she had any genuine human emotions left, she kept them buried very deep.

And then she turned and looked at me. It wasn't a look of anger, not even hatred; there was something else in that stare, something dark and implacable, something hungry which would never be satisfied.

I shivered.

What Next?

'Your lawyer's here,' said the policewoman as she pushed open the door to the holding cell. Then she laughed, the nasty, crowing laugh of the professional bully. 'Maybe you should've got someone better, eh?'

She looked at me with her piggy little eyes and waited for me to cower like the broken woman she assumed I was. I held her gaze and smiled, filling my look with dark promises, until she turned her head away, stepping aside to let Simon pass. 'Murdering bitch,' she muttered under her breath as she pulled the door closed.

Simon Argyle had been my personal lawyer for a very long time – I looked after him well and he worked exclusively for me.

As he walked into the interview room he avoided my gaze, his eyes flicking all around the cell. I suspected he was much more upset than me about the verdict. He would be questioning where his next mortgage payment was coming from after all. Even a day earlier, he'd tried to convince me there was a good chance of acquittal and I knew he expected me to be furious with him.

That was the thing about lawyers; however good they were, they could never make a realistic appraisal of the odds facing them. It was always in their interests to convince their clients that the chances of success were better than they actually were. Misguided hope and false optimism kept the fees rolling in.

Unfortunately, after years of gilding the lily, it seemed that every one of them lost the ability to look at reality even when the facts were spread out in front of them, as glaringly obvious as shining diamond rings in a jeweller's window.

I'd seen the truth days earlier as soon as the new evidence was introduced. Everyone wanted to find me guilty – they just needed enough justification to legitimise their decision. What was the point of pretending? In any case, it wasn't Simon's fault, it was mine. I'd let my guard down and there were consequences.

I wasn't intending to fire him, neither did I have any intention of spending years behind bars. All that the guilty verdict meant was that we had work to do.

'Hello, Julie,' he said, finally looking me in the eye. 'I'm so sorry. I really thought …'

'Save it, Simon. It's what it is.' I looked at his pale face and watched his left knee shaking. 'Pull yourself together,' I said. 'I'm not going to fire you, although if you don't stop shaking I might be tempted.'

'Thank you, Julie,' he said, visibly straightening. 'I won't let you down again.'

'Good,' I said. 'We've only got fifteen minutes. How long are they going to give me?'

'It depends a lot how sympathetic the judge is. If we're lucky …'

'Can we cut the sugar-coated bullshit for once?' I said. 'We've both been sitting in that courtroom for weeks now. Is there anything to suggest that the judge, or anyone else for that matter, is going to show me any sympathy whatsoever? If we were back in the day, there'd be a lynch mob outside the door. We're not going to be lucky. Just tell me how long.'

'The sentencing guidelines specify nine to sixteen years,' said Simon. 'But they can make exceptions. If you want my honest opinion, I think this judge will play to the crowd and go for an exceptional life sentence.'

There was something chilling about the idea of a life sentence. Even though I knew most people were released much earlier, those words still made me shiver.

'How long will I actually serve?' I said.

'If we don't win on appeal … at least ten years,' said Simon. 'Probably more.'

'You'd better get to work on the appeal, then,' I said. 'Because one thing's for sure. I'm not rotting away in here for the next ten years.'

As I watched Simon walk out, I felt the anger steadily building inside me like steam in a boiler. For a while, there had been something masochistically fascinating about my arrest and the subsequent prosecution, but enough was enough. The amusement was long gone.

Relief

The ordeal was almost over.

I could hear shouting from outside. Thousands of spectators had turned up to jeer Julie Martin on the way to her sentencing. We'd been waiting for over an hour and there was still no sign of Julie or the judge.

Daz squeezed into the seat beside me, breathing heavily. He'd gone outside twenty minutes earlier to see what was happening and we'd started to worry about him.

'So?' said my dad.

'Give us a sec,' said Daz. 'It's a bloody zoo out there.'

'What's going on?' I said, not feeling even slightly patient.

'They can't get the van past the crowds,' said Daz. 'There's some sort of anti-privacy group running a flash mob. Loads of them blocking the street. All sorts of conspiracy theory stuff – Julie is the Anti-Christ – she's stolen all our souls – it's the End of Days. God knows, I think she's an evil bitch, but that's giving her a little too much credit.'

'Maybe?' I said, remembering a few things Julie had said when she was feeling boastful.

'Anyway.' Daz stood up and took off his coat. 'They couldn't get the van past until a few more cops showed up. She's through now. Shouldn't be long.'

Right on cue, a wave of silence swept across the courtroom and every head turned towards the side door. She walked in flanked by two policemen, one of whom had a fresh-looking band-aid stretched over his temple. Although her arms were handcuffed in front of her, Julie strolled in like a lioness, a small smile playing at the corners of her mouth – she might have been going shopping. The smile deepened as she caught my eye. What was going on behind those dark pupils? Was she so confident of overturning the conviction on appeal? The memory of the cold dark look Julie had given me the day before wouldn't go away. She always had another trick up her sleeve and I knew she'd never forgive me for what I'd done to her. No point worrying about it though. This was a day to celebrate victory, not to wallow in "what-if" conjecturing.

The noise returned to the room only to fade away again as the judge took his seat and the Clerk of Court opened the proceedings.

All eyes were on the bench as His Honour Judge Davison picked up the stack of papers in front of him and began to speak in a slow, mellow baritone:

'Janice Cargill (also known as Julie Martin and Jacqueline Daniels) you have been convicted, on overwhelming evidence, of causing grievous bodily harm with intent, contrary to section 29 of the Offences against the Person Act 1861, by throwing a corrosive substance at Police Constable Jason Hall in Carrington Street, Mayfair in the early evening of Saturday 26th March 2011.

'You are a British citizen of good character, aged fifty-two.' That was a joke. There was nothing about Julie that could allow her to claim good character.

'Until recently you were the owner and founder of one of the world's largest personal identification companies.

'Having presided over your trial I am sure of the following facts.

'In 2011, you were a committed anarchist, living amongst a small group of non-violent activists. At the same time, you had become associated with a more radical fringe group, linked to the so-called Black Bloc groups of violent extremists. It is my understanding that you were eager to impress your peers with your willingness to do "whatever it took" to help them to achieve their anti-society goals.

'You decided between you, and in order to advance your extremist cause, to attack a number of police officers during the TUC-sponsored March for the Alternative which was due to take place in Central London on 26th March 2011. Your intent was to cause the police officers serious bodily harm and disfigurement and, as a result, to generate maximum media coverage for your cause. You were aware that the chosen methods of attack had the potential to lead to the deaths of one or more of the victims.

'The planning took place over a period of time. In the weeks prior to the march, you and your fellow-extremists filled ten glass light bulbs with a highly corrosive ammonia-based substance. The day before the march, these bulbs were divided between three of you. You were allocated four bulbs.

'On the day of the protest, you took the ammonia-filled light bulbs in a borrowed backpack and joined the march together with your girlfriend Fabiola Carlantino and your other moderate friends. You proceeded as though everything was normal and it was only once you reached Piccadilly, after three or four hours, that you separated from them and disappeared into the crowd.

'We have seen extensive video footage showing how you lured PC Hall to chase after you by breaking windows along Shepherd Street with a hammer and, as he turned the corner to follow you into Carrington Street, you were waiting for him. You threw the first of the glass bulbs into his face at close range and then, as he fell to the ground, you threw a second one, again at his face. You then placed a note on the ground beside him before running off. Video footage shows that you then hid in a waste container on Bruton Lane until the early hours of the following morning.

'Although we have heard from witnesses who were privy to the details of the plan, it has not been possible to identify the other two chosen attackers. However, as there were no other attacks, it must be assumed that, unlike you, they came to their senses and aborted their planned assaults.

'PC Hall was 28 years old, had joined the police force in 2002, and was a well-liked, outgoing and popular personality. He was a diligent professional policeman and was due to be promoted to Sergeant within a few months of the attack. He was a keen club footballer and had also recently become engaged to be married. In March 2011, he was doing his duty and had done absolutely nothing to deserve what you went on to do to him.

'The attacks left PC Hall blind in both eyes, facially disfigured and in constant pain. Tragically, just nine months later, he took his own life.

'As is clear from their moving Victim Personal Statements, the consequences of the attack, its brutality and the publicity, have had a severe and lasting impact on those close to PC Hall.

'In addition, Dr Julia Prince, the police psychologist assigned to support PC Hall during his recuperation has stated that, in her professional opinion, the trauma and injuries following the incident were directly responsible for his subsequent decision to commit suicide.

'Despite the three decades which have passed since this tragedy, I don't believe that you have any real insight into the enormity of what you did, nor any genuine remorse for it either – your only regret seems to be that you have been finally apprehended and brought to justice before the courts. I am sure that many of those in court today, including myself, regret that it has taken so long.

'I note that you have not submitted any pleas in mitigation and I have not been presented with any evidence of other mitigating factors. I would also note that you have continued to deny your involvement in this act despite the compelling evidence against you.

'In different circumstances, I believe you would have been brought to trial for murder. However, as the prosecution explained in their opening statement, the length of time between the attack and PC Hall's death precluded that course of action.

'The prosecution submit that the offence falls within Category 1 of the Sentencing Guidelines and the counsel for the defendant does not disagree. The prosecution also submit, however, that this is an offence of exceptionally high seriousness, with a significant degree of planning or premeditation and which occurred while PC Hall was providing a public service or performing a public duty. As such, they submit that you are a dangerous offender and that it would be open to the court to exceed the current sentencing guidelines of nine to sixteen years and consider a life sentence which is the maximum allowed by law.

'In light of the evidence, I am convinced that there was malicious intent behind this crime and believe that the prosecution submissions are both well founded and just and proportionate.

'There is no mitigation, and whilst to state the obvious, this is not a murder case, it is nevertheless one of those rare cases where not only is the seriousness exceptionally high but the requirements of just punishment and retribution demand a commensurate penalty. Accordingly, I propose to impose the maximum sentence.

'Janice Cargill. I therefore sentence you to life imprisonment with a minimum term of fifteen years.'

Granny hadn't been in court.

When the trial date was originally set, she'd reminded us all of how "that woman" had already caused too much pain and heartache for our family; she had no intention of allowing her to steal another three months of her life.

Even though she made a good point, I couldn't have sat back and waited to know what was going to happen to Julie. In any case, Daz and I were important prosecution witnesses and the option wasn't available.

After the judge dropped his sentencing bombshell, we waited in the courtroom for the mob to leave. Julie hadn't reacted to the life sentence – it was as though she'd put herself into a trance – and she walked out with the same cool nonchalance as before. There had been no repeat of the stare which had chilled me so much the day before.

Eventually we slipped past the press cordon, found our car and set off back to The Old Vicarage. Traffic was light by London standards and in less than two hours we were settled around the big garden table giving Granny a blow-by-blow update of the day.

'But, what does that actually mean?' Granny said. 'Will she be in prison for life or for fifteen years?'

'It's quite confusing,' said Liz. 'Probably somewhere between the two. The good thing is that it will be at least fifteen years, which is more than we could have hoped for.' Liz Simpson had once been a senior police officer and had helped as much as anyone to bring Julie to justice. She was, like all of us present, a victim of Julie's malice and vindictiveness – the blinded policeman, Jason Hall, had been her fiancee.

Granny shook her head and drew a sharp breath. 'I suppose I'm the only one here who finds all of this deliberately confusing?' she said. 'Never mind. The important thing is that it's all over and that woman is getting what she deserves.' She looked around the table, her eyes still sharp despite their wrinkled setting. '… And that is thanks to all of you. I know this last year has been extremely difficult, but it seems to be over at last and I wanted to say how proud I am of everyone here, especially you, Sam.'

I didn't know what to say. Granny wasn't known for speeches and certainly not for sharing her feelings.

'Some of us aren't able to be here to celebrate today,' she said, 'but I'm sure that Fabiola and John would be equally proud if they were still with us.'

My dad was sitting next to me and I felt his hand squeeze my shoulder. That was the moment, surrounded by family and friends, when I realised that the nightmare was really over. I'd been going through the motions of rebuilding a normal life; now I could stop treading water and get on with living for the future.

Darkness crept in, almost unnoticed. Lights came on, candles were lit and gradually the table emptied as people slipped off to bed one-by-one.

The last-but-one to go was Daz, discretely leaving ten minutes after Liz as though their bedtime journeys were unrelated. Sixty-year-olds really shouldn't behave like teenagers – it wasn't as if they were fooling anyone.

That left me and my dad, sipping our drinks and looking up at a fat orange moon. I knew he would be thinking about Mum and how some things couldn't be fixed. I needed to put the past few years behind me. Maybe it was time for him to move on as well.

'What now?' he said as the moon slid behind a cloud.

'I dunno,' I said. 'I've got shedloads of work to do with the new launch. That'll keep me busy. I'm also still fiddling around with the idea of a novel. But beyond that …'

'Not sure what I think of your novel idea,' he said. 'It doesn't sound much like moving on. D'you remember what I said to you when you were flying out to LA that first time? When you were so hyped up and excited?'

'Yeah,' I said. 'I do.' I remembered his advice all too well, and I also remembered the ease with which I'd dismissed it.

'You've changed, Sam,' he said, eyes shining in the candlelight. 'That was only a few years ago, but you're a different person now.'

I felt a tiny spark of anger flash. Of course I'd changed after what I'd been through. What did he bloody expect? I kept it hidden, though – he was just being my dad.

'I know,' I said. 'I can feel it. I'm harder now … and much more cynical. I'm finding it tougher to trust people these days.'

'That's not such a bad thing,' he said. 'It happens to most of us at some point. No, that's not what I'm talking about. It's more that you seem to have forgotten how to be happy. You don't smile and laugh like you used to.'

I looked up at him. 'I don't think I've forgotten, Dad,' I said. 'It's different. It's more like I don't feel as though I deserve to be happy.'

'That's a stupid thing to say. Why wouldn't you deserve to be happy just as much as anyone else?'

'I never said I was being rational,' I said, more sharply than intended. 'I'm struggling to put things in perspective. I really thought I was going to die when Julie locked me in that safe room. I still wake up in the middle of the night struggling to breathe.'

'It must be horrible …'

'… And that's not the worst nightmare,' I said. 'You weren't there, but I can't forget the time after Daz and I first met Liz and she told us who Julie really was … and about what she did to her father when she was a teenager. She castrated him with a kitchen knife, for Christ's sake! Can you imagine what it was like going back and getting into bed with her after that? I must have been mad. Just the thought of it makes me want to curl up in a ball and whimper.'

'I guess we've not managed to find the time to talk about these things properly,' Dad said.

'Or we've both tried to pretend they didn't happen? I don't know.

All I know is that I've been holding it all together by focusing on the trial, and now it's over, I don't know how I'm going to move on. I feel like such a naïve and stupid idiot. Just having fun and being happy seems a long way away. And there's Mum, of course ...'

'Mum? How do you mean?'

'Before Julie, I guess I'd managed to find a place to keep Mum in the background and get on with life. I was only two when she died after all. But with all I've learned, with her diaries and everything we've found out about her and Jax, she's become much more "alive" to me – I miss her even more now if that makes sense?'

He nodded.

'And I can't ignore what Julie did to us – to me – it's not easy to push away those feelings. She must have been planning to draw me in and seduce me for a long time, possibly my whole life. It's more than creepy. What sort of person does that? How could I not have suspected something?'

'The experts seem to have decided she's a full-blown psychopath,' he said. 'I'm not convinced about all of these labels though. Trying to put people or ideas into fixed boxes never really works. As to how you could have been fooled, it appears that she has an exceptional ability to charm and manipulate people ...' He laughed. '... And, let's face it, it's not that difficult for a beautiful woman to lead an average young man by his dick, is it?'

'You make a good point,' I said, happy to change the mood. 'While we're on that topic, have I ever told you how she ended up seducing me?'

'No,' he said, leaning forward. 'I'm guessing it wasn't just an ordinary grope and fumble?'

'Oh, no. Nothing ordinary about it at all.' Looking at my dad, perked up and keen to hear the story, I was filled with an urge to tease him, just like I'd done since I was in my teens. 'But it's late,' I said, covering my mouth in a mock yawn. 'I'll tell you another time.'

It was great to see the smile spread across his face as he realised what I was doing. Life had been much too serious for much too long.

That's a Surprise

Dave hadn't been able to make the end of the trial. He'd been dragged off to a MySafe board meeting in New York. They were finalising the integration of the Pulsar legacy infrastructure into the MySafe network and they expected their Product Development Director to be there in person.

It had been three weeks since Julie's sentencing and I hadn't seen him since. I was excited to catch up.

'Professor Bukowski's running a little late, Mr Blackwell,' said Gina, his assistant. 'Would you mind taking a seat? He won't be long.'

'No problem,' I said, settling into the white leather sofa and picking up the Financial Times.

I wondered if Dave had realised what moving from academia to the business world would actually entail. At twenty-nine, he'd been the youngest tenured professor at Imperial College ever and, in that strange academic bubble, he'd been the maverick American wunderkind, free to do whatever he wanted.

Taking his unique new technology to MySafe had destroyed Pulsar and made the thirty-six-year-old Professor Bukowski very wealthy and influential overnight. The Time Magazine cover had done nothing to dampen the raging furnace of Dave's ego and he'd even been childishly flattered when they labelled him "The Bad Boy of Tech".

Everything comes at a price however and, although he'd taken enormous pleasure in being the instrument of Julie Martin's destruction, his new corporate persona came with more strings than he was used to; prima-donna behaviour tended to be frowned upon in the board rooms of listed companies.

Dave hadn't forgotten my role in his meteoric rise, and the share option package that came with my new role as Head of Product Marketing made me many times richer than I'd ever expected to be. The job was great fun with plenty of travel and eye-watering budgets. I was, as usual, completely out of my depth, but young and inexperienced were apparently core competencies for most positions in the tech sector and I wasn't alone. Luckily there were plenty of experienced people in my department and I was smart enough to know when to listen.

At ten-thirty, two men in dark suits walked out of Dave's office, followed by Dave who stood in the doorway grinning from ear to ear. He waved me in, pulled the door closed and lifted his arm for a high-five.

'Well done,' he said, slapping my hand as hard as he could. 'You got the bitch. I was in a very stuffy meeting when I heard the news and I had to sneak out to the bathroom for a little dance and a fist pump. They gave her life. That's so cool.'

I unravelled myself from the hug and stretched out on his Eames lounger. 'She'll probably only serve the fifteen years,' I said. 'But that's much more than we'd hoped for. It's a great result.'

'She got what was coming to her,' he said. 'Especially after what she did to your mother.'

Dave's sister had been an early victim of online bullying while she was at school. After years of self-harm, she'd taken an overdose and they'd found her too late to save her. When I'd told him how Julie had driven my mum to suicide, he'd taken years of pent-up fury and channelled it in her direction.

'No doubt. We just have to hope she can't get to us from inside,' I said. 'You should have seen the look she gave me when she was convicted. Like a cat looking down on a trapped mouse. We know she's not going to forgive or forget.'

'Don't worry about that,' he said. 'I've taken on Milinsky Labs to look out for us. They'll monitor our digital footprints for anything out of the ordinary.'

In retrospect the way the world's population had thrown every detail of their lives online was reckless to say the least. The mass of uncontrolled and uncontrollable data had spawned two massive industries – legal, semi-legal and downright criminal businesses which looked for every possible way to exploit all of those soft data underbellies, and an equally profitable raft of firms offering services to defend against that exploitation. Milinsky Labs were the new stars of the Data Safety industry with a client base that read like an invitation list for Davos.

'Thanks, Dave. Hopefully we won't need it,' I said. 'Anyway, how was New York?'

'Same old. Same old,' he said. 'If those guys quit mouthing off so much, they'd actually get something done. It's like they're trying to slow us down on purpose.'

'But you got the launch date agreed?'

'Damn right, I did. October 24th for the US and we roll out worldwide over the following three months.'

'Nice one,' I said. 'And you'll be ready in time?'

'If they leave me to get on with it, no problem. How about the marketing?'

'All on track. I've got a good team.'

'Nothing to worry about then.' He stood up and moved to the door. 'Look, I've got a couple more meetings. How about we meet up after work for a drink?'

'I can't. I've got my dad coming round to see the flat.'

I'd just moved into my new flat. It wasn't exactly Julie's Knightsbridge palace, but it was a long, long way from the damp dump I'd shared in Acton. And I didn't have to worry about a flatmate any more. Even though Karl was a decent enough bloke, he was a selfish git and he'd been a pain in the arse to live with.

The flat might not have been a palace, but in many ways it was much better and definitely suited me more. And there was one unique feature which, from my perspective, made it a million times better than Julie's over-ornate mansion.

I met the CEO of PixelFilm, Sacha Kaspersky, at a tech

conference and we spent the evening drinking caipirinhas and swapping bullshit stories. I'd given up trying to avoid talking about my time with Julie – everyone I spoke to wanted to find out more, and to share their opinions. At least my saga was more gossip-worthy than anyone else's and I got bought a lot of drinks.

To be fair, Sacha had his fair share of entertaining war stories and we'd had a great evening. I'd been telling him how excited I was about the flat which was in a new block overlooking the river next to Chelsea bridge. It wasn't huge but was achingly modern and cool. Minimalist alloy and solar glass were showing no signs of going out of fashion.

The evening was topped by the email Sacha sent me the next morning asking me if I wanted to be a beta tester for the newest PixelFilm product. The PixelWall wasn't due to be launched until the end of the year and, although he'd tried his best to describe it to me, I hadn't quite grasped how amazing it was. I was never going to refuse and he sent over a couple of engineers a week later. By the time they'd finished playing around, I was one of twenty trial owners of a PixelWall.

On first look, there was nothing special about my living room – a large flush-mounted TV screen, some contemporary artwork, sharp white walls, downlighters – a mirror image of a thousand other modern flats in cities around the world. Look a bit closer or call out a few voice commands and the differences became clear. Every surface of the room except the floor was covered in PixelFilm, a smooth ultra-high-resolution video display material. The paintings, the lighting, the wall colouring, the TV screen – all of them were video images and could be configured on demand. It must have been the coolest thing I'd ever seen.

I made a point of not telling my family and friends about my pixellated miracle. The experience was difficult to describe and there would be so many more opportunities to show off once they were actually standing in the room.

Dad was my first guinea pig. He'd been banging on about coming up to see the new flat and, now that the trial was over and the PixelWall installed and (mostly) debugged, it was time. I wasn't brave enough to cook dinner at home, so we'd agreed to meet at the flat after work and go out for something simple nearby.

After my Michelin-star-filled life with Julie, I'd lost the taste for expensive restaurants and nothing gave me greater pleasure than sweet and sour chicken or a mixed grill at our local Turkish bistro. It was partly my desire to lock that nightmare away in an airtight box and partly the sad truth that fine dining tends to disappoint when you've been used to very, very fine dining.

Dad was fifteen minutes late and I was struggling to contain my excitement as I waited. Just like waiting in a darkened room at a surprise party or playing hide-and-seek as a child. My heart was in my mouth and time had slowed to a geriatric crawl.

The PixelWall came with a bunch of presets and the ability to add personal configurations. When I eventually heard the door buzzer, I switched the room to "Acton Flat", smiled as I watched the transformation and went to let him in.

'Very posh location,' he said, giving me a firm handshake and a hug. 'I'm impressed.' The handshake was more than firm and I needed to squeeze my knuckles back into shape when he eventually let go.

'Are you deliberately squeezing harder when you shake hands these days?' I said, grinning. 'So that people don't think you're old and weak?'

'Of course I'm not,' he said, even as a flicker of self doubt wrinkled his smile. He closed the door and appraised the hall with his estate agent eyes. 'Very nice indeed,' he said. 'Come on. Show me the rest.'

I gave him the tour, leaving the best until last and kept my eyes glued on him as he pushed open the living room door. The surprise and confusion froze his features; he managed to squeeze out a muffled grunt before running out of steam and standing still in the doorway, head slowly turning from side to side.

Acton Flat was probably a little extreme. I'd gone for magnolia walls, cracked paint, damp patches, cheap Athena posters and a poxy little TV, but I couldn't hide the German bi-fold doors or the balcony giving on to the river. It looked horrible, but not realistic.

'Activate: Normal.' I said and watched as the room transformed itself. Dad even took a step backwards and lifted a hand to his mouth. There are times when childish slapstick pleasures are unbeatable and this was one of those times.

'Bloody hell,' he said. 'What was that?'

'Let me get you a beer,' I said, 'and I'll show you.'

We cycled through all the preset options and even spent ten minutes playing Doom in full surround. Even though VR goggles had been frighteningly realistic for years, they still hadn't fixed the vertigo issues. Standing in the middle of the room, however, watching as aliens scrabbled towards you from all sides was a whole different experience. The fact that some of them were coming from behind the sofa didn't make it any less terrifying.

However, like all gimmicks, the extreme and funky features were more amusing than entertaining and it wasn't long before the two of us were settled on the sofa watching Wimbledon. I was pleased to note that even my cynical old-fashioned father was forced to admit that expanding the screen to cover an entire wall did enhance the tennis-watching experience.

The match was only moderately interesting, half way through the second set and no real tension, so we were happy to chat with half an eye for the screen in case anything exciting happened. We'd caught up on family, work and the fact that I still didn't have a girlfriend when my dad got up and walked out to the hall.

'There's something you need to see,' he said, sitting back down and pulling a sheet of A4 paper out of a folder.

'Sounds serious,' I said.

'Read this first and then we'll talk.'

I felt my hand shaking as I reached over to take the paper. Although I was feeling a lot better, I still had the odd panic attack, and a night without at least one nightmare was a rarity. I didn't need any more excitement.

I felt the warmth of my father's hand closing over mine. 'Don't worry, boy,' he said, his deep, familiar tones calm and steady. 'It'll come as quite a shock, but not in a bad way. Go ahead …'

16ᵗʰ June 2042

Dear Rupert,

I am sorry to write to you out of the blue like this, but it is important and I urge you to read what I have to say carefully. I have written and re-written this letter so many times over the past few weeks – hopefully you will take it seriously.

My name is Joe Taylor and I knew your deceased wife, Fabiola, many years ago. A long time before you met her. She was the love of my life, but I was older, already married and a father of two. I was also her schoolteacher. With the simple clarity of hindsight, the end of our sorry story was as inevitable as the setting sun, but I was still young enough and naïve enough to believe that love would conquer all.

It was only following her tragic death – I was there at her funeral, but you wouldn't have seen me – that I learned her most precious secret. After we were discovered, torn apart and each thrown to a different set of wolves, she left Bedford and went into hiding before going to university. I don't know where she went, but I now know why.

It turns out that Fabiola was pregnant with our child. Soon after her funeral, I found out that she'd given birth to a daughter, Nicki, who was eleven at the time of Fabiola's death and living with her adopted parents.

The way I found out, and what happened next, is so bizarre that I struggle to believe it myself, but truth can be stranger than fiction.

It's a truth that has been hidden until now as I was weak and allowed myself to be bribed and intimidated. I gave my word that I would never tell anyone – including Nicki – about her mother and everything that happened. I have kept that promise until now, but circumstances have changed and I need to unburden myself of this secret.

I can't say any more over email, but will tell you the whole story face-to-face. Please come and see me as soon as possible. I am not well enough to travel – pancreatic cancer, unfortunately – but I'm not too far from Oxford.

I think you and I should agree on the best way to explain this to Nicki and your son and I don't intend to tell her anything until we have spoken.

I don't have that much time. Please come soon.

Best wishes,

Joe

Quite a shock. That was an understatement. I didn't speak until I'd got to the end. My brain was trying to cope with dozens of simultaneous ideas and imaginings without success.

'Bloody hell! You're saying I've got a sister?' I said eventually, still staring at the sheet of paper as though it would change something.

Dad plucked it out of my hands and put it back into the folder. 'Let's not get carried away,' he said. 'That's what Joe's saying. We don't actually know if he's lying or mad. Or both.'

'Why would anyone make something like that up?'

'I don't bloody know,' he said. 'With all that's happened over the last year, anything's possible. I didn't know whether I should tell you. Joe was insistent that I didn't.' He stood up and turned to face me, the evening sun painting a golden aura around him. 'The thing is that we've been living with so many secrets and lies and it has to stop somewhere. You and I need to trust each other completely, to know there's nothing hidden between us.'

'You know I agree,' I said. 'I made you a promise and I intend to keep it. Anyway, of course you had to tell me. It affects me more than anyone.' I took a gulp of my beer as I gathered my thoughts. 'Is he for real?'

'I think so. I spoke to him this afternoon and I knew all about your mum's schoolteacher scandal anyway – it was why she fell out with her family. You can imagine how that went down in an Italian community.'

I'd also known about Joe Taylor for years. The news articles filled the first pages of any search for Fabiola Carlantino and there'd been a time when I'd been obsessed with finding out more about my mother. I'd never discussed it with my dad and there didn't seem much point in changing that. 'Poor Mum,' I said. 'She didn't make brilliant choices did she?' Dad's eyebrows raised and he shrugged. 'Until you, that is,' I followed up quickly and we both laughed. 'And he wouldn't tell you anything else over the phone?'

'No,' Dad said. 'He was evasive, cagey, almost rude. As though he was afraid someone was listening in. He didn't sound great either. You probably don't remember, but your great aunt died of pancreatic cancer – very quick and very nasty.'

'So. Are you going to see him?'

'On Thursday.'

'I'm coming.'

'No, Sam. That wouldn't be smart. It's bad enough that I've told you about it, but I've no idea what he'll do if we both rock up. He might refuse to say anything.'

'I don't care. I was hoping for a little peace and quiet to get my act together ... and now this! I'm coming.'

Staying Ahead

'Good morning, Julie.'

Simon sat down opposite me, his maroon velvet jacket clashing with everything else in the drab interview room. His face was round as a golf ball, shining spots of red glowing on his cheeks. He was clearly a man living the good life.

'I've lodged the appeal, Julie,' he said. 'The evidence was always thin and I expect them to push us up the list.' He shuffled the stack of papers in front of him with restless fingers. 'It'll be at least three months, though. Could be as long as six. I can't make it go any faster.'

'Calm down,' I said. 'You're doing what you can, and it was on the cards I'd be in for a while.'

I could never understand why people worried about things they couldn't change. It distracted them from dealing with everything else. Did he think I was going to blame him for the inefficiencies of the system? What would be the point in that?

'Do you know where they're sending me?' I said.

'Not a hundred per cent yet,' he said, 'but it's looking like Downview.'

'You'll make arrangements?' I asked.

'I'm already on it,' he said. 'You'll be looked after.'

'Good. Anything else?'

'Yes,' said Simon, looking over to the door and lowering his voice. Official visits were supposed to be privileged and eavesdropping was illegal, but it didn't hurt to be careful. 'You asked me to keep an eye on the girl's father.'

'I did. Is there a problem?'

'He sent an email to Sam's father, Rupert, yesterday. Joe's dying of cancer, apparently. Doesn't seem to think he's got anything to lose any more. Probably feels braver after your sentencing.'

'Shit. He was always a weak link. What did he say? Did he mention me?'

'Not in the email. But he's told him about Fabiola, which is bad enough. He also asked Rupert to come and see him, and I'm pretty sure he'll tell him everything when they meet.'

'That can't happen.'

'But ...'

'... it can't happen.'

'Understood,' he said, looking at his shoes. 'What do you want me to do?'

'You remember David Wilson, the security consultant we worked with a few years ago? When we had the issue with Nicki's adopted father?'

'Not so easy to forget.'

'Have you still got his details?'

'Of course.'

'Well, call him and explain the situation. He'll know how to stop Joe blabbing. Do it straight away and tell him what I just said.'

'OK,' said Simon. 'I'll call him as soon as I'm out. And I'll start chasing the appeal.'

'Good. But before you do that, email Nicki Taylor the letter I drafted. Even if we keep Joe quiet, Rupert will tell Sam he has a sister. It's only a matter of time before they contact Nicki directly. I need to keep ahead of them – to control the narrative.'

'That makes total sense. I'll get it done.'

'Of course it makes sense, Simon. I wasn't asking for your bloody blessing. Just make sure it happens. Then give it a couple of days and tell Nicki Taylor to come and visit me.'

He got up and turned to leave. 'One last thing,' I said. He turned back, and I stared at him until he was forced to look down and away. 'Lay off the sauce, Simon. I mean it.'

Is It True?

Joe was living in a small village just outside Brighton and Dad picked me up on the way. We'd arranged to be there at eleven-thirty after Joe's morning sleep while his home care nurses were out for a few hours.

Unsurprisingly, traffic wasn't co-operating and we ended up sitting in a jam on the M23 going nowhere fast.

It could have been worse. The sun was shining; we had the roof down on Dad's Mini and a great playlist. We left a message for Joe and then there was nothing to do but wait.

'I never did tell you how Julie seduced your poor innocent son, did I?'

'You know you didn't,' said Dad. 'Is this just phase two of the wind up?'

'No,' I said. 'If you want to hear it, I'll tell you now. It's definitely going in my book, anyway.'

'We've nothing better to do,' he said. 'But go light on the gory details, eh.'

'I'll do my best,' I said, taking a deep breath. 'Right. Let's give you a bit of context. I'd been working at Pulsar for about four months and was beginning to get the hang of the routines. Julie travelled non-stop and I'd usually tag along. Most of the time she was busy and I ended up kicking my heels. Julie would send for me at any time day or night – whenever she had a free moment – and we would talk about the company. The most fascinating part was looking back at the twenties and learning how close the world was to collapsing.'

'I remember,' said my dad. 'And I read your Pulsar book.'

'Of course you do,' I said. 'Anyway. Sometimes we would go out for dinner, usually in groups, but occasionally just me and Julie. On that particular night, there were six of us. Julie was about to kick off a massive fundraising and had invited the two founder partners of GB Capital, the largest venture capital fund in the US. It wasn't only a dinner invitation; she'd flown them and their wives to Kanazawa in Japan, the town which has more Michelin stars per square metre than anywhere else.

'We were eating at the Suginoi Ryotei which had recently earned its third star, after slumming it with only two stars for decades. The building was old – Meiji era – and, from our second floor dining room, we looked out onto the river and the rows of cherry trees lining its banks. They were in full bloom, of course. Julie left nothing to chance.

'It wasn't hard to figure out that the dinner was important for Julie and that I was expected to shine. The food was amazing – a multi-course Kaiseki dinner – and the exotic delicacies kept on coming, each tiny plate accompanied by its own perfectly matched, thimble-sized cup of sake.

'I hadn't met any venture capitalists before and no-one had warned me that most of them are pompous, self-satisfied gits. Luckily the guys from GB Capital were an exception – not up themselves at all – and we had a real laugh. It turned out that the pair had met each other on the Harvard rowing team and one of their wives had been a Rhodes Scholar at Oxford, so we had loads to talk about.

'When they eventually stopped bringing us food and drink I remember being surprised that I didn't feel bloated or drunk, even though we must have been through thirty courses or more. Although I felt good, I was definitely ready for my bed and I think we all felt the same.

'We'd taken all four rooms at a beautiful ryokan – a Japanese inn – just up the road. It was very traditional, proper beds were not an option, and the down-stuffed duvets and futons gave a totally new perspective to crashing on the floor. I can't actually remember what the ryokan was called or how we made it back, so I might have been

157

a little more pissed than I thought.

'After we'd said goodnight to her guests, I could tell she was happy. I was becoming familiar with the charm aura she projected when she needed to, and I'd seen her turn it on or off like there was a physical switch in her pocket. I'm not saying I was immune to that controlled charm, but this was something different. Maybe she'd had a sake too many? Maybe the fundraising was more important than I knew? Whatever the reason, Julie was genuinely excited, skipping up the narrow wooden stairs like a young girl.'

I picked up my phone. 'I'm gonna read you the next bit from the draft chapter of my book. Less embarrassing that way,'

Dad nodded, grinning like an idiot and probably feeling as awkward as me. Although we were good friends as well as father and son, I wondered if telling him this story was crossing some sort of invisible line.

'OK. *I walked Sonja to her room* – Sonja is Julie, right?'

'I'd never have guessed,' he said.

'Right. So. *I walked Sonja to her room, and she turned to face me. That look! Her eyes were deep burning pools of black oil, swirling in spirals and speckled with flakes of gold. Then, after she closed the door, I crossed the hallway to my own room, head spinning. There was no way I was getting to sleep in a hurry.*

I don't know how long I'd been staring at the ceiling, watching the moon shadows play on the wooden beams, when I heard a soft rustling from the corridor outside. I sat up, ears straining to pick out the sounds. There was nothing for a few seconds until I heard the mouse-quiet squeak of wood on wood.

I watched breathless as Sonja slid open the paper shoji doors and stood in the entranceway, the moonlight limning her hair and picking out the sharp folds and soft curves of her kimono. It was as though she was etched onto ink-black lacquer.

'Are you awake,' she said, her whispered words cutting through the silence.

'Yeah,' I replied. 'Couldn't sleep.'

'Me neither,' she said, and stepped into the room.

There was just enough light for me to see as she slipped the kimono over her shoulders and let it fall ...'

I took a deep breath and turned to my dad.

'And that, dear father, is how your poor innocent son was seduced by the arch bitch, Julie Martin.'

He looked at me and snorted with laughter. 'Sounds like a Mills and Boon novel,' he said. 'You don't think you're overcooking it a tad? Limning? Really?'

'Work in progress,' I said. 'Seriously, you think it's too much?'

Dad nodded, raised his eyebrows and grinned

'OK. Maybe I'll tone it down a bit,' I said. 'In the book I describe what happened next. Should I go on?'

'Whoah. No thanks,' he said. 'That'd be way too much information.' The traffic had eventually started to move and he turned back to the road. 'You're seriously going ahead with the book thing?'

'Why not? I'm going to make all the characters fictional, but it's a great story. I might as well write it?'

'I'd have thought you'd be wanting to forget that entire episode,' he said.

'That's never happening, Dad. I think writing about it may help. If it doesn't, I can always just put it in a drawer and move on. Anyway, at the rate I'm going, it'll be years before I've even got a first draft.'

It was after twelve by the time we arrived at The White Barn. We'd needed to reverse a hundred yards back up the single track lane because of a delivery van which didn't help. I hated being late for anything and this wasn't exactly a normal visit. I could hear my pulse pounding insistently behind my ear.

My dad had been an estate agent all his life. He wasn't smarmy or untrustworthy or anything like that, but he'd picked up a few bad habits. One of these was a compulsion to value every house he saw. As we got out of the car, super agent Rupert leapt into action:

'Mid-seventeenth century, four bedrooms, maybe five, commutable to London or Brighton, about half an acre of gardens, very charming building and location, must be worth at least two million euros.'

'Very clever,' I said. 'Is this really the right time to be playing your valuation games? We're late and I'm stressed out enough as it is.'

'Not a game,' he said. 'Answer me this. How does a divorced schoolteacher who hasn't had a proper job for years get to live here?'

'You checked up on him?'

'Of course I checked up on him,' he said. 'Didn't you?'

I suddenly felt like a teenager again, perpetually impetuous and often regretting it.

'No,' I said, mumbling and looking down at my shoes. 'Probably should have though.'

'Never mind,' he said, as we walked up the rose-lined path. It was all very twee and English country garden. 'The thing is that he doesn't own it.'

'So he's renting then? What's the big deal?'

'Probably nothing, although I couldn't find a rental agreement on the national database and he couldn't afford this place on a teacher's pension, anyway. The house is registered to a blind trust in the Caymans. Something doesn't smell right.'

'OK. OK,' I said. 'You've made your point, but you could have bloody told me all of this in the car. Anyway, it doesn't change anything. We're here now. Let's go in. I hate being late.'

'All right. Keep your hair on,' he said, stepping forward and pressing the doorbell. I heard the buzzer echo down the hall, but there were no other sounds.

'Try again,' I said. 'He might be asleep.'

We tried ringing and knocking for ten minutes with no response and I was beginning to wonder if the whole thing was someone's idea of a sick joke.

'Let's go,' I said. 'There's no-one here.'

'Hang on,' said my dad. 'We've come all this way, we should try round the back first. You wait here.'

Dad was in his element. I watched as he strode across the lawn to the side gate, his confident strides making it appear as though he was the owner. More estate agent habits I supposed. After he'd pushed through the gate and disappeared, I felt exposed and out of place, as though I was about to be caught doing something illegal. I looked up the lane, but there was no sign of life.

I stood by the porch for what seemed like an age, shuffling from one foot to another, until I heard someone fiddling with the latch on the front door. This was it. He was in. In a few minutes, this man was going to give me a sister.

The door opened and my heart sank as I saw Dad standing there alone in the low, black-beamed hallway. 'Very strange,' he said. 'There's no-one here. The lock on the back door was broken, so I walked straight in.'

I pushed past him. 'Joe,' I shouted. 'Joe Taylor. Anyone at home?'

'He's not here,' said my dad. 'You were right. We've wasted our time. Let's go home.' He turned to the open doorway.

'Hang on,' I said. 'Maybe he's had some sort of medical crisis. A heart attack or something. Have you checked upstairs?'

Dad shook his head and I started up the narrow stairs. The ceilings were even lower on the first floor and we both had to watch our heads. For some reason, neither of us spoke. Dad pointed towards the front of the house, shrugged and opened the nearest door. I turned and moved down the corridor which angled around to the right. The house had an unloved feel about it; there were paintings where there were supposed to be paintings, knick-knacks sitting on a desk in an alcove, nothing out of the ordinary. I just had the feeling that they'd been put there by an interior decorator. No-one cared about them.

I reached the end and opened the final door. Nothing to see, another unused guest room looking as though the only guests it remembered were the cleaners who visited once a month.

'Sam!' I heard Dad's voice echo down the narrow passage. 'Sam! Come here. Now!'

I ran back to where my father was framed by an open doorway, facing into the room and slumped sideways against the door. I looked over his shoulder and saw a middle-aged man stretched out on a single bed, eyes open and staring at the ceiling.

'Is he...?' I said.

'Yes,' said my father. 'But not for long.' He turned to face me. 'His body's still warm.'

When the police arrived, we were standing in the front garden. I'd been afraid that we would be stuck waiting around for hours, but the whole process was very relaxed and informal. The two young policewomen checked our IDs, took contact details and brief statements – why we were there and how we'd found the body – and then told us that we could go.

They told us they'd spoken to Joe's doctor; apparently the cancer had been very advanced and the doctor wasn't surprised to hear that he'd died in his sleep. Apparently, if the police needed to ask any more questions, we would do that at our local police station.

Neither of us had much to say as we drove down the narrow lanes. Joe had told my father that Nicki didn't know anything about his secrets. If she didn't know, had they died with him? Maybe there were some documents which could help? I had a gut feeling that there wouldn't be and, in any case, how would we access them?

'So, what do we do?' I said, as we reached the M23. 'Nicki knows nothing about me or her real mother. She's just lost her father. Are we going to track her down and drop those bombshells? I don't see that going down well.'

'Such bad timing,' said Dad. 'I'm sure he had something important to tell us. If he'd been able to hang on just a little longer …'

'It is what it is,' I said. 'Nothing we do is going to change that. What about Nicki?'

'You're right, of course,' he said. 'We can't simply rock up and dump this on her. Especially not now. Shall we see what Daz and Liz have got to say about it. You were planning on telling them about her at dinner tonight, weren't you?'

'That was the plan,' I said. 'And I agree. Let's talk about something else for now. I can't really think straight at the moment.'

Uncle Daz and Liz were an odd couple to say the least. The committed anarchist and psychiatric nurse and the retired detective superintendent. No stranger than Daz becoming good friends with my grandmother I supposed. Everyone loved Daz.

They were pretending to be just good friends and the rest of us had, by unspoken consent, decided to play along with the charade. Why they bothered was beyond me – it could have been because Liz was a few years older than him, or maybe because they felt sorry for me and my dad for being such sad loners without partners.

It was Liz's birthday and we were meeting around the corner from her flat. Red Pepper on Formosa Street was a great little Italian trattoria which served the best pizza in London. Always overbooked and generally overpriced, it had been a Little Venice institution through three generations of the Citterio family. The legend was that since the restaurant opened in nineteen sixty-four there hadn't been a single service without at least one family member on duty.

Giving statements and talking to the police had delayed us enough to ensure that we hit rush hour on our way back to London; sitting in the car had started to become a bit old by the time we finally found a parking space in Little Venice. Dad had been brought up properly and, once he knew we were going to be late, he'd called the restaurant and ordered a bottle of champagne for Daz and Liz with his compliments. Maybe he was an estate agent slimeball after all?

Daz squeezed the last two half glasses out of the bottle as we sat down. At least he and Liz seemed happy.

'OK Sammy Boy,' said Daz, after we'd toasted the birthday girl. 'You've been mumbling about some sort of secret since last week. and now you and Rupert roll up half an hour late and looking very sheepish.' He turned to my dad. 'Thanks for the fizz by the way. Much appreciated.' And then his focus was back on me. 'Time to share, Sam.'

I let Dad start by explaining about the email from Joe. Uncle Daz didn't react as I'd expected.

'Poor Fabiola,' he said. 'This must have all happened just before Uni. Right before we met. She must have been so lonely.' He looked around the table as though he would find answers in our eyes. 'Why did she never tell anyone?'

'I don't know,' said Dad. 'There was always something dark and sad hiding deep inside her. This must have been it. I always assumed it had something to do with Jax and you guys; she was never very forthcoming about any of that.'

'That figures,' said Daz. 'You know what? Knowing this makes me feel that I started letting her down right at the start. She never had the lucky breaks, did she?'

'Aren't we missing something?' I said.

'Of course,' said Daz. 'We need to look at the positives. We're not gonna change the past. You've got a sister now. There's another little piece of Fabiola out there.'

'Well, half sister,' I said. 'And we only have a dead guy's word for any of this.'

'It shouldn't be hard to find out more,' said Liz. 'They won't share adoption records, but your sister must be mid-thirties now. She'll have a big social media footprint.'

'Not as much as I expected,' said my dad. 'What I managed to find was very limited and didn't tell me a lot. I'm not an expert, but it looks managed. She works for a company called Odell Services, some sort of political consultancy. Maybe they control their senior people's profiles?'

'Odell? That name rings a bell,' said Daz. 'Isn't that the name of the place where Fabiola died?'

'Yes,' said my dad. 'Weird isn't it?'

'Why not just pick up the phone to this Nicki?' said Daz.

'Firstly, she's probably hearing about her father's death right about now,' I said. 'It may not be the best time.'

'All right,' said Daz. 'No need to be quite so sarky. Some of us are trying to catch up.'

'And secondly,' I continued. 'What's she going to say if I turn up with nothing but an email sent to my Dad? We're basing everything on the fact that Dad believes Joe was telling the truth.'

'Telling the truth, and frightened of something,' said Dad.

Liz sat up straight like a meerkat. 'You're not suggesting ....?'

'No. Of course not,' said Dad. 'I just believed him and, from what he implied, there's more to this story than we know.'

'There's a fairly simple solution,' said Liz after we'd proceeded to talk ourselves round and round in ever decreasing circles for half an hour. 'We can't do anything now – the poor woman's just lost her father – so we use the next couple of weeks to find out more.'

'How exactly?' I said.

'I know someone. Used to be a colleague and a good friend. She runs a small investigation agency. They're not cheap, but they're very good. Let her poke around discretely for ten days or so and see what she turns up. At least that way you'll know a little more about Nicki before you get in touch.'

'That sounds like a good idea,' said my dad. 'Liz's friend can try and get to the bottom of Joe's money situation as well. I thought that was strange.'

'I'm not sure,' I said. 'Isn't this all a bit creepy and intrusive? What will Nicki say when she finds out? Not a great start to a relationship.'

'Why would she find out?' said Liz.

'Because I'll tell her, for starters,' I said. 'I'm not going to lie to her.' I looked around the table at the three scheming faces. Why couldn't they see that poking around in Nicki's life was wrong?

'All right,' said Daz. 'We might be getting carried away here.' He looked over to me. 'The thing is, Sam … you've been in the press a lot recently and there are lots of dodgy people out there. This could be some sort of scam. We're just trying to look out for you.'

'I know,' I said. 'I just don't want to do anything underhand.'

'Neither do we,' said my dad. 'You know us better than that. How about we agree to limit the investigation to checking that Joe was telling the truth?'

'OK,' I said. 'Then I'll be able to tell her what we did, and why.' I felt my niggling irritation fade as quickly as it had arrived. 'Dad and I will meet up with Liz's investigator, tell her what we know, and we'll meet back here in a couple of weeks to discuss the results.'

Looking at the three people nodding their agreement in front of me, I saw my closest family and friends, people who would be there for me no matter what.

I couldn't help imagining that, in a few weeks or months, there might be one more.

Revelations

Nicki looked terrible as she walked into the visiting room. I had arranged for us to be alone, but the guards had still insisted on a screen between us.

She slumped into the chair, arms crossed, looking more like a rebellious teenage goth than a thirty-eight-year-old CEO. I could see that her eyes were red and swollen.

'Hi Nicki,' I said, smiling. 'I was sorry to hear about your father.'

'Thank you,' she mumbled into her lap, before lifting her head and staring at me with defiant eyes. 'What the fuck's going on Julie?' She was almost shouting. 'One minute you're my boss, then you're in prison for murder and now … now I don't know what the hell you are.'

'You read the letter then?'

'Of course I read the bloody letter. I can't say I understood half of it, but I read it a hundred times.'

'It must be a hell of a lot to take in …'

'No shit, Sherlock.'

'Nicki!' I snapped. There were limits. 'I'm trying to be supportive here, but remember who you're speaking to.'

I genuinely felt awash with sympathy as I watched her crumple back into her chair. 'I'm sorry, Julie,' she said. 'I just don't know what to believe any more. I'm still trying to get to grips with my dad dying. I knew he was ill, but he was supposed to have six months or more. He could be a plonker sometimes, but he was a good dad. He did his best.'

'Of course he did. I know it's tough, but don't take it out on me.

Did you cross check the timings?'

'Of course. It all fits. Everything makes sense now, except for why no-one ever told me the truth – and how you come into it.'

'I tried to explain that in the letter and, as for me, if you'd known your mother, you'd understand. Anybody who had Fabiola in their lives felt the same way, including your dad. She was wonderful, even when she was being a spoilt pain in the arse. Have you ever watched a small child stroking a lamb?'

Nicki nodded without speaking, her anger and confusion seemingly evaporated.

'Everyone who was with Fabiola would have that look on their faces. Innocent, unquestioning adoration.' I said, looking down at the floor. 'Although she left me and broke my heart, I would still have done anything for her.' I lifted my head and smiled at Nicki. 'After she died, looking out for you and Sam was all I had left of her.'

She probably thought I was laying it on a bit thick, but it was all true. Looking around a room just after Fabiola walked in (or walked out for that matter), you'd see it on every face – eyes glazed, bottom lips hanging loose, every head pulling itself imperceptibly towards her. Fabiola had traipsed through her short life unconsciously dragging a trail of disciples behind her like tin cans on a wedding car.

Nicki wasn't convinced. 'It still doesn't make sense. You helped fund my schooling and you've supported my career. I just about get that.' She looked over her shoulder at the guard before whispering. 'I know you've got enough money, so why not? I even think I understand why you changed your name and kept your past hidden from both of us.' She leant forward, fingers splayed out on the metal shelf and nose almost pressed against the glass. 'But you had an affair with Sam, who's apparently now my half-brother. You actually slept with him. How does that fit with the whole godmother/mentor thing? … And then there's all this business with my mother's phone and her suicide. Something stinks.'

Finally, we were getting to the nub. In my experience, truth was a fluid and slippery thing. By the time this conversation was over,

Nicki needed to be convinced of my truth. Convinced in a way that no revelations of half-brothers or water-cooler scandals would shake. The difference between my truth and Sam's truth was that I had been nurturing Nicki for a quarter of a century, and poor Sam hadn't even met her yet.

'OK,' I said, smiling a young girl's smile and lowering my eyes. 'I couldn't explain this in a letter. Apart from anything else, I feel so foolish. My relationship with Sam was clearly a mistake and I regret it now. I started off trying to help his career, just as I have been helping yours. It was totally professional and then … then it just happened. I could see how attracted he was to me and, trust me, as you get older, that feels pretty good. We'd been working late, had a glass of wine too many and …' I continued to avoid her gaze and allowed the silence between us to swell and grow.

The shadows shifted on the steel counter as she pulled back from the glass and sank back into her chair with a sigh. 'I guess it's not the first time that sort of thing has happened,' she said. 'But still … it's not right.' Acceptance and understanding would do. I wasn't expecting approval. But she wasn't finished. 'And anyway, that doesn't explain what you did to his – I mean, our – mother.'

No room for playing the blushing ingénue here. She was on the back foot and needed to see her mentor and boss. 'How long have you been working for Odell?' I snapped.

'Almost five years.'

'… And you still believe everything you read or hear in the media?'

'No, but …'

'The basic explanation for that story is that it's not true,' I said. 'None of it. As much as anyone can, I understand how deeply Fabiola's death affected Sam – there's always been something missing in his life – but I've never understood why he turned it into such a vendetta. It's never added up.'

'So you didn't put spy software on Fabiola's phone?' Nicki said, her voice oozing sarcasm. 'Sam just made all of that up?'

As I thought back to that time, it wasn't difficult to fill my voice with sadness and tears. 'No. He didn't make it up.' I took a deep breath before continuing. 'I did install the software, but her husband did too. We were both worried about her. She became very fragile after Sam's birth. The rest of it – the stories of persecution and manipulation – were all in Fabiola's imagination, I'm afraid. There's a reason why the police never investigated that story – there was nothing to it.'

'I don't buy it,' said Nicki. 'Why would Sam go to so much trouble to pursue you?'

'Take a step back and open your eyes. Imagine you're vetting a new client. What's the first rule I taught you about modelling a politician's behaviour?'

'Forget the noise. Follow the money.'

'Exactly,' I said. '… Exactly.' I leant forward and lowered my voice. 'And that's what you need to do now. I've been successful because I've always kept tight, tight control on my strategy and plans. That's how I managed to keep one step ahead of the competition. I've only let my guard down twice – once with Sam and once with Dave Bukowski. I shared my vision with them and look at what happened. Dave's now a billionaire and Sam's not far behind.'

Nicki's eyes widened, her lips forming a perfect "O". 'Are you saying that the two of them manufactured those accusations to destroy your reputation and take Pulsar from you?'

'Not exactly – it's much more complicated than that. But I am saying that you should do your homework before you make assumptions. And they didn't just take Pulsar from me. They took it from both of us.'

'What?'

'Wake up, Nicki. Who else would be my successor? … Who?'

I had waited a long time to drop that bombshell, and could tell from her blank expression that everything she had previously imagined about her life and her future had been vaporised, wiped out by a few, simple words. It would take a while for greed and resentment to seep in to fill the space, but they would.

'You'll still have Odell,' I continued. 'But you were supposed to have so much more.'

I looked at the still figure in front of me and was surprised by my sudden urge to give her a hug. I didn't do hugs – ever – but Nicki looked so confused and alone.

'Nicki,' I said. 'I know you're still in shock about your dad … And this is the last thing you need to be dealing with. Go home and rest. Look after yourself for a few days, grieve for your loss, and we can pick this up another time. OK?'

She nodded and stood up.

'One last thing,' I said. 'I'd place a big bet that your dad contacted Rupert or Sam before he died. They'll be looking for you now. When you hear from them, promise me you'll come and see me.'

'All right. I'll do that.'

'Before you meet them.'

'Yes.'

One In – One Out

Life often seems like one of those complicated Scottish dances where people spin round, dip between arches of raised arms, twirl behind a back or two and end up hand-in-hand with a new partner. One in, another out.

I had started to believe that I might be gaining a sister but, before I'd even met her, I found myself needing to consider the possibility that I might lose my last remaining grandparent. Granny had been rushed into hospital and, although the consultants were still waiting for the biopsy results, the prognosis didn't look good.

'She'll be all right, Dad. It's Granny. She's the toughest.'

'I'm not sure this time,' he said, sadness creeping into his voice. 'I saw her yesterday, and she was different. As though she'd shrunk – withered into herself. The doctors didn't say much to make me feel better.'

I realised I was holding the phone away from my ear. In a futile attempt to dilute his words?

'Can I see her?' I said. 'I could come up for a few hours tomorrow.'

'Leave it until the weekend. She'll be back home on Friday and I know she'd rather be in her own space. Hospitals are such awful places.'

'OK. I'll come up on Saturday morning, first thing.'

'Great,' he said. '... And for now, don't worry too much about your granny. We'll know more in a few days.'

'I'll try,' I said, noticing how empty most words of comfort tended to be.

'What about that private investigator lady?' he said. 'How did it go? Sorry I couldn't be there, but now you know why.'

'That was actually why I called,' I said. 'I know you've got a lot on your plate, but I was going to ask if you could write to Nicki sooner rather than later.'

'I thought we agreed to wait?'

'We did, but Liz's PI friend is still on holiday and her assistant said the earliest we'd have any feedback is in three or four weeks, at best. I'm actually thinking of not bothering with the whole investigator thing.'

'That's a bore,' he said, 'but go and see her, anyway. Even if you meet Nicki before you hear from Liz's friend, it's still worth making sure.'

'All right,' I said. 'Anyway, it's been ten days since Nicki's father's funeral and I think we should contact her before she stumbles across a copy of the email Joe sent you ... or something else which mentions Mum or me.'

'Why don't you just call her? It's you she'll want to meet.'

'I guess for the same reasons Joe contacted you first, rather than me. You can act as a buffer ... it'll give her a chance to go through her thoughts and feelings ahead of time. I know I'd prefer that.'

'Yeah. There's some sort of logic there, I suppose. Leave it with me. I'll use Joe's address. I'm sure that'll get to her.'

Iona Stevens was Liz's investigator friend, and she wasn't a lady to be messed with. That was clear the moment I walked into her office; the woman was a pocket-sized bundle of sharp angles and nervous energy, not more than five foot tall, cropped black hair and bossy as they come. Without Dad to add a bit of moral support and gravitas, we passed a frosty first five minutes. I was half-expecting her to tell me to leave and stop wasting her time – in fact, I'd have taken bets she'd have done exactly that if Liz hadn't been calling in a favour from the past.

The conversation eventually settled down and become more relaxed, but there was never any question about who called the shots. When it came to the actual nitty gritty, and I handed her the details I had, a look of weary despair washed over her face. It was the kind of look I hadn't seen since I was a school kid and Mrs Hibbert was handing me back a particularly poor Religious Studies essay.

'So this is it?' she said, leaning forward and waving the single sheet of A4 paper in front of my nose. 'An email from her deceased father to your father, a reference to a sordid scandal from forty years ago, her name and her father's address? That's what I have to go on?'

I shrunk back in my chair. She may have been tiny, but she was very frightening. 'I'm sorry. That's it,' I said. 'That's why we wanted your help. We don't want you to dig too deeply, nothing intrusive. We just want to know that it isn't some sort of scam.'

Her world-weary shrug and rolling of eyes looked well practised.

'... Oh. And there's the stuff my dad discovered about her father's house and the offshore company ...'

She nodded and shrugged her shoulders.

'... And that's it really ...'

The silence grew uncomfortable before she unrolled her paper sword, straightened out the fold and stood up.

'OK. Thank you Mr Blackwell. I'll see what I can find out.' She gestured towards the door. 'My assistant will have explained our fee structure?'

'Yes. Thank you,' I said.

'... I'll have something for you in three weeks,' she said, as I made my escape. 'Not before.'

I could see what my father had meant about Granny. She was a different person from the one I'd seen just a few weeks earlier.

Even in her own kitchen and wearing normal clothes, she looked frail – less substantial and much older. Exactly as Dad had told me, she'd withered into herself like a plant in need of watering. It was as though she'd already decided the tests would come back negative and mortality had suddenly caught up with her.

Granny had always played the dominant role in our family, the ultimate arbiter of all things and especially what was socially acceptable and what wasn't. There had never been room for the concepts of weakness or frailty in her world.

She looked up and smiled as she saw me walk in. 'Pour yourself a cup of tea and sit down,' she said. 'I've been waiting for you.'

I poured the tea and sat down next to her. 'Sorry to hear you're under the weather,' I said. 'Hopefully, they'll get everything sorted soon enough.'

'Sorted *out*,' she said. 'Not "sorted". If you're going to be a writer, there's no room for sloppiness in your language. In any case, I'm not convinced that they'll be able to sort anything out, I'm afraid.'

'Don't be so negative, Granny,' I said. 'I'm sure …'

'… Oh, I'm not negative,' she said. 'Quite the opposite.' She took a bird-like sip of her tea. 'Do you remember the conversation we had a couple of years ago? Sitting right here? It was right after that terrible time when that witch Julie Martin locked you up and left you to die.'

'Of course I remember,' I said. 'I try to forget about those days, but without much success. You were trying to take all the blame for what happened to Mum.'

Although she was frail and her voice was weak, there was nothing wrong with her mind and her personality hadn't changed.

'You know that's not quite accurate,' she said. 'I wasn't taking all the blame. I was just acknowledging the fact that I wasn't as kind to Fabiola as I might have been and that I believe my behaviour may have contributed to what happened.'

'OK, Granny,' I said. 'I was only teasing. I remember what you said.'

She looked at me with eyebrows arched. 'Do you think there might be better times and better subjects for your humour?' She didn't look angry, but I wasn't quite sure.

'I'm sorry,' I said. 'Anyway, why were you thinking about that conversation?'

'A scare like I've just had makes its mark. Maybe this one will turn out to be a false alarm, but if it's not this one, something else will be along soon. I'm eighty-four and I'm not sad that I'll be seeing your grandfather sooner rather than later. I would have liked to meet your children, but we can't have everything, can we?'

All I wanted to do was to tell her that she was wrong and that she was going to be fine. In a rare flash of mature insight, however, I understood that she didn't want to hear those platitudes and my straw-clutching optimism wasn't going to change a thing.

'... And Mum? How does she figure in your thinking?'

Although her brain was still working, she was obviously exhausted, and it took her a few moments to gather her thoughts.

'Oh, yes. I remember,' she said, as the pennies dropped into place. 'D'you know what? I'm excited to see Fabiola again. I'll be able to apologise at last, to tell her what a wonderful man her Sam has turned out to be, and I'm actually looking forward to finding out if she's ever forgiven me.'

Luckily my dad chose that moment to come back into the kitchen, noisily banging the kettle onto the Aga and offering more tea. I took the opportunity to slip out into the garden for five minutes and gather myself.

How strange it must be to have such a simple, almost childlike faith? I found it impossible to believe in an afterlife where everyone you had ever known would be waiting for you, unchanged? How did it work, this faith which could override all logic?

Plan B

Nicki was looking a lot better than a few weeks earlier. Joe's funeral would have helped her to draw a line, and she was made of strong stuff.

'I had a letter from Sam Blackwell's dad yesterday,' she said, as she sat down. 'Just like you said I would. It was an old-fashioned handwritten one and he told me that my father had emailed him and that Fabiola was my mother. He wants me and Sam to meet.'

She shrugged her shoulders and leant back in her chair. 'I promised to come and see you first … and here I am.'

Our previous meeting had ended abruptly with Nicki apparently broken and overwhelmed by the onslaught of conflicting information piling on top of her. She must have felt as though she was standing in the middle of an earthquake watching the buildings collapsing around her.

Although true empathy may not have been my strongest talent, I still had a sense for how people would respond to external factors – when it was right to push forward, and when it was better to stand back and wait. I'd known that Nicki would benefit from some time to process everything she'd heard about me, to look into the available facts and to draw her own conclusions. She'd also appeared to be genuinely grieving for Joe. He'd been a waste of space, but he'd been her waste of space.

I couldn't have planted my seeds better, they'd been well fed and watered, but Nicki was backed into a corner and would soon be coming under pressure to take sides, to choose who and what to believe. I was confident that I'd done enough to stay in control, but nothing was certain.

'When are you meeting them?'

'Friday morning,' she said. 'But I'm worried about Damocles. It's been out there for a week now, and things will start to happen soon. What if I end up liking Sam? Should I warn him?'

'You will like him. He's charming and funny. That doesn't change anything.'

'But now I know he's my half-brother ...'

'And?' I said. 'You understood the situation well enough before you found that out. Has anything really changed? Sam still helped to destroy Pulsar and put me here. Are you going soft on me?'

'No. Of course not. It's just ...'

'Listen to me. When you meet him, you need to play dumb – act totally surprised and embrace your long-lost family. You don't know me. You worked for Pulsar for a few years, but only in a junior role. Give them the usual public-facing vanilla bullshit about Odell. Meanwhile our private project is moving forward one way or another. Falling on your sword won't help anyone.' I rested my fingertips on the glass between us and looked into her eyes. 'Just remember what he took away from us.'

'I know. I know you're right,' she said, her hand reaching out towards mine. 'I've been thinking a lot about what you did for me as a child. How you helped me to get out of that home and have a good life with my dad. It means a lot ...'

Our fingertips met on either side of the glass.

'And just because he and I have the same mother,' she continued. 'That doesn't change anything. I've never even met the guy.' Her mouth hardened and I saw determined resolution in those familiar dark eyes. 'As you say, he's only getting what's coming to him.'

I watched her leave with a sinking feeling. She was still loyal to me, and the fact that she was the one who had created and launched Damocles would be difficult for her to explain away. But the prison wouldn't allow me another social visit for weeks and meanwhile Sam would be turning on that boyish charm. Nicki had no other family and she would be tempted to embrace her new one.

If I left the two of them to their own devices, it was only a matter of time before my plans crumbled into dust. I needed to take back control and I couldn't do that from behind bars.

Simon glared at the guard until she took a couple of steps back closer to the metal door. Josie was a walking sackful of bitterness and resentment. I'd been in Downview for two weeks and every time I saw her, she had the same scowl plastered over her fat face. She looked dangerous and the word was that she'd half killed a young girl who'd upset her in some way. Nothing had come of it, of course. The wardens protected each other, whatever happened.

As Simon leant forward towards me, I could see that the red blotches on his cheeks were gone and the purple veins on his nose were fading. He'd apparently taken my "suggestion" on board. Paying him too much had its advantages after all.

'She's meeting him on Friday,' I said.

'You knew it would happen.' He shrugged his shoulders. 'And you've spoken to her?'

'Yes. Two weeks ago and again yesterday. I've done what I can for now.'

'You'll have heard that the other business went off as planned?' His voice had dropped to a bass murmur.

'Of course I heard.'

'Well, you should be aware that it was tight. Only ten minutes to spare. No reason why that should cause complications, but it's best that you know.'

'Bloody right,' I said. 'That's sloppy. What happened?'

'I couldn't reach David for twenty-four hours. Apparently he was heli-skiing in the Caucasus.'

I'd learned from years of experience that money could buy almost anything. There was a slight caveat to that. If people were given too much money, they tended to enjoy spending it, which made them less available when I needed them. That was why, as a general rule, I always replaced my key operations people on a regular basis. There were some downsides, but it kept them hungry.

Simon was an exception; he'd been my lawyer for over ten years. Although I'd often wondered if I could have done better, motivation was often as much about sticks as it was about carrots. Simon wouldn't have wanted anyone to find out about the jobs he'd commissioned on my behalf.

'Next time – if there is a next time – take a bit of initiative, Simon. When I say something is urgent, I'm not blowing hot air for the sake of it.'

'Yes. I will,' he said, beads of sweat glistening like tiny pearls on his forehead. 'Now, about the appeal hearing …'

'… Will we have a date in the next four weeks?'

'Not a chance.'

'Then it's not important. We need to move to Plan B.'

I hadn't allowed for Joe's cancer. Without the knowledge of his imminent death, I doubted he'd have had the courage to defy me, whether or not I was in prison. We would have had time for the appeal and the odds of overturning the conviction were more than evens. Unfortunately all plans were subject to unknown rogue factors – it was foolish to believe otherwise. The trick was to have contingency plans and I always made a point of having plenty of those.

'Plan B?' Simon said, his voice little more than a whisper. 'I see.'

'Is there a problem?'

'No … well …no … there's not a problem.'

'Good. I'm thinking two weeks at the outside.'

'Two weeks,' he said. 'That's not very long.' His voice was shaky and I watched the dark patches of sweat spread inexorably across his pink shirt. White would have been a more sensible choice.

'You're not filling me with confidence, Simon,' I said. 'Is everything ready?'

'Sorry, Julie. You just threw me for a minute.' He pulled out a linen handkerchief and wiped his face. 'Don't worry. Two weeks is fine. The plan is in place. I just need to finalise a couple of details.'

'Excellent,' I said. 'I'm sure you won't let me down. Now, there's one other thing …'

Siblings

'You sure you're up for this, Dad?'

'Of course I am. This is a massive day for you. I couldn't let you down.' He turned to look at me, red-rimmed eyes blinking furiously. 'Besides, what else am I going do?'

Dad had spent most of the night at the John Radcliffe hospital holding Granny's hand; I doubted he'd slept at all.

We sat in silent solidarity as the train trundled painfully slowly through the sprawl of West London. I stared out of the window, the thick glass cool against my forehead. There was one graffiti tag which appeared again and again at the side of the tracks, usually in seemingly unreachable locations. It appeared that Ajax – whoever he or she might be – was equally happy hanging upside down from a bridge or balanced precariously on tiny ledges no wider than my thumb.

Why? So random people going by on a train would know that Ajax existed? Once again. Why?

Dad had arranged for us to meet Nicki in the lobby of the Park Lane Hilton. She'd wanted somewhere public, and the hotel was what they'd come up with. When he'd told me about the meeting a couple of days earlier, I wouldn't have minded if the rendezvous had been set in the middle of Oxford Circus.

I'd been so excited to have a firm date. My thoughts whirled like a cloud of helicopter seeds falling from a sycamore tree, each spinning in one direction for a few seconds before jolting randomly onto a completely different trajectory. Before I'd heard about Nicki, I'd begun to see a stable, predictable path stretching out in front of me.

Not any longer. My future had been thrown up in the air again and the wait to see how the seeds would fall was both thrilling and agonising.

I'd been reading about families who reunited with long-lost relations; a lot of them talked about the sense of a physical bond which was pulling them back together despite having been stretched almost to breaking point. I understood the feeling. Although I'd never really known my mother, discovering a living connection to her was a wonderful and unexpected gift.

For all I knew, we might end up hating each other, but my gut feelings told me that being in the same room as my sister would be enough. Enough to satisfy that ache which, only a few weeks earlier, I hadn't even known I had.

The euphoria had lasted until a few hours earlier when life threw me another curve ball and the thrill melted away leaving nothing but a bad taste on the roof of my mouth. My Granny had died at three o'clock in the morning and all of my fears about "one in, another out" had come true in a moment of dark inevitability.

Both Dad and I had been there at the end, along with Uncle Daz and, as far as I could tell, she didn't suffer. She wasn't really conscious – there were no final words – she just stopped *being* from one moment to the next.

The doctor said that it looked as though she'd decided it was her time. He tried to explain how the power of a patient's desire to live could keep them going and how, when that desire fades, the patient so often fades away as well. I wasn't really listening, but the snippets which had slipped through reminded me of my final conversation with Granny.

She'd known.

Dad was holding up surprisingly well. In a place deep inside, I suspected he'd also known. He'd told me he didn't feel anything was left unsaid or unresolved between them. He would miss her, but there was no itch which couldn't be scratched, no sense of "if only …" or "I should have …".

'Granny was ready, wasn't she,' I said, as the train started to slow. 'She was tired and bored of being old.'

'I think so,' he said. 'I think she was also impatient to see your Gramps again.'

'Yeah. She talked a bit about that with me last week … Strange to have such certainty.'

'It's what kept her strong,' said Dad. 'She believed things with such conviction. Not only religious faith, everything. She was infuriatingly dogmatic and intransigent, but she believed in family, loyalty and honour as much as anything else. That can't be so bad.' He stood up and pulled his coat from the rack above us. 'I only remember her doubting herself once – when your mother died. It was the one time I can remember when she questioned her beliefs about anything.'

I looked up at him and smiled. 'We talked about that last week as well,' I said. 'She told me that she was looking forward to seeing Mum as well. To find out if she'd forgiven her.'

Dad's eyes lost focus for a moment. 'I can believe that,' he said. 'She was never afraid of anything.'

As we stepped off the train into the flow of people, he took hold of my shoulder, leant towards me and whispered hoarsely in my ear. 'I'd put money that your Granny knew the truth when she spoke with you. She knew how unlikely it was that Fabiola was going to forgive her – or any of us for that matter. Your mother was from the South of Italy. Gorgeous, passionate, kind, but not really the forgiving type.'

We took a taxi from Paddington. Despite decades of doom-and-gloom merchants forecasting its demise, the traditional London Black Cab was alive and well, as much a part of the city's soul as the Tower of London or Buckingham Palace.

Luckily, we didn't have a chatty driver and slipped back into silence as we drove along Bayswater and down Park Lane, sandwiched between massive buildings and the green lung of Hyde Park. I wanted to rekindle my former excitement, but the combination of losing my grandmother and being reminded of my mother had settled over my thoughts like a damp, grey fog. The timing couldn't have been worse.

The taxi pulled up outside the Hilton, I paid the driver and we stepped out into the bright sunshine. My dad wrapped his arm around me and steered me towards the hotel entrance.

'Come on, boy,' he said. 'Enough of this sadness. I'm excited. You must be boiling over. Let's go and meet your sister.'

The next ten minutes passed in a blur. Most people will only ever know a handful of truly life-changing moments; the birth of a child; an unexpected diagnosis or maybe the loss of a loved one. It's fortunate that there are usually only a few, as our bodies and minds inevitably struggle to cope with the emotional overload.

I could remember how close I was to being sick as we walked through the lobby, our footsteps echoing plaintively on the marble floor. I could remember the uncertainty of a handshake which transmogrified into an awkward hug, I could remember trying to take in everything all at once – her eyes, mouth, body, hair, clothes, everything – and I could remember trying and failing to control the tears which threatened to overwhelm me.

Somehow – probably thanks to my dad – we ended up sitting in comfortable armchairs around a small round table, cappuccinos and glasses of water in front of us. I looked at Nicki. She was nine years older than me and I think I'd expected her to be slightly frumpy – almost middle-aged. I'd seen enough photos of our mother to have known better. There was nothing whatsoever frumpy about her – she was beautiful with a gorgeous confident smile and dark, laughing eyes. She wasn't from a different generation at all; we could be friends as well as siblings.

My dad was managing the conversation while I sat slack-mouthed and punch drunk and probably sporting a pathetic grin.

'... And you knew nothing about your real mother until I wrote to you?'

'Nothing,' she said. 'My dad refused to talk about her. He wouldn't even tell me her name. I pushed him a few times, and he'd just tell me that I'd had enough parents already and I didn't need any more. One time, when I was sixteen, I refused to let it drop.' She looked at me and then back to my dad. 'You know what teenagers can be like?'

We both nodded. There were plenty of memories to pick from.

'Anyway, I managed to wear him down, eventually. After three days of me sniping at him, he grabbed me by the shoulders and shouted at me. "She's dead. OK? She's dead." He then spun around and stormed out. He didn't come back until the following day and I remember realising how much he must have loved her.'

'I'll show you the letter he wrote me at some point,' said my dad. 'Whatever I might feel about the circumstances of their relationship, I'm sure he loved Fabiola.' He smiled. 'Trust me. It wasn't difficult.'

'And she never told you anything about me?' Nicki asked my dad. 'You didn't suspect?'

'No,' he said. 'She wasn't a secretive person but, considering that, it appears she had an awful lot of secrets. I only found out that she'd been part of an anarchist group after Sam was born and, as for the fact that she spent five years in a relationship with a woman right before I met her …'

'Yes. That must have come as a surprise,' said Nicki with a smile. 'When I got your letter, I knew the names were familiar. It didn't take me long to figure out that you, Fabiola and Sam were linked to the Julie Martin case.'

'You don't know the half of it,' I jumped in. 'Even from behind bars, she had the media running scared.'

'… but she still claims she was innocent, doesn't she?'

'Believe me,' said my dad. 'Innocent isn't a word that can ever be linked to that woman.'

'Can we not talk about Julie, please,' I said. 'Those are not memories I want to drag up. I'll tell you the whole story at some point, but not right now. Is that OK?'

'Sorry,' she said. 'You don't need to tell me anything if you don't want to.' A waiter interrupted her to ask if we wanted more coffee. She waited until he was gone before continuing in a low voice. '… But I do have to tell you that I actually worked for Pulsar for a few years.'

I turned to my dad; his shocked look must have been mirrored by my own. We blurted out our surprise in unison.

'No!'

'Seriously?'

'When?'

'I left about four years ago. They sponsored me through my MBA and then offered me a job.'

'… And you met her?' I said, images – good and bad – flashing unbidden in front of my eyes.

'A few times,' said Nicki. 'I never saw any sign of the person they've been describing in the papers. She always came across as a charismatic, visionary leader. Most of her staff would have taken a bullet for her.' She laughed. 'Not a real one, of course.'

I didn't know what to say. That bitch had even managed to stick her bloodstained fingers into this moment.

Nicki was smart enough to sense the mood. 'Anyway, enough about me,' she said. 'I want to hear about you, Sam … and about Fabiola.'

Two hours and several cappuccinos later, all thoughts of Julie had faded away. I was over my initial paralysis and was convinced that the two of us would become friends. I wasn't sure how Dad would fit in – I couldn't see them having any sort of parent-child relationship – but we had a common bond. Mum might be dead, but she was still the glue holding us all together.

After half an hour or so, there was an unspoken agreement to stop asking each other serious questions, and we sat and listened to my dad talking about our mum. A new and fascinated audience had inspired him to dig deep into his memories and, although I'd heard most of the stories before, the pictures he painted of the young Fabiola Carlantino were almost as fresh to me as it must have been to Nicki.

Nicki had to leave for a lunch meeting and we all stood to say goodbye. There was no more awkwardness in our hugs and Dad and I waited and watched as she walked out towards the entrance. As she stepped through the double-height glass doors, she looked back at us and smiled, her hand lifted in a half wave, before slipping out into the bright afternoon.

I slumped back into my chair, feeling the nervous exhaustion overtake me, melting every bone in my body and leaving me sagging like an under-stuffed scarecrow.

'Phew,' said Dad.

I managed a feeble chuckle. 'It's two thousand and forty-two, Dad. Who actually says "phew"?'

'Don't be a smug smartarse,' he said. 'It's not funny and it's not clever.'

'I'll try,' I said. 'As long as you try not to be too much of an old fart.' I punched him on the shoulder. 'So …?'

'I thought it went rather well,' he said, grinning. 'She's lovely.'

'Yup,' I said. 'She's great. Wonderful. But bloody Pulsar, eh?'

'You should have seen the look on your face.'

'And yours,' I said. 'I guess it's not such a huge coincidence. They've got over thirty thousand employees.'

'I suppose not,' he said. 'Six degrees of separation and all that.'

He was probably right, but "coincidence" didn't sit well alongside Julie Martin any more than "innocent" did — however hard I tried, she still visited me every night in my dreams.

I needed to get that woman out of my head and made a mental note to bite the bullet and do something about it. I'd been putting off going to a counsellor for months — I didn't have a high opinion of psychiatry — but it was long past time to deal with my issues.

'I'm turning into a paranoid idiot, aren't I?' I said.

'Give yourself a break,' my dad said. 'It's probably just the six cups of coffee starting to kick in.'

'Seriously, I thought Nicki was amazing,' I said. 'I'm sure we'll get on and I can't wait to find out what Daz thinks of her. I'll figure out how to put my paranoia back in its box before then.'

We'd arranged to meet for dinner a couple of weeks later, after Granny's funeral. She would have loved Nicki. I knew it.

Gossamer Threads

I couldn't face going straight to the office after meeting Nicki. I needed time to myself, to think and to allow the adrenalin to find a way out of my system. I crossed Park Lane and started wandering aimlessly through Hyde Park.

Dad had gone straight back to Oxford. There were funeral arrangements to make and Daz was waiting for him at the Old Vicarage. As soon as it had become clear that Granny wouldn't recover, he'd booked a week off work. As I thought about Dad and Uncle Daz, I wasn't sure who would have been the most upset out of the two of them.

Daz never talked about his family and had made it clear he preferred not to. Maybe they were all dead, or there had been a massive family bust-up. Whatever the story, I had the impression that he'd learned to fend for himself from an early age.

As to how and why Daz had adopted me, my father and my Granny? That was bizarre. He was different – from Granny especially – in every way, but he really had become like a second son to her and no nephew could have had a better uncle than I did.

I stopped and sat on a bench in the rose garden. There was no-one else there apart from two pretty Latin-looking girls chatting and laughing together. One of them reminded me of my mother and I took a sharp breath as I realised how much influence she continued to have on all of us, even a quarter of a century after her death.

Nicki, Daz, Julie, my family; all of us were joined by gossamer threads of Fabiola's making. Disparate souls caught in her sticky web.

I sat on the bench for a long time, watching the grey squirrels run fearlessly along the upside-down arches of the rope swags and half-noticing the people passing by: mothers (or nannies) with prams; energy-conserving park keepers pretending to work; an ancient, wrinkled couple walking hand-in-hand; a group of teenagers who should surely have been in school.

My thoughts wandered without purpose, darting from place-to-place like so many dragonflies shimmering on a lily pond. I thought about my Granny, each memory bundled together by the joy and love in those sharp blue eyes. And I thought about Nicki – what I'd anticipated and what I'd found.

I hadn't known what to expect, but each time I thought back to our short time together, I couldn't help smiling. She was much more than I'd dared to hope for and I knew we'd become close friends.

I was jolted back to reality by my phone which was buzzing in my pocket like a trapped bluebottle. It was Lucy, Dave's assistant.

'Will you be in later?'

'I was planning to taking the day off. I thought Dave knew.'

'Yes. Sorry to hear about your grandmother. It's just that we've got the Three-Sixty pre-launch meeting at half-past four and Dave needs you there if at all possible.'

I looked at my watch.

'Of course, Lucy.' I stood up. 'Thanks for reminding me. Don't worry. I'll be there.'

I still had plenty of time to go home, change and read through the meeting notes, but I couldn't believe I'd completely forgotten about the meeting. Ever since my dream – or nightmare as it turned out – job offer from Julie, I'd allowed my personal life to swamp everything else. I'd almost forgotten what a work ethic was.

That imbalance couldn't continue. MySafe had a huge product launch coming up in just a few weeks and, even if my team did most the actual work for me, I needed to be around. There was also the possibility that I had a useful contribution to make. Someone needed to be in charge after all.

I was in good time for the meeting. There were only six department heads in attendance, three of whom had flown in from New York, and I shivered when I imagined how it would have looked if I hadn't shown up. I owed Lucy a massive bunch of flowers.

Luckily no-one needed to know I was behaving like an unprofessional moron. The meeting went well – I'd been right to trust my team and product marketing had its ducks neatly lined in a row. Our Texan operations manager even went so far as to say that the campaign was 'mighty impressive'.

I was halfway out of the door when Dave called me back.

'Close the door behind you, Sam.'

As I turned back to face him, he wrapped his arms around me and hugged me.

'Sorry to hear about your Gran,' he said. 'She was a great lady.'

'Thanks, Dave,' I said. 'She was great, but she was also eighty-four, which is a pretty good innings. I think she was ready to go.'

'Eighty-four?' he said. 'That's impressive. I can't see either of us making it that long.'

'Not unless they perfect those cloned liver transplants.'

We both laughed and sat down.

'So,' he said, eyebrows arching. 'How was it?'

'You mean Nicki?'

'Of course I mean Nicki, numbskull. What was she like?'

'Well one thing's for sure,' I said. 'You're gonna like her … in fact, I'm thinking of making sure you two never meet.'

'Cute, huh?'

'I thought she was gorgeous … as well as charming, witty and sharp as a tack,' I said. 'But, then again, I might have a bit of a bias.'

'Got any photos?'

'A couple.' I took out my phone and scrolled down. 'Here you go.'

'Oh yes. Definitely see what you mean.' Dave took the phone from me and held it closer. 'Hang on,' he said. 'I've met her before.'

'What?' I felt my stomach lurch sideways. 'How could you possibly …?'

'It was with Julie,' he said. 'Three or four years ago. I only saw her for a few minutes, but it was definitely her.'

My stomach settled. 'I suppose that makes sense,' I said. 'She told me she worked for Pulsar for a few years.'

'This was after she left Pulsar,' he said. 'They were having coffee in Zak's. They seemed pretty close considering Nicki was an ex-employee. She said she worked for some consultancy. I wondered if they might have been an item for a second or two. Something about the way Julie looked at her.'

'Stop winding me up, Dave,' I said. 'It's not funny.'

'I'm not. I met her with Julie in Zak's just like I said.' He looked straight at me and I couldn't see any signs he was lying. 'It was only for a couple of minutes though, so don't read anything into it.'

Dave stood up, went over to his desk and picked up a slim folder.

'I got the first report from Milinsky Labs,' he said.

'And …?'

'There isn't anything specific … but there's not nothing, if you get what I mean.'

I suspected that my expression gave a clear indication of how much I got what he meant and he handed me the folder.

After flicking through it and reading the summary, I was slightly clearer.

'Let me see if I understand,' I said.

Dave nodded.

'They're certain that Julie hasn't got any online access, and all communications from the prisons she's been in are clean?'

'Uh-huh.'

'But they've observed thousands of minor incursions to our personal and social media accounts. Nothing serious, all completely unrelated and untraceable. They say they've never seen anything like it.'

'That's about it,' he said. 'Nothing specific to worry about at the moment, but it can't be a random coincidence. Something is going on and it smells like Julie. Milinsky are the best, so I think we just need to wait and see what they come up with.'

I slumped forward, squeezing my face in my hands. 'It's never going to end, is it?' I said. 'She's never going to let us go.'

'Of course it will,' said Dave, his big confident voice almost convincing. 'She's safely behind bars. Maybe she set up something before she went away, but it can't do that much harm. We've taken all the right precautions and, as soon as the lab figures out exactly what's happening, they'll shut it down.'

He walked over to the tiny replica jukebox on the windowsill and pulled on the front. It swung open to reveal two perfectly frozen shot glasses and a small, opaque bottle. He placed the glasses on the table and ceremoniously poured the clear, oily liquid.

'Come on,' he said, handing me a glass. 'What better way to toast your Granny than with a shot of grappa?'

As the cold hit the back of my throat and the fire reached the roof of my mouth, I couldn't help thinking that Granny would have been able to think of many, many better ways.

St Peter's was decked out like the Great Pavilion at the Chelsea Flower Show. Every possible surface, nook or cranny overflowed with bright blooms – freshly cut flowers from cottage gardens mixed riotously with the paler pastels of Oxfordshire's wild flowers. No sombre, formal wreaths and funeral bouquets in sight. Granny had been very specific in her will.

We'd all dressed up as she would have expected with no need for posthumous instructions. Even Daz was sporting a haircut and neatly trimmed beard to go with his brand new suit and tie, which was both touching and mildly amusing. Although he'd made the effort, he still managed to look like a Dickensian street urchin, scrubbed clean and crammed into unfamiliar clothing against his will. I imagined Granny looking at him and tut-tutting before striding up to adjust his tie, straighten his collar and push his hair back over his ears.

He walked into the church arm-in-arm with Liz who was police-officer-smart in her black dress and hat; the pair of them were a perfect example of how some odd couples can appear so perfectly matched. I was also happy that they'd stopped trying to hide their relationship. Like most of their close friends, I was tired of being treated like an idiot.

'Look at all those flowers,' said Dad. 'I'll bet St Peter's has never seen as many.'

Dad and I were standing to the side of the font, watching the church filling up. There wasn't going to be room for everyone to be inside. Where had all of these people come from?

'I always thought that Gramps was the flower ladies' favourite,' I said, 'but they've really pulled out all the stops for Granny, haven't they?'

'I'm not a bit surprised,' said Dad. 'Mummy always let Dad play the front man, and he was a real charmer. People loved that, but when anyone actually needed something, it was Mummy who turned out and did what needed to be done. You should see the condolence cards I've been getting. So many, and from all over – not just locals.' His voice cracked, and he looked down to the floor. 'You spend a lifetime living close to someone and it's only after they've gone that you understand who and what they really were.'

I nodded, looking at my own shoes.

He straightened up and slapped me on the shoulder. 'Let's try not to let that happen to us, eh?'

I didn't know what to say. The concept of my father's mortality wasn't something I wanted to acknowledge, especially not at Grannie's funeral. 'No. Of course not, Dad,' I said. 'We'll carry on popping down to the pub for a couple of beers and a chat. What's better than that?'

I looked at the simple cream-coloured coffin, sitting elegantly in front of the altar. In spite of Granny's unswerving faith, I'd never come close to being religious, and neither had my dad. There was something about churches though. It was as though centuries of thoughts and prayers, tears of sadness and tears of joy had been absorbed into the fabric of the building itself. I wouldn't want to go too often, but from time to time, it felt good to piggy back on the stored belief of all of those generations of worshippers.

Before people had started to arrive, Dad and I had walked over to the edge of the churchyard to visit Mum's grave. I made a point of going every time I was home, but always found it difficult to make the connection between that cold grey marble headstone and the beautiful smiling young woman who I only knew from photos and a diary.

Over the years, I'd struggled so hard to find a true memory of her. However brutally I dug into my mind, I could never be sure if those elusive half-remembered hints of a voice or a smell were real, or if they were wishful fabrications constructed from the stories and images which survived her.

There was one memory I wanted to believe was true. All I could see were her eyes, with their distinctive almond shape. She was looking down at me and love and laughter were dancing in the infinite blackness of her pupils. Real? Made up? I would never know, but at some point I'd decided to accept the memory as true and would draw on it for comfort whenever I needed to.

It's Complicated

Red Pepper was almost empty – not such a surprise at 12:15 on a Tuesday lunchtime. Daz and Liz were first there again and, as Liz lived just around the corner, I was tempted to be mischievous and ask Daz if he'd moved in with her already. I resisted the impulse, feeling quietly impressed by my own mature self-restraint.

My father hadn't reached my level of maturity.

'Short walk here is it, Daz?' he said, grinning and slapping Daz on the shoulder. 'From the new love nest?'

'Grow up, Rupert,' said Liz. 'You're behaving like a fifteen-year-old.'

Liz would have needed to work hard to assert her authority as she fought her way through the ranks. Whatever they might claim, the police were still known for their male-dominated culture and rumours of endemic freemasonry were never far away. Even so, as I watched her slap my dad down like a naughty puppy, I wondered if she'd found it challenging at all.

'Why the short notice?' I said. 'We're all having dinner with Nicki next week. There wasn't anything worth discussing in the investigator's report. It could have waited.'

'Not really. There were a few things we thought were important,' said Liz. 'What did you think of Iona by the way?'

'She's definitely a piece of work,' I said. 'Not someone to cross.'

Liz laughed. 'Well spotted. I decided years ago that keeping on the right side of Iona is the smart move,' she said. 'That said, she's bloody good at what she does.'

I lifted my copy of Iona's report. 'Yes. This is exactly what we needed. Thanks for the introduction – and for convincing me to do it in the first place.'

'Not a problem,' she said, picking up her own copy of the report and looking over to Daz. 'Daz? Do you want to take this?'

Something wasn't right. The three of them, even my dad, were sharing shifty looks and avoiding direct eye contact with me.

'What's going on?' I said.

Daz cleared his throat. 'You know we agreed to limit the investigation to the basics?'

'Yes,' I said. 'And that's what the investigator gave us.'

'That's what she gave you,' he said. 'I wasn't comfortable and asked Liz to give her friend a call …'

'Why?' I said, although I could see what was coming.

'We asked her to dig a little deeper,' he said. 'Just in case. We weren't going to tell you originally, but now I think we have to.'

'You did what?' I said, pushing my chair back with a screech and hearing my voice squeak up an octave or two. 'You knew what I thought about it and carried on behind my back, anyway?'

To give Daz his dues, he looked ashamed, as did the others. 'Yes,' he said, 'but when you hear what she found …'

I stood up. 'I don't want to know what sordid little secrets you dug up,' I said, stomping towards the door. 'I don't care. She's my sister, not yours. I won't let you ruin everything.'

The door slammed behind me as I ran out.

I'd almost reached Paddington Basin by the time Dad caught up with me.

'Sam,' he said, gasping for breath. 'Hang on a second. You're behaving like a bloody infant.'

'And what about you lot?' I said. 'You're all treating me like a child, so don't be surprised if I behave like one.' I glared at him. 'Did you know what they were up to?'

'Not until this morning,' he said. 'They gave me a heads up just before you arrived.'

'Why didn't you stick up for me, then?'

'I tried, until they explained what Iona found. I'm sorry, but I think you have to hear it.'

I turned away, tears pricking at my eyes. The last thing I wanted was to fall out with my closest friends and family.

'And then what am I going to tell Nicki?'

'I have no idea,' he said. 'But you can't just stick your head in the sand. Come back and listen to what Daz has to say and then we'll figure out what to do next.'

What choice did I have? The problem was that I couldn't stop myself picturing the look of betrayal on Nicki's face when she found out I'd been spying on her. I knew how it would make me feel.

When we got back to Red Pepper, Daz was standing in the doorway. 'I'm really sorry, Sam,' he said, handing me his – much thicker – report. 'Read this and then we can talk.'

I sat at an outside table, flicking though the document which was clear and to the point. With each passing paragraph I realised that Daz and Liz were right. However much I wanted things to be simple, life rarely was. And in this instance, there were too many unanswered questions to ignore.

Once I'd finished reading, I walked back inside with my head bowed. 'OK. I get it. What now?'

Daz pointed at Liz. 'I think Liz should talk us through the main points, if everyone agrees?'

We all nodded. She was the only one who knew what she was talking about.

'OK,' said Liz, opening the report in front of her. 'The way I see it there are a number of key facts – each of which throws up a bunch of unanswered questions.' She looked around the table – presumably to make sure we were all paying attention. 'These are, in no special order: the arrest and prosecution of Nicki's adopted father, Damian, which led to her being taken into care; Damian's sudden death ten years later; Joe conveniently appearing on the scene just as Damian is prosecuted; the source of Joe's money; Joe's sudden death; and finally, the fact that Nicki was a Pulsar Scholar and worked for Pulsar for five years.' She took a deep breath. 'Have I missed anything?'

'I don't think so,' said my dad. 'One thought, though. You imply that Joe kept the relationship secret until Nicki was taken into care. There's another possibility … maybe he didn't know? Maybe Fabiola never told him about Nicki?'

'If that was true,' said Daz, 'how did he find out about Nicki after Fabiola's death? What changed?'

'We don't know,' said Liz, 'but that doesn't mean it's not a possible scenario. We have to consider the possibility that Joe didn't know about Nicki.'

'It does make more sense in some ways,' said my dad. 'If he'd known before, would he have sat back and accepted the adoption?'

I held up the report. 'Before we get carried away with wild conjecture,' I said, 'what about the last paragraph of the summary? Listen to this! "*I have never seen such a spotless data signature. In my experience, it isn't possible for someone of Nicki Taylor's generation to have such a vanilla digital profile without highly skilled and pro-active management. This may have been carried out by her current employer, Odell Services, which is itself extremely good at limiting publicly available information.*" I know that Nicki is some sort of artificial intelligence expert, but this must be important. There's nothing tangible, but what about the spaces where things are supposed to be. Isn't that suspicious?'

Daz nodded. 'I thought the same,' he said. 'It made me think of when I was a kid. We had a big tree at the end of our garden, a massive old oak. It was the first thing I saw out of my window every morning. One night when I was maybe eight or nine, there was a huge storm – thunder, lightning, the works. I was curled up in bed too scared to sleep.

'When the storm stopped, I got up and went to the window. It was pitch black, but something was wrong, something was missing. I couldn't see a thing, but I knew the tree was gone.'

It was the first time I'd heard Uncle Daz speak about his childhood. He'd had a house and a garden. Maybe his upbringing had been more conventional than I'd thought.

He continued. 'Sorry, Sam. Rambling on. I'm just agreeing with you that missing things leave a mark on what stays behind – or something like that. We can't ignore the things which aren't there, but are supposed to be.'

'Yes,' I said. 'That's exactly my point.' I closed the report and placed it face down on the table in front of me. 'What are we saying here? That these aren't simply coincidences? That someone else has been involved in Nicki's life?'

The waitress came over to our table with two huge pizzas and we sat in silence while she cut them into segments, crunching the pizza wheel from edge to edge with long practised strokes. Once she'd gone, it was Daz who spoke first.

'Look,' he said. 'We all know what everyone's thinking. This smells of Jax, or Julie, or whatever you want to call her. Nicki is Fabi's daughter and, if Jax knew about her, that could easily give her reason enough to interfere.' He took a deep breath. 'Let's face it, none of us believe that her latching on to Sam was a coincidence. For Jax, it's all about Fabiola and always has been.'

'If that's true,' said Liz, 'then anything's possible. Literally anything.'

'And we have no idea if Nicki knows anything about this,' I said. 'Let's face it. I lived with Julie for two years and didn't have a clue that she and Jax were the same person. If I hadn't found that phone with pictures of her and Mum together, I still wouldn't know.'

The pizzas sat untouched on the small table and I could see from the grim faces in front of me that we were all drawing the same disturbing conclusions.

I knew I should tell them about Dave having met Nicki and Julie together, and the Milinsky report with its implication that Julie was co-ordinating some kind of cyber attack against me, even from behind bars. I knew that I should, but it would only feed their suspicion and paranoia about Nicki and I couldn't face any more of that.

'No. We don't know if Nicki knows anything,' said Liz. 'In fact, we have no evidence – apart from our own suspicions – that there is anything to know. There is no indication that Julie Martin is even aware that Nicki is Fabiola's daughter, let alone evidence that she's sitting like a spider behind some macabre scheme to manage her life.'

'We have to tell her what we know,' I said. 'We have to tell Nicki.'

Although I wasn't surprised that neither my father, Daz or Liz agreed with me, I hadn't expected such passionate resistance and we argued in ever-diminishing circles for half an hour as the pizza quietly morphed into cold, soggy cardboard.

I'd known they would be afraid to tell Nicki about the investigator, and I understood why. Even so, I couldn't help being frustrated by their failure to see my point of view and to appreciate the conflicts which raged inside me. How was I supposed to bond with my new sister while hiding all of these ugly worries and suspicions?

She'd need to know at some point, and every day that went by before she did was another turn of the rack, stretching any hope of trust to breaking point and beyond.

We were all exhausted by the time we gave up arguing, paid the bill and left. As we turned down Formosa Street towards Warrington Crescent, Daz put a hand on my shoulder.

'Got another ten minutes, Sam,' he said. 'Maybe we could grab a pint at the Warrington? Just the two of us.'

'Sure,' I said. 'Just a quick one though.'

We said goodbye to the other two and walked along the soft curve of white stucco houses to the pub. Once we were settled at one of the outside tables, Daz turned to me.

'I get that you feel you're between a rock and a hard place,' he said. 'And it must look like we're ganging up on you. But I need to you to understand a few things. It's up to you how much you actually accept, but do me a favour and hear me out. OK?'

'Of course,' I said. 'I can't promise I'll change my mind though.'

'That's up to you,' he said. 'I'll start at the beginning.'

His eyes glazed over and an unfamiliar frown spread over his face. 'I'm the only one of us who actually knew Jax before she became Julie,' he said, speaking slowly and carefully, almost as though he was in a trance. 'You saw glimpses, but by the time you met her, she was already the polished article with years of experience of hiding the raw malice underneath. Even after everything you've been through, I can see that you, and even Liz and your dad, are shying away from believing the worst. You don't want to live in a world where that kind of evil exists.

'It's not actually evil – I don't believe in that sort of thing – it's something worse. Jax is a high-functioning psychopath. She has no concept of empathy, she simply doesn't care and that's the part that normal people can't grasp.

'Not only did I spend years in her circle when she was younger, I've also been working in mental health my whole life and I've worked with hundreds of psychopaths. They're quite different from the other patients; they don't have an illness as such, they have a fundamental personality disorder which, unlike most mental illnesses, can't be cured or improved.'

'So psychopaths are never released back into the community?'

'Actually quite the opposite, but that's a failing of the system,' said Daz. 'They tend to be better at gaming the assessment processes and charming the decision-makers, so a lot get out. That doesn't mean they were cured though, and they tend to re-offend.'

'If you're right, why didn't her lawyer claim some sort of diminished responsibility?'

'You're not getting it, Sam,' said Daz. 'Jax doesn't see herself as flawed or damaged, she believes she's a superior being. She would never allow her legal team to use that argument. She's in a completely different league from any patient I've ever known.

'She sees the world in a totally narcissistic way and there's no point in trying to identify with her or to double guess what she's going to do. For Jax, reality is in a state of flux, constantly changing with her always at the centre. She has a simple concept of right and wrong. Whatever she decides to do is right, and that's it.'

I found myself struggling to take in what Uncle Daz was saying. For hours I'd been listening to older people telling me how I should think and I'd reached some sort of limit.

'We've talked about this before,' I said, trying not to sound rude. 'And I've lived a lot of it. Whatever you believe, I really think that I do understand what she's capable of and she terrifies me … but she's safely locked up now.'

'… As she was when Nicki's father died suddenly. Just when he was about to tell you more about Nicki.'

'You don't seriously think …?'

Daz looked at me and shrugged.

'… But she couldn't have known we'd be going to see Joe …'

He shrugged again.

'But …'

I decided to assume that Uncle Daz was allowing his paranoia to get the better of him. Although he was probably right about the kind of person Julie was, that didn't mean she had anything to do with Nicki. I wondered if he'd been reading too many crime thrillers. Or maybe he and Liz just fired each other up?

Even assuming he was right, it still made sense to tell Nicki the truth. That would bring everything out into the open and I didn't see what more I could do to protect myself from Julie. With hindsight, I was relieved that I'd kept the whole business with Dave and the Milinsky report to myself. It wouldn't make a difference one way or the other

After a string of back-and-forth emails, I managed to reach a compromise with Dad, Liz and Daz; they accepted that I was going to tell Nicki about our investigation and I agreed I wouldn't say anything until after we'd finished eating, and then only if I still felt it was a good idea.

Nicki lived in North London and had suggested a hot new Italian restaurant on the corner of Almeida Street in Islington. In normal circumstances I wouldn't have had any problems getting there on time. The London transport system had other ideas, however, and I was a hot and sweaty twenty minutes late by the time I arrived.

I took a second to watch Daz, Nicki and my dad from across the room – they seemed to be having a good time. Liz had decided not to join us – she hadn't really known Fabiola.

'Apologies for being late,' I said walking up to the table and leaning down to give Nicki a kiss. 'Sorry, Nicki.'

'Not a problem,' she said. 'We've been having a nice time. We just ordered drinks and I was about to ask Daz to tell me about Fabiola.'

'Perfect,' I said. 'You carry on.'

Nicki smiled and turned to face Uncle Daz.

'So, Daz,' said Nicki. 'You knew Fabiola at university? When she was … what?'

'Eighteen or nineteen,' said Daz.

'Can you tell me about her? It must have been less than a year after I was born.'

'Ah,' said Daz. 'She was amazing – a goddess, come down to Earth – I'm sure Rupert will agree. Fabi was the love of my life from the moment I met her.' He grinned at the memory and scratched his beard. 'Describing what she was like though. That's not so easy.'

'Please try,' said Nicki.

'She genuinely had no idea how special she was. Any room would go quiet the moment she walked in, but she never noticed.' Daz looked more ill at ease than I'd ever seen him. He kept shifting around in his chair and wouldn't stop picking at his fingernails. 'I don't know, Nicki,' he continued. 'How can words, or even pictures explain who a person was, once they're gone? Fabiola was kind, happy and natural – watching her change and fade in those years before her death was unimaginably painful.'

'Thanks, Daz. I know it can't be easy,' said Nicki. '… And you knew Julie?'

'Yeah. I knew Julie,' said Daz. 'She was Jax when I knew her, though. I was there when she and Fabiola first got together. We were at a march in Germany.'

'And you were all friends, back then?'

'In the same group, but never friends. If it hadn't have been for Fabi, I don't think Jax would have given me the time of day … and I'd have been a lot happier that way.'

'OK. Julie Martin certainly doesn't have any friends in this room,' said Nicki. 'Maybe we shouldn't talk about her.' She smiled and touched Daz on the arm. 'One thing I did want to know. Did my mother ever mention my father?'

'Only one time,' said Daz. 'Someone at uni came from Bedford and recognised her, so Fabi gave us her version of the scandal. I guess she thought she needed to justify herself.'

'But nothing about me?'

'God, no. No-one had any idea that she'd ended up having the teacher's baby.'

'And how about you, Nicki?' I said. 'Did you know about the affair?'

'Yes,' she said. 'These things always come out. One of the girls at school found out about it when I was thirteen. For a while I had lots of new friends because all the girls wanted to meet my dad.'

'That must have been awkward,' I said. 'And you never asked him about the timing?'

Nicki laughed. 'Not the sort of conversation you have with your dad when you're thirteen, is it? I just assumed he found someone else soon after. He was a good-looking man when he was younger.'

My father reached over and poured Nicki another glass of wine. 'But you didn't meet your father until you were eleven?' he asked. 'You were adopted. Sorry to be nosey, but how did he find you, and what happened to your adopted parents?'

'Don't worry,' said Nicki. 'It's OK to be nosey, but I actually don't remember much about that time. Just before and after I went to live with Dad, I went off the rails a bit. I was definitely a more obnoxious teenager than average.'

'But you remember your adopted parents,' I said.

'Of course I do,' said Nicki. 'I remember being very happy with them and then my world exploded. My dad was suddenly arrested for some awful stuff, my mum went to pieces and I was taken into care. I met some bad influences, and I suspect I was well on my way to becoming a bad influence myself.

'After a year or so of living with my real dad, I started to improve. The school made me see a counsellor which really helped. One of her strategies was to teach me techniques to help me to stop thinking about what might have been, and to focus on looking forward. She called it "Piafism" which I always found funny. Anyway, I tried it and it worked.' She shrugged. 'I've tried to live that way ever since.'

'Piafism?' said my dad. 'Never heard of that.'

'Keep up,' I said, laughing. 'Edith Piaf? Je ne regrette rien?'

'Oh,' he said, slapping his forehead like a circus clown. 'Just being a thicko.' The sheepish look on his face was hysterical and I watched Nicki press her lips together as she tried not to laugh.

It was an ideal moment for the food to arrive. Nicki might have been happy enough to answer personal questions, but the atmosphere around the table had intensified as she talked about her childhood. We needed to take a break from the questions and answers.

I heard Dad muttering to Nicki as he poured the wine:

'Sorry. I'm not usually that dense,' he said. 'Your mother was the sharp one, though. Always a step ahead.'

Nicki smiled and raised her glass. 'Let's hope I got some of that, then.'

A phone vibrated on the table. It was Daz's.

'Give us a sec,' he said, standing up. 'It's Liz.'

I saw his shoulders tensing as he strode outside, leaving the door to slam behind him. A sudden chill sent shivers down my back. Had something happened to Liz?

Uncle Daz had been single ever since I'd known him – having eventually found a perfect soulmate, it would truly be Sod's Law if she was sick.

No-one spoke as we watched him pace up and down outside the window like a cornered animal. I'd never seen him look so angry. By the time he eventually walked back into the restaurant, his eyes were bulging and his fists were clenched into balls; something was very wrong.

'You're not gonna believe this,' he said, hands pressed over his mouth in an apparent attempt to push the truth back inside. 'It can't be happening.'

'What?' we shouted as one.

'Julie Martin's bloody escaped,' he said, slamming his hand on the table. 'She's disappeared.'

We all picked up our phones to check the news feeds, no-one ready to respond until they'd seen it for themselves. As I skimmed the reports, I glanced up at Nicki. She was scrolling down her screen open-mouthed like the rest of us. Whatever Daz might suspect, this was as big a surprise to her as it was to us all.

As the truth took shape, bit by bit, word by word, I felt the walls closing in and crushing me. I couldn't breathe. My throat was pinched tight and cloth bands were wrapping themselves tightly around my chest threatening to mummify me alive.

I heard the sound of my chair clattering onto the hard floor as I jumped up and ran outside. I needed air. Fresh air. Outside. Space.

As I stood on the pavement, doubled over, gasping and coughing, I felt a hand on my shoulder.

'Slow, deep breaths,' said my dad, the soft richness of his voice evoking memories of a lifetime's comfort and support; unbroken links in a chain which stretched back into my misty beginnings. 'It's OK. You're OK. Just breathe.'

'It's happening again, Dad,' I said. 'I know it is. She'll come after me. She'll come after all of us.'

'Maybe,' he said. 'Maybe they'll catch her straight away. The news reports said that the police didn't expect her to get far.'

I tried to laugh and doubled up again in a fit of uncontrollable coughing.

'You don't really believe that, do you?' I said, once I'd recovered. 'Next, you'll be telling me she might decide to leave us alone. I know your glass of water is always half full, but there are limits.'

'What do you want me to say?' he said. 'I'm doing my best.'

'I know you are, Dad,' I said, turning and hugging him. 'I'm sorry.'

I was facing the plate-glass window of the restaurant and could see, through the reflections, Nicki staring out at us, white-faced and tense. She was probably wondering what sort of crazy family she'd inherited.

Who could blame her?

A Rocky Road

None of us wanted to talk about Julie's escape. What was there to say?

Daz and my dad left early to meet Liz – apparently she was trying to squeeze some details out of her former colleagues – and I offered to walk Nicki home. Over the course of dinner I'd decided to delay telling her about the investigation. When we heard the shocking news about Julie, I changed my mind – I had no choice.

'Nicki. You need to understand who Julie Martin really is,' I said, as we walked slowly along Halton Road. 'If she knows you're my sister, you could be in danger.'

'What?' she said. 'That's ridiculous.'

'No … It's not,' I said. 'Julie isn't who, or what, you think she is.'

'But still …'

'… Anyway. Before we talk about her, I've got a confession to make.'

'Go on …'

'I'm not proud of this, but, before we met, after Dad got the letter from your father, I hired a private investigator to check up on you.'

'Nice!' she said, looking down at the pavement, her hair falling forward and hiding her expression. 'And you didn't think to mention this last time we met?'

'We didn't have the report then,' I said. 'I probably should have done though.' We stopped at a traffic light and I put my hand on her shoulder. 'The thing is … the thing is … we agreed to keep it very basic – a simple identity check – but Daz is completely paranoid about Julie and he asked the investigator to dig deeper without telling me.'

She shrugged my hand away, still hiding her face, 'It doesn't make a difference,' she said. 'The principle's the same.' She stopped talking as we crossed the road. 'What did they find? I really don't think I've got anything to hide.'

'No-one's saying you have, but there are things in there, things which don't fit together, questions which don't have answers. I think you'll probably feel the same way.'

'Like what exactly?' Nicki snapped, stopping and turning to look at me, eyes on fire.

I handed her my copy of the report. 'You'll have to see for yourself,' I said. 'But haven't you ever wondered where your father got the money to live like he did?' I waited as a smartly dressed couple walked past us. About my age, they were like something out of a TV advert – beautiful, tanned, laughing together – a caricature of a perfect, normal life and about as far from mine as I could imagine.

I wasn't sure if Nicki was actually taking anything in – all I could see was anger and resentment – but I carried on anyway. 'Now you know who your birth mother was, don't you find it an amazing coincidence that you chose the career you did, and then went to work for your mother's former lover?'

'No. I haven't thought about it,' she said. 'The world's full of coincidences. Maybe I'm not as devious as you lot all seem to be?'

I couldn't hide my frustration at the way she was brushing me aside without listening. 'I wasn't like that until my mother's former lover seduced me ... and then tried to kill me after I discovered her nasty secrets,' I said. 'She forced me into her safe room at gunpoint and disabled the air systems, for Christs's sake.'

'But Julie told the police where to find you before the air ran out, didn't she?'

'Yes,' I said. 'But only because Daz caught her and threatened to break her arm.'

'Or so he claims,' said Nicki.

I couldn't speak. If I'd opened my mouth, all that would have come out would have been an anguished scream of frustration. I knew I was right, but it seemed that nothing I could do or say would convince Nicki.

After a few deep breaths, I calmed down enough to reply. 'You don't have to believe me or Daz,' I said. 'Just look at the facts. It's not hard to conclude that I'm telling the truth and to see that Julie's been manipulating me all my life.'

'Now you're being ridiculous,' said Nicki.

'I'm really not,' I said as we stood on the pavement glaring at each other. 'I know you've only just met me, but I'm not making this up or being a drama queen. Julie Martin is obsessed with anything to do with Mum. I don't really understand it, but she is. I can't believe she employed me by accident. Nothing Julie ever does is by accident. If Fabiola told her about you why would that be any different? It would certainly explain a lot about your career choices and the Pulsar Scholarship, wouldn't it?'

'Stop! Enough!' said Nicki, holding the report tight to her chest like a shield. 'I think you're a good person, Sam. I really do. And I believe you mean well. But I hardly know you and I'm not going to listen to any more of this. Julie Martin was a good boss to me, and Pulsar gave me an incredible start. I won't stand here and let you turn her into some sort of crazy, obsessed psychopath.'

'But that's exactly what she is?' I said. 'She drove your mother to kill herself. Isn't that enough proof?'

'According to you,' she said. Was that a shadow of doubt in the back of her eyes? 'Look. I said I didn't want to carry on discussing this and I meant it. You don't need to come any further. I'm just up the road.' She waved the file at me. 'I'll read this and then I'll call you.'

'OK,' I said, realising I wasn't being given a choice. 'Sorry again.'

She half-lifted one hand in half-recognition of my apology, turned and walked away. No thought of a hug, not even a handshake.

As I made my own way back to the Tube, I allowed myself to wallow in self-pity and misery, imagining her anger and disgust and realising that she'd probably never call.

As happened every night, Highbury and Islington station had transformed over the few hours while we'd been having dinner. There were no more bright-eyed workers hurrying home to their clean, safe houses. Every doorway, every shady corner, every bench had been claimed by the Fausts – their blank, uncaring looks a chilling reminder of the desolation inside them.

We'd all played around with synths when I was in my teens – all-nighters wouldn't have been the same without a tab or two. But it changed when Solar 99 came along – for a year of so, it was all anyone could talk about, the way everything burned brighter and longer and the sense of power and immortality which lingered long after the effects of the drug had worn off.

I only tried it once, and that was enough to smell the danger. The sensations were great, fabulous even, and I felt – no, knew – that I could do anything I wanted. The entire world had belonged to me for a few short hours.

Luckily for me, and most of my friends, it was expensive, we were poor schoolkids, and we'd been brought up with just enough street smarts to know that the road to heaven was never going to be that easy to find. Many of those with more money than sense weren't so lucky, and S99 had been on the streets for over a year before the first reports started to come in.

Conservative estimates put the number of victims in the UK alone at over a hundred thousand. Anyone who'd taken the drug more than five or ten times was affected eventually, sometimes years afterwards. Their bodies would wake up one morning and it was as though their souls had been torn out of them during the night. They were left as shells, physically normal, but empty of all thoughts and feelings.

Even the richer countries still hadn't figured out how to cope. At least the UK hadn't gone down the route of establishing isolation camps, but there were still no systems in place to manage the volume of vulnerable victims, and many thousands had found themselves on the streets.

Apparently, Fausts were almost never violent, but that didn't stop them from being frightening as shuffled slowly around. In search of what? I hurried past the vacant faces and into the station.

When I heard the alarm, I stopped and turned. There was no-one else in sight. The alarm didn't stop. Its insistent beep was urgent and demanding. The barrier in front of me was closed and a big red help button was flashing. I didn't have time for this. If I missed the last train, it was a long way back to Chelsea. I punched the button.

The disembodied voice which answered from the metal grill was predictably harsh and distorted.

'Can I help you?'

'Yes,' I said. 'There's something wrong with the barrier. The alarm's going off and I can't get through.'

'Which station are you at?'

'Highbury and Islington.'

'One moment.'

After a few seconds of waiting, the alarm stopped. It was as though a weight had suddenly been lifted off my chest and I could breathe again.

'Hello?' The voice was back.

'Yes. I'm still here.'

'I'm sorry, Mr Blackwell, but you don't have any credit on your account.'

'That's ridiculous,' I said. 'I've got a monthly pass.'

'Which was cancelled earlier today,' said the voice.

'No, it wasn't,' I said. 'Why would I do that?'

'I don't know, sir. All I know is what's on the screen in front of me.'

'Well, that's no bloody use to me, is it?' I shouted.

'I would appreciate it if you didn't take that tone with me, Mr Blackwell. We have a very strict abuse policy and all calls are recorded.'

'I'm sorry,' I said. 'I just don't understand what's going on and I need to catch the last train. Is there any way you could open the barrier …?'

'I'm sorry, sir. I'm not authorised to …'

I turned and half-ran back up the steps. I was getting nowhere. I'd need to get an Uber which might take an age in North London.

I walked the gauntlet of blank stares, and as soon as I was far enough away from the Fausts, took out my phone to request a car. No data signal. I walked another hundred metres. Still no signal. This was becoming ridiculous.

It was only eleven o'clock. I could call my Dad and get him to come and pick me up. It would be just like old times.

The phone rang once. Another metallic robot voice:

'It has not been possible to connect you. Your phone is only authorised to make emergency calls. Please dial 100 to speak to an operator. Operators are available between 09:00 and 17:30 Monday to Friday.'

What was going on? It was like all the systems were down. Surely Julie couldn't be behind it? She'd only been out of prison for a few hours. Daz's warnings started to fill my mind as stood alone on the dark street and I switched my phone into full lockdown mode just in case.

It didn't take me long to realise that I was out of options. How ridiculous was that? A few technical problems and I was stuck. Luckily, I was young and fit and it was only about five miles back to Chelsea. It wouldn't take much more than an hour to walk.

I ended up walking for almost two hours and my cool new shoes had managed to gouge a nasty crater into my left heel along the way. For the last half hour, every step felt as though someone was driving a knife into my foot. I couldn't get Julie's face out of my mind. That last stare she'd directed at me after she was found guilty. For the first time, I understood how my mother must have felt as her grasp on reality weakened.

The automatic door opened, and I hobbled into my flat. At least my Pulsar Trust was still working – for a moment I'd worried that I wouldn't actually be able to get inside. My TV didn't come on though and, by the time I'd realised that and found a blister plaster, I'd managed to get spots of blood all over my new cream-coloured carpet. It was turning out to be a nightmare day.

I only managed to see the funny side of the evening as I reached the bottom of a large whisky. I was determined not to believe that Julie was behind my technical issues and thought back to my dad telling me stories of the early days of digital technology and how clunky everything had been. I'd never experienced that. My entire life had been based on tech not being a big deal. All the hidden chips and codebases operated seamlessly in the background. Things just worked. By the time I became an adult, the concepts of cash, or maps, or keys, or passports were already clunky hangovers from another world.

During those two years with Julie and Pulsar, I'd come to understand more than most about the web of technology which supported our daily lives, and how each individual filament was both essential and fragile. Even knowing that, I never applied that knowledge to my reality. In my world that web was unbreakable.

Until something actually did break.

I finished a second whisky and hopped to my bedroom. My phone was still dead; hopefully I'd be able to find out more tomorrow in the office but, if the system crash was global, stock markets would go crazy the moment they went back online. There should be plenty of opportunities for MySafe if we got our PR spin right.

I set my alarm for five-thirty. I would need to be in early.

The moon was still up as I walked along the Chelsea Embankment to the MySafe offices. When we took over Pulsar, we'd moved everyone out of Shard Two – the Board had wanted to distance itself as much as possible from Julie Martin. Making a clean break was easier said than done though – over seventy per cent of our revenues still came from Pulsar legacy products and subscriptions.

Shard Two was amazing, but it was worth moving to be able to walk to work – especially since the new garden trackway had been completed. London was definitely regaining its place as one of the top cities in the world and, on a normal day, I'd have relished those fifteen minutes of peace and quiet. After the events of the previous night however, I found myself looking over my shoulder as I walked, imagining Julie lying in wait for me dressed in some clever disguise. A stupid thing to worry about. She'd be long gone by now. She wouldn't forget about me, but she'd look after herself first.

Nothing appeared out of the ordinary as I walked – my phone was still out of action and I'd been expecting to see some sign of the system meltdown. At least that was one positive development. The problems had probably only affected a few people, and I'd been hyping myself up for no reason.

After ten minutes in the office and a quick talk with Johan, our IT manager, I realised exactly how few people had actually experienced technical issues. It had been one … Me.

Why had I assumed anything different? Julie was free and the whole world seemed to be conspiring against me. I left Johan to figure out what had gone wrong and went up to see Dave.

We began by sharing our stunned amazement – and closet terror – about Julie's escape, and then I caught him up on the disastrous end to the dinner with Nicki. Dave had already read the investigator's report and was, if anything, even more suspicious than Uncle Daz.

'Methinks the lady doth protest too much,' he said in a truly cringeworthy attempt at an English accent.

'What?' I said.

'Come on, Sam,' he said. 'Wake up and smell the doughnuts. Your new sister's an AI expert working for a secretive political consultancy. D'you think she didn't run checks on you as well? Even if she didn't, there's no way she's actually surprised or upset by the fact that you did.'

Crass and insensitive perhaps, but he probably had a point. 'So, what are you saying?'

'How should I know?' he said. 'I wasn't even there … but something smells like a trawlerfull of rotting halibut.'

I always found it difficult to know when Dave was being smart or incredibly stupid and, while I was trying to figure that out, there was a knock at the door. It was Johan from IT.

'Sorry to interrupt,' he said, leaning his head around the door before stepping half into the office. 'I've got the results for Mr

Blackwell's system outage. He said it was urgent.'

'What system outage?' said Dave.

'I'll explain in a minute,' I said, turning to Johan. 'What did you find?'

'Your TV, phone and a number of your other accounts have been locked for non-payment,' he said. 'Technically, your systems are fine.'

'Non-payment?' I said. 'But that's not possible.'

'I'm sorry,' he said. 'I've dug as far as I can. You'll need to check with your bank.'

As Johan sidled out of the door, I reached over and picked up Dave's datapad.

'Can I borrow this for a sec?' I said.

'Sure,' said Dave. 'Knock yourself out. And then you tell me what's going on, right?'

'Of course,' I said, barely listening and already in the process of logging in to my bank.

As I looked at the words on the screen in front of me, something snapped and my pent-up stress and frustration erupted.

You have attempted three logins with an incorrect password or username. Your online access is now locked. Please contact your account manager by telephone on ....

'... and now they've locked me out of fucking online banking,' I shouted, looking for something to throw or break. 'I'll have to sit in a phone queue for hours. Just what I bloody need.'

I got up and stormed out of Dave's office, leaving him sitting wide-eyed and speechless.

'Just take the datapad if you want ...' he said.

Dave was in meetings all morning and I'd calmed down by the time I saw him again.

'What was that all about?' he said, as I handed him back his datapad.

'All of my direct debits bounced,' I said. 'Because I transferred ten thousand euros out of my current account which left it massively in the red.'

'Why did you do that?' he said.

'I didn't, obviously,' I said. 'That's what's disturbing. The bank has an instruction from me, asking them to move the funds to my deposit account.'

'And you didn't make that instruction?'

'Correct,' I said. 'It appears to have come from me, but I had nothing to do with it. I must have been hacked. Can you call your guys from Milinsky?'

Dave and I looked at each other without speaking. I knew what he was thinking. Surely she couldn't have moved that fast? It must be a coincidence.

It had taken me hours to unravel the mess caused by a simple bank transfer. Hours of my life I'd never get back. Each supplier I spoke to had automatically moved me to a bad debtor list and consequently treated me almost like a criminal. I shuddered as I imagined what life must be like for all those people who actually couldn't pay their bills every month.

When my phone eventually blinked back into life, I saw three missed calls – one from my Dad and two from Nicki. I slumped down into my chair with a sigh. Thank God for that. I'd really thought that she was going to give up on me. My Dad could wait ...

'Nicki?'

'Hi, Sam. You took your time.'

'Sorry. I've had problems with my phone. You OK?'

'Yes. I'm fine. And I'm sorry about last night. I shouldn't have reacted like that.'

'I get it. It's all been a bit much, hasn't it? If it helps, I'm sorry too.'

'Thanks,' she said. 'Let's put it behind us. Anyway. I'm about to get on a plane, so can't talk more right now. I'm only away for a couple of days. Shall we get together when I'm back.'

'Absolutely. Where are you going?'

'Italy. Rome. A new client. I decided to go a couple of days early. Take a bit of time and space to think.' The phone was silent for several seconds. 'I read the report by the way. Thanks for sharing it with me.'

215

'Anything you didn't know?'

'Let's wait and discuss it face-to-face. I'll message you.'

I found myself almost giggling out loud as I leant back in my chair and stretched out my arms. Maybe things would work out after all.

Running Free

I'd been in police custody of one kind or another for over a year and, despite my best efforts, institutional influences and prison habits had crept up on me. For the first few days after I got out, I found myself stuck motionless at odd moments, waiting to be told what to do or where to go next. It was the strangest feeling, almost like I was being operated by remote control.

It didn't take me long to flush that poison out of my system though and, by the time I was south of Lyon, I was myself again. The Autoroute du Soleil stretched out in front of me, almost empty at four in the morning. The mid-range BMW saloon wrapped me in a smooth cocoon, and I had plenty of time to think as the kilometres flashed by.

Getting out of Downview had been easy. Prison walls and locked gates could always be opened with the right inside help and I'd learned many years earlier that anyone who claimed to be incorruptible was simply someone who'd not yet been offered a large enough bribe. As Winston Churchill once said: 'Madam, we've already established what you are, we're just discussing the price'.

Sophie, the guard on my floor hadn't been terribly expensive as it turned out. A small satchel with fifty thousand in cash had done the trick. She'd brought in the wig, some make-up and a tiny, clever device which very few people knew existed. We'd developed the Pulsar Trust identity cloner as a proof of concept and I'd kept hold of the only three examples ever made.

I'd left Sophie unconscious on my bed – the poor girl had believed she wouldn't be suspected of involvement if I drugged her

– and then I walked out unchallenged. I looked like her, I was wearing her uniform and, most importantly, all the security door scanners checked my newly cloned Pulsar Trust ID implants and confirmed that I was indeed Sophie Talbot.

Simon had a car waiting and, within the hour, I was stepping onto a forty-foot yacht moored on the Hamble river. It was a clear, warm night, and I sat outside on the deck, sipping a glass of Cristal as the lights of Portsmouth faded behind us. The sails went up once we cleared the Needles Channel and the engine noise stopped with a sweet sigh. I'd given instructions that the crew were not to speak to me and all I could hear was the wind filling the sails and the oil-black waters surging against the hull.

I'd been in no hurry. We would take two days to sail around the coast of Brittany and down to La Rochelle. There would be warrants out for my arrest everywhere in any case and they'd probably be looking for Sophie Talbot's ID as well. Fortunately, the woman who arrived three days later at La Rochelle had been someone else entirely.

The whole process had been seamless; I made a mental note to give Simon a bonus, or perhaps a special gift. He'd earned it.

Dawn was a sliver of mother-of-pearl on the horizon as I drove past Aix and I felt a brief moment of melancholy when I pictured my old Provence house. It had been almost perfect. No use crying over spilt milk though and, in any case, the Peschici villa was just as beautiful in its own way.

I reached for my sunglasses and drove onwards into the rising sun.

I didn't need to be in Rome for two more days and took my time, following the coast road all the way along the French and Italian Rivieras from Cannes to Santa Marinella. I had plenty of places to stay as Simon had rented six holiday villas, staggered out along my route. Even with my freshly cloned identity, we both felt private rentals were a safer bet than hotels. The police still used facial recognition and my disguise wasn't perfect. Better safe than sorry.

My meeting was set for Monday lunchtime and I spent the

Sunday night in Talamone on the southern coast of Tuscany. The Villa Presidio was an old Spanish castle, set at the end of a long single-track road and looking out over the cliffs. It had been used as a set for a number of well-known movies which made it feel strangely familiar as I drove in through the massive stone gate pillars.

The keys were where they were supposed to be, the fridge was well stocked and I spent a quiet evening on the terrace, looking out over the Med and working out what I was going to say the next day.

I would find it more difficult to avoid cameras and police in Rome and I couldn't help thinking back to that moment eighteen months earlier when that bloody police captain had walked up to me and arrested me. Captain Roberto de Alfaro was definitely in my little black book and would pay his penance in due course.

The morning chill from the thick stone walls and marble tiles made me shiver as I sat doing my make-up in front of the ornate, gold-framed mirror. I'd allowed an extra twenty minutes to make sure my temporary disguise was just right, and I rubbed the last touch of foundation into my cheeks, wincing at the thought of the surgery I had planned.

I hated the thought of going through all of that again. When I'd changed from Jax to Julie, I really had believed it would be the last time and my fists clenched involuntarily with anger and resentment when I pictured all the idiots who had interfered with my plans.

Beauty wasn't only skin deep – they would break bones and stretch, pull and tear until a different person appeared – that was the point after all. But that person would be a stranger and, after enough changes of name and appearance, it became hard to keep a grip on reality.

I didn't mind the pain – there were drugs for that. My struggle was with something deeper, something which tore at my soul. I'd been there before and it was harder every time. The moments of shock when I saw myself in the mirror for the first time would haunt me for months and even years afterwards.

It had to be done, unfortunately. There could be no mistakes this time. I would keep a low profile at the Peschici villa until the work was complete, and I had healed. Then I would emerge into the autumn sunshine, iridescent wings glinting in the low light. It would be hard, but I would still have Nicki. And I would still have my revenge …

We were meeting at a small trattoria in the EUR district, much more relaxed than the centre of Rome and easy to reach from the coast. Being back in Rome, in Italy, felt like coming home. I arrived early and as I sat drinking my first coffee of the day, I was struck by a wonderful revelation – I was going to be happy here. I would settle in to the villa in Peschici and stay there. My days of global travelling were over and I wouldn't miss any of it. Anyone or anything I needed could come to me.

I smiled, leant back in the chair and rolled my shoulders in the warm velvet air. Then I reached for my coffee cup and stopped, fingertips almost brushing the porcelain handle. No hint of a tremble; I felt good and was certain the meeting was going to go well. Even after four days of freedom, my pallid skin still looked as though I'd been freshly dragged from an open grave, but a few days of Southern Mediterranean sun would soon fix that.

Nicki must have been wondering who her mysterious new potential client might be. Simon had arranged for my Italian lawyers to set up this meeting on behalf of a "major industrialist" who was considering running for the 2043 presidential elections. Politics in Italy hadn't changed much in my lifetime – priorities had little to do with governing the country, and plenty to do with protecting wealth and power. Fertile territory for Odell and worth a personal visit from Nicki. Besides, the enigmatic Signor X had insisted on meeting the boss.

I watched her arrive from my vantage point in the far corner of the small terrace. The waiter pointed towards me, Nicki turned, took one step and stopped. With the sun behind her, I couldn't see the expression on her face which was a shame. I would have loved to know if she was delighted, surprised, horrified, or a combination of all three.

She gathered herself quickly, half-ran over to the table, sat down and leant close to me.

'Julie!' she whispered, eyes flicking from side to side as though she expected me to be arrested at any second. 'What the hell are you doing here?'

'It's lovely to see you too, Nicki,' I said, with a grin.

Nicki's cheeks reddened as she reached across the table to take my hand. 'I'm sorry,' she said. 'It's amazing to see you. I was surprised. When I heard you'd …'

'… I got bored of being in prison,' I said. 'My appeal was going to take at least six months and I didn't want to wait.'

'But … but aren't you in danger?'

'Are you planning on turning me in?'

'No. Of course not.'

'Then I don't think I'm in any danger.'

She relaxed back into her chair and listened as I told her a sanitised version of my escape. It wouldn't do to reveal all of my secrets, even to Nicki. Once I'd brought her up to date, we ordered drinks and talked about Rome – it was Nicki's first time and she'd spent the weekend wearing holes in her shoes as she tried to do the impossible and see everything all at once.

It was great to see her again face-to-face, with no filthy glass or perspex between us. She seemed genuinely pleased to see me and not especially disturbed by my decision to cut short my time spent serving at His Majesty's Pleasure.

'So … you've met Sam?' I couldn't wait any longer.

'Yes,' said Nicki. 'A couple of times now.'

'… And?'

'Just as you told me, he seems like a great guy.' She shrugged her shoulders. 'But we had a big fight last week.'

'Oh?' I leant forward and swallowed my smile.

'I found out that he, or rather Daz, had hired an investigator to check up on me,' she said. 'I didn't react well.'

'Why?' I said. 'Surely you investigated him?'

'Of course I asked our guys to poke around a little,' she said. 'But that's different. It's what I do. They recruited some grubby private eye to look into me.'

'I'm not surprised,' I said. 'And I don't blame you for being pissed off. 'Maybe that helps you see that he's not quite what he seems.'

'Maybe,' she said. 'Although I'm beginning to understand why they did it. They're all very friendly, but they really hate you, especially Daz.'

'There's a reason for that,' I said. 'It goes back a long way.'

'Go on ...'

'You don't want to know.'

Nicki looked at me without speaking.

'OK. It's not a big deal, really,' I said. 'Short version. Daz and I went out for a while in the first few weeks of uni. He never got over me dumping him for Fabiola. You know what blokes are like?'

'Jeez,' said Nicki. 'That explains a lot.'

I nodded my head. 'Anyway, you've met Sam now. I hope it doesn't change anything. You haven't forgotten what he did?'

'No. Of course not,' said Nicki. 'But I'm sure you get that it's complicated.'

'Of course I do,' I said. 'Which is why you need to stay strong.' I took a sip of my wine. 'That's delicious, by the way. You sure you won't have any?'

'I'm fine.'

'And Damocles?' I continued. 'You launched it weeks ago and I haven't heard anything. Shouldn't it be starting to kick in?'

'It's actually only been two weeks and the virus is designed to take its time and leave lots of false trails. Makes it seem more human. I thought that's how you wanted it?'

'It is,' I said. 'I'm just impatient.'

'Anyway, it has started – Sam told me that he had to walk home after our fight last week. Some cock-up with his bank had blocked his credit rating and locked his phone and a bunch of other accounts. It must have been Damocles.'

'Good,' I said. 'And you're right. It'll be better if it takes its time.'

'One other thing you should know,' said Nicki. 'I think Sam and Dave have got external cyber security in place – probably Milinsky Labs.'

'Shit,' I said. 'That'll be bloody Dave. Is there going to be a problem?'

'No. Don't worry. Damocles might take a little longer to find a way around their defences, but there's nothing anyone can do to stop it. It'll keep on worrying away until it achieves its mission.'

Even though I hadn't been nervous before the meeting, I'd been tense. With no visible results from Damocles, I'd been afraid that Nicki might have bottled out and delayed the launch. I sank back into my chair with a sigh. 'You know what, Nicki?' I said. 'You are a very clever girl. Very clever indeed.'

Nicki laughed. 'Hardly a girl,' she said. 'But I'll take it as a compliment.'

We talked about Odell for an hour or so, but I could tell that Nicki wasn't fully engaged. That awful habit of digging her thumbnail into her fingertip was back.

I reached over and straightened out her fingers gently. 'Something's bugging you,' I said. 'What is it?'

'I've got a couple of questions,' she said.

'Go ahead.'

'Sam gave me a copy of the investigator's report about me.'

'And?'

'There were a number of issues which stood out. Things like where my dad's money came from and how he found me. You explained everything to me in your letter, but unless I tell Sam about your role in my life, he's bound to be suspicious. And if he isn't, Daz and Rupert definitely will be.'

'You can't tell him about me,' I said. 'It would be a disaster.'

'So what do I do?'

'Accept things as they are and leave Damocles to do its job.'

'I'm not sure I can do that,' said Nicki. 'All these lies are eating away at me.'

'OK. Leave it with me,' I said. 'I'll figure something out. I promise. Now, let's just enjoy the rest of our lunch and save the boring, serious stuff for another time.'

'OK,' said Nicki. 'As long as it's soon.'

I'd been wrong to relax. Even though I always put so much effort into thinking objectively, threads of wishful thinking seemed destined to weave their way into my thoughts and actions. Just as the gold-flecked idea of being part of a family was weaving its way into Nicki's mind.

I'd assumed that Damocles would be enough leverage and couldn't see what I was missing. Nicki had released the virus, it couldn't be recalled and it would destroy Sam's life. How was she planning on explaining that?

However much that made sense to me, I could tell that she wasn't going to drop this and I would need to find another way to manage the situation. I wasn't going to be able to sit back and enjoy watching Sam and Dave suffer as I'd hoped.

It was only a matter of time before Nicki told Sam about me, and her guilty conscience would probably drive her to tell him about Damocles as well. That couldn't be allowed to happen.

A shame, but there were many ways to skin a cat, after all.

I'd planned to arrive in Peschici after dark; it was best for no-one to see me arrive. The drive from Rome should have taken less than five hours, but traffic was a pig and it was after eleven by the time I finally slipped the BMW through the huge wrought-iron gates and into the garage. The car would be fine, locked away here until it was safe to take it to the crusher.

As the gates swung soundlessly closed behind me, I slumped forward over the steering wheel, hands covering my face and eyes. The last week had been thrilling, but I was glad it was successfully over and I'd arrived. There was definitely such a thing as too much excitement. From now on, I would have no reason to go out until my surgery was completed, and the only people who knew about the Peschici villa were Simon and the young couple who looked after the house and the garden.

Although I hadn't met Signor and Signora Russo, they'd been sourced from a very special and exclusive agency and I knew I would be able to trust them. People tended to associate the Sicilian mafia with drugs, prostitution and extortion, but there were three families which provided other services, one of which was arranging trusted staff for clients who needed one hundred per cent guarantees of discretion and privacy. By the time the owners of every luxury villa and super-yacht were added together, they controlled a huge global market.

The service was extremely expensive and survived entirely on reputation. For the duration of their employment, the staff were allowed no contact with anyone they knew, and afterwards would never say where they'd been or who they'd been working for. They all had extended family back home in Sicily and the consequences of betrayal would be extreme.

I'd requested that the Russos live in town and so had the villa to myself when I arrived. A glass of Barolo on the balcony was tempting, and I went as far as picking a bottle and finding the corkscrew before accepting that all I wanted to do was to bury myself in soft Egyptian-cotton sheets and close my eyes.

My bedroom shutters were open and a cool breeze filled the room as I lay on my back listening to the night and the sea sounds drifting up from the base of the cliffs.

I woke to the smell of coffee and followed my nose down to the kitchen. Signora Russo was standing by the stove, a short slim woman with long dark hair pulled back from her face. She would have been pretty if it hadn't been for the dozens of pockmarks dotting her cheeks. She introduced herself briefly with a smile and a curtsey before leading me out to the balcony where a simple breakfast of fresh fruit and pastries had been laid out under the shade of the vines. As she poured my espresso – black and thick as crude oil – she pointed to her husband who was down by the cliff edge, raking the gravel path.

They were both young – probably early thirties – and he looked fit and strong. I knew he could double as a trained bodyguard if required – it had cost me an extra ten thousand, so he should be good. I hadn't expected to need protecting, but now my plans for Nicki and Sam were changing, those extra skills would come in useful.

Signora Russo was also well trained and, before I'd taken the first sip of my coffee, she'd faded back into the kitchen. My instructions had been very clear. I was happy with my own company and had no desire to build a relationship with the staff.

The view was as spectacular as I remembered. This part of the Adriatic was never still. Fishing boats were coming home, day boats and yachts were setting off to the Isola Tremiti and, further out, cruise liners and rusty freighters ploughed their way up to Venice and Trieste. I'd been told that it was possible to see Dubrovnik from the Peschici cliffs on a clear day.

It was almost ten o'clock; I'd been bone-tired and had slept the sleep of the dead until the first rays of morning sun started to find their way through the shutters. For the following hour, I'd lain splayed out like a newborn, revelling in the first moments of my new life.

I sipped my coffee and, once the caffeine kicked in, I got down to business, revising my plans and working out exactly what to tell Nicki. As the next steps became clear, I remembered that the villa had a stone wine cellar, carved deep into the rock. That would be ideal.

I typed the email to Nicki, feeling the familiar pleasure of seeing the future with crystal clarity, and watching a solution take form. One step at a time. The original plan had been good, but this one was even better.

Dear Nicki,

It was wonderful to see you on Monday. I've realised that you really are the only person in this world who I trust and I hope you've forgiven me for keeping so many secrets from you for so long.

As promised, I've been thinking about what you said and I think I've come up with a solution.

I'm now convinced that the only way we're ever going to resolve these issues is for me to speak to Sam face-to-face and tell him the truth about what really happened to his mother. His thoughts have been poisoned and I can only hope that, by meeting him alone and talking things through, I'll be able to convince him that I loved Fabiola and would never have done anything to hurt her.

I'm not saying that I'm going to forgive him for what he did to us, and he may decide not to believe me, but at least everything will be out in the open and you'll be able to stop lying.

I can't travel at the moment and he won't come here if he knows it's to meet me. I do, however, have an idea which I think will work.

If you were to tell him you want to find out more about your mother, I'm sure he would be pleased. Tell him you've tracked down some of Fabiola's family – that her brother has actually moved back to their family's home town – and you should be able to persuade him to come to Italy with you.

We can then meet and I'll tell him everything. Don't forget! He mustn't know he's coming to see me, or he won't come.

Let me know what you think and, if you think it's a good idea, I'll send you some more details.

All my love,

Julie

Reunited

My dad had been dropping all sorts of hints to Uncle Daz about my new flat and eventually it was his turn to enjoy the PixelWall experience. I sat him down with a beer and took him through what was becoming my standard routine – it was sad how even the most amazing things could quickly become repetitive and commonplace – but, when we got to the main show in the living room, Daz barely reacted. I flicked through the full range of presets, from North Pole in Blizzard to Eiffel Tower Panorama with no response. The only time I saw a flicker of excitement was when I switched to Shark Tank and we were catapulted into the middle of a huge aquarium surrounded by circling sharks.

'Ah. That's nice,' said Daz. 'I like sharks. I've always thought I should learn to scuba dive, but I guess it's a bit late now.'

I switched the room back to Modern City Apartment and threw the controller onto the sofa.

'I give up,' I said. 'You really don't give a damn about technology do you?'

'Not so much,' he said. 'I get that it's very clever and all that but …' He shrugged his shoulders and walked over to the balcony where he could see the sun setting behind Battersea Bridge. 'Now that,' he said. 'That's impressive.'

He had a point. Sunsets never got tiring while even the PixelWall had quickly become ordinary. He could have humoured me though. A couple of 'Ooohs' and 'Aaahs' would have been enough. Looking at Daz's studied nonchalance, I suspected my dad had set him up, and the whole thing was a wind-up.

'Did I tell you what happened to me after dinner last week?' I said, realising I'd got as much out of him as I was ever going to get.

Daz shook his head, still apparently transfixed by the fading orange sky.

'Well first I got into a huge fight with Nicki.'

'Oh, yeah? What about?'

'Three guesses,' I said. 'On second thoughts, don't bother. It was about the bloody investigator of course.'

He turned to look at me. 'Ah,' he said. 'And what did Nicki have to say about the findings?'

'I don't know,' I said. 'I gave it to her, she stormed off, and I've not seen her since.'

'Sorry to hear that,' he said. 'She'll come round when she reads it.'

'Maybe,' I said. 'I'm seeing her again on Friday, so I'll know soon enough. That wasn't the high point of the night though.'

Daz listened patiently while I told him about my credit collapse and the long walk home.

'And you've not figured out what happened?'

'Not really. It's very strange, actually. Dave and I are being targeted by thousands of minor hacking attempts. Most are being blocked, but this one got through. Our security company can't trace them back. Every hack is coming from a different unique IP address. They've never seen anything like it.'

'You know this is Jax, don't you?'

There was still a massive gulf between what I knew and what I wanted to believe. 'She'd only been out of prison for a couple of hours,' I said. 'And, besides, the attacks started a week earlier.'

'It's still her,' said Daz. 'And, if you knew you were being hacked nearly two weeks ago, don't you think it might have been an idea to share that with us at the time?'

I avoided his gaze. 'Of course I should have. I'm sorry.'

'I guess it wouldn't have made any difference,' he said, shaking his head. 'All we can hope for is that the police get her soon.' Then he grabbed me by the shoulders, fingers digging into my flesh, and forced me to look at him. 'Otherwise she won't stop with a few online hacking games. You understand that, don't you?'

'Yes,' I said. 'I think I always have.'

'How was your trip?' I asked Nicki as we walked along the banks of the Serpentine. It was a grey, dull day, and I felt heavy and tired. I'd never been a great sleeper and the past few weeks had been worse than ever.

In contrast, Nicki seemed totally buoyant, fizzing with energy and jabbering away about anything and everything.

'Rome was amazing,' she said. 'I went early and spent the weekend on my own, just walking and walking. It was my first time, and I loved it. I shouldn't have been surprised, what with all that history, but I didn't expect the ancient buildings to still be there – and everywhere. Have you been?'

I nodded. 'Julie was a big fan,' I said. 'We went every few months. It really is a beautiful city.' I thought back to those trips and stopped walking as my memories blurred into a single flowing montage: image after image, memory after memory, perfect moments. Horse-drawn carriages at dusk, lunches on sun-kissed terraces, laughing through mouthfuls of gelato and long afternoons stretched out together on crisp white sheets. Like many times before, I allowed myself to be led like an innocent child into that impossibly idyllic paradise until, with a tearing graunch of seized cogs, the montage froze. Then, like a film stuck in an old-fashioned projector, black holes spread out over the images like plague pustules, their flaming, melting edges tearing everything apart …

'Are you OK?'

I looked up with a start to see Nicki standing in front of me, eyes wide with concern.

'I'm fine,' I said, feeling the acid burn in my throat as I swallowed back bitter bile.

'You don't look fine,' she said. 'You went white as a sheet and I thought you were about to collapse.'

'Honestly, I'm OK. I just woke up with a bit of migraine. The painkillers will kick in soon.'

I was never the world's best liar and could see that Nicki wasn't convinced. I reminded myself once again that I needed to see that counsellor. I was a mess.

We walked on in silence until we got to the cafe.

I made the stupid mistake of buying a slice of cake to go with our coffees. Thirty seconds later, Nicki and I were neck deep in a war of waving hands, flapping wings and spilt cappuccinos. We fought bravely, but it wasn't long before we were forced to accept defeat and I moved the cake to another table where the three predatory pigeons could feast in peace. I could have sworn I saw smug satisfaction in their beady little eyes.

'Did you read the report I gave you?' I said, once we were settled back at the table, sipping what was left of our coffees and pretending that we hadn't wanted cake, anyway.

Nicki nodded.

'And?'

'And what?' she said, grinning. She must have known how awkward I felt and she was still teasing me. I probably deserved it.

'You know exactly what,' I said. 'Did the findings surprise you? Open up unanswered questions?'

'Not really,' she said. 'There was nothing in there I didn't already know.'

I was lost for words. She wasn't lying – that was clear. Why had I assumed that she would be surprised?

'I've still got lots of things to tell you,' she continued. 'And I'm sure you have plenty as well. I don't think we should have unrealistic expectations though. It will … it should … take us time to get to know each other. Don't you agree?'

She had such a beautiful smile. How could I not agree? I felt like an idiot. Why had I ever allowed Daz to fill my mind with his suspicions and paranoia? Nicki would figure out who Julie really was soon enough. It wasn't as though she was after my money. Or anything else for that matter. From what I'd seen, she was a lot better off than I was.

'Of course I agree,' I said. 'And I'm really sorry about the investigator. I shouldn't have allowed myself to be pressured into agreeing to that. I should have put my foot down. You're my sister, not theirs.'

'It's OK,' she said. 'I really do understand.'

'Excellent,' I said. 'I owe you one.' I stood up and took a step backwards. 'Shall we put it all behind us and start again?' I stepped forwards and stretched out my arm. 'Hi Nicki. I'm Sam.'

She took my hand in a firm, businesslike grip. 'Hi Sam. Pleased to meet you.'

We both laughed, and I felt the tension in my shoulders ease away. It was going to be all right after all.

'In your email, you said you wanted to talk through something,' I said. 'I assumed it was to do with the subject which we've now forgotten about, but I guess it wasn't.'

'No,' she said. 'My idea is much more constructive, and it's about getting to know each other ... and our mother.'

'Go on ...'

'Well. I've done a bit of digging,' she said, 'and I've tracked down quite a few of Fabiola's relations, the ones who are still alive. Did you know that her older brother, Roberto, moved back to Italy five years ago?'

'No,' I replied. 'I don't know anything about her family. Dad said that none of them came to her funeral and it was always a no-go subject at home.' I couldn't see how a bit of family research was going to help us to get to know either each other or my mum. 'Are you thinking of giving her brother a call? I don't think they'd spoken for years before she died. Not since the scandal ...'

'Exactly.'

'You think ...?'

'Yes,' said Nicki. 'Maybe they knew about me?'

'But they wouldn't have ...'

'Who knows? Proud Italians. Shame on top of shame. Whatever happened, something was serious enough to split the family completely,' said Nicki. 'Anyway, I think we should go and see Roberto. Find out what he's got to say about it.'

'What? But you said that he'd gone back to Italy.'

'Yes. And we should visit him, take a trip to Puglia together, find out what we can about our mother and what really caused the rift with her family … and take the time to get to know each other on the way.'

'Oh. I see.' She was actually serious. Half an hour earlier, I'd been expecting to find out she didn't want to see me again. And then we were going on holiday together. 'And when are you thinking we might do this?'

'I've provisionally booked us flights for next weekend. Going out to Bari late on Friday and coming back Tuesday afternoon. You'd need to take a couple of days off work. What do you think?'

I'd agreed to go, of course. No-one who knew me would have been even slightly surprised. If there was ever a crazy impulsive decision to take, I could be relied upon to be there, ready and waiting to leap headfirst into whatever mess was sitting in front of me.

Dad wasn't impressed. For some unfathomable reason, he still expected me to learn from my mistakes.

'Are you sure this is such a great idea,' he said. 'I can't see you finding much of a welcome.'

'Why?' I said. 'You did when you went to Puglia.'

He slipped seamlessly into the far-away look which usually appeared when we talked about Mum. 'That was a long, long time ago,' he said. 'I was with your mother … and you were so cute. Most of those people will be long dead by now and, charming as you are, I doubt anyone will be queueing up to pinch your chubby cheeks this time round.'

I did my best to look hurt and offended.

'I suppose you might try and look up her uncle, Alberto?' he continued. 'He was the only one who wrote to me after Fabiola died. If he's still alive, he must be in his eighties by now.'

'Thanks, Dad. I'll see if I can track him down.'

'And what about Nicki? Don't you think it's a bit weird, her wanting to go off with you like this?'

'Maybe,' I said. 'I don't know. There's nothing normal about this situation, but I've decided to put my suspicious thoughts to one side. They haven't been getting me anywhere. And I don't want any more advice on the subject from you or Uncle Daz.' I noticed his expression and replayed my words. 'Sorry. That came out wrong. You know what I mean?'

'Yup,' he said. 'I know what you mean.'

Details

'Hello? Nicki?'

'Julie?'

'Yes. Can you hear me?'

'Only just. It's a terrible line.'

'I've routed the call via St Helena. It's one of the few places no-one bothers to monitor. Better safe than sorry. Doesn't do much for the call quality, unfortunately.'

'It's OK. I can hear you now.'

'Good … So? How's it going?'

'It was harder than expected, but we got there eventually. Sam and I fly into Bari on Friday.'

'Excellent. I knew you'd figure it out. It'll be good to resolve this … one way or another.'

'How do you mean? One way or another?' It was difficult to read the tone of her voice through the crackle and echo, but Nicki sounded uncomfortable and on edge. Not her usual confident self.

I shivered as I realised that our relationship was as fragile as it had ever been. The final goal was only a few steps away but, for now, everything was in balance like a swaying tightrope walker stuck halfway across the Niagara Falls.

'Nothing,' I said. 'I'm just looking forward to clearing everything up.'

'Me too,' said Nicki. 'I'm not enjoying lying to Sam.'

'They're white lies, Nicki. You know that he wouldn't come here if you told him the truth?'

'I know. I'm sure you're right. It's not so much that. It's

Damocles. From what Sam told me, the incursions are ramping up. Apparently Milinsky Labs have now got a team of five engineers working full-time trying to protect Sam and Dave.'

'That's what you designed it to do. You must be pleased?'

'I know … I am … but …'

'But what?'

'… Nothing. It's nothing really. I'm just finding it more difficult than I thought I would. Don't worry about me. I'll be fine.'

'OK. Well, let me know if you need anything from me. There'll be a car waiting for you at Avis. You'll find a phone in the glove compartment. Use that to reach me. Just dial Head Office.'

The Old Country

I couldn't believe I was actually doing this.

I'd met Nicki three times in my life and suddenly there we were, walking through the immigration scanner and out into the noise and bustle of Bari airport. I was cruising on autopilot – every time I tried to work through the mess of the past few months, I felt a sharp, stabbing pain in my right temple and my brain turned to mush. Better to simply go with the flow.

Nicki and I hadn't spoken about anything serious since I met her at Heathrow, apart from to discuss what she'd found out about Roberto and Mum's other relations – which wasn't a lot as it turned out. It seemed that disaster was never far from their family, or rather our family.

Having escaped from the grinding poverty of post-WWII Puglia, Fabiola's grandfather, Nonno, had forged a good life for them all in Bedford – by rights there should have been a growing dynasty of British Carlantinos building a future on the back of his hard work.

It hadn't panned out that way; a combination of bad luck, infertility and tragedy had cursed that vision. Roberto's wife had died young, as had his younger brother and sister and, by the time he was seventy, Fabiola's older brother had been the only one left. Perhaps not surprising that he'd decided to spend his last days back in Puglia.

It was only as Nicki was describing this sad story that I realised the man we were planning to see was actually our uncle. It felt unreal.

The last time I'd travelled abroad had been with Julie for the book launch. We'd travelled in her usual style, arriving at Nice by private jet before being whisked effortlessly by speedboat to the Hotel Eden Roc in Antibes. I'd made myself a promise to avoid being corrupted by the outrageous luxury of those years but, when I met Nicki at Gatwick, it had been difficult to ignore the contrast. We weren't even travelling at the budget end of the spectrum – we'd flown BA and were renting our car from Avis – but, after forty-five minutes queueing at the Avis counter, I was beginning to struggle. How long could it take to fill out a form?

It didn't matter. We had plenty of time and, only forty minutes later, we had our car keys and walked out into the glare of the midday sun. My phone vibrated in my pocket, but the sun was too bright for me to see the screen. By the time I'd stepped behind a bus shelter to read the message, Nicki was well in front of me, disappearing into the shade of the Avis car park.

I couldn't believe what I was reading. The nascent migraine stabbed an icepick into my skull as I strode after Nicki. No amount of wishful thinking was going to wash this away.

I reached her just as she was pulling open the boot of our rental hatchback 'Nicki?' I shouted, grabbing her shoulder and pulling her roughly around.

She recoiled like a startled cat, eyes blazing and claws raised. 'What the hell!'

I lifted my hand like a policeman in traffic. 'Stop,' I said. 'Save your bullshit. I've just had a message from Daz.'

'And ...?'

'He says you visited Julie three times in prison. Before and after the sentencing.'

'Does he now?' Nicki was almost shouting, but I could tell she was shocked.

'You're saying he's lying?'

She stared at me for a second or two before slumping forward and looking down at the oily concrete floor. 'No. Not exactly,' she said, eventually. 'But it's not what you think.'

'Trust me,' I said, still fighting an almost uncontrollable desire to break something. 'You have no bloody idea what I think.'

I couldn't remember how we got from the airport to our hotel in Bari. Nicki told me she could explain, and she needed to show me something. She said we would be better off talking at the hotel rather than in a car park, and I suppose she convinced me. Beyond that, the drive into town, parking the car, checking in to the hotel and walking up to Nicki's room … they all must have happened, but I might as well have been somewhere else.

She closed the door behind her, opened her handbag and took out an envelope. She looked at it as though it were something living before taking out a crumpled sheet of A4 paper and handing it to me.

'Here,' she said. 'Read this.' Then she turned and walked out to the balcony.

I unfolded the paper, smoothed it out and began to read:

17th June 2042

Dear Nicki,

If you are reading this, then your father is dead. I am sorry to hear that and you have my sincere condolences. He was a good man.

You will be wondering why I am writing to you and how I know your father. That is what I will try to explain in this letter.

I am not just your boss and professional mentor. We have a longer story which I have hidden from you. I have actually been involved in your life since you were a little girl.

It's complicated, so bear with me and try to forgive me for keeping all of this secret from you for so long.

I am sure that by now, you will have heard of Fabiola Carlantino, my former lover, who committed suicide when you were only eleven. Everything I have to tell you revolves around Fabiola – everything.

Fabiola was the love of my life, but she was also the love of your father's life and – there's no easy way to tell you this – Fabiola was your mother.

She told me that she'd had a child, a baby girl, while we were together. She only mentioned you once – when she was drunk – and I'm certain she just needed to tell someone. It was before she went to Uni and she was only seventeen. She left you in the Royal Free Hospital in Hampstead because she didn't know what else to do. Your father was her economics teacher, Joe Taylor.

I didn't really think much about it until after Fabiola died, when I had a call from your dad out of the blue. Joe had found out about you – Fabiola had written him a letter to be opened if she died and she'd told him that, if anyone could track you down, it would be me. And so he came to me for help.

I was happy to try. I would have done anything to bring Fabiola back, and watching over her children was the next best thing.

It wasn't easy, but I found a way to hack into the adoption databases and found you after three months of trying. It was in the nick of time as the police were on the point of arresting your creepy adopted father, Damian.

You were only eleven and being uprooted from your home by social services was bad enough; Joe didn't want you caught up in the history of the old scandal or the tragedy of Fabiola's death as well. So he asked me to create a false data trail for your mother. A short affair after his wife had kicked him out. Joe told the authorities that he'd received an anonymous phone call and used a private investigator to track you down.

Because of that, we agreed that neither of us would ever tell anyone that you were Fabiola's daughter and I couldn't be directly involved in your life. But I've been watching from a distance – like a fairy godmother – and I'm sure you've wondered where your father got all of his money …

Joe asked me to tell you the truth if anything happened to him, which is why I'm writing to you now. It is unfortunate that this is happening when I'm in the middle of my own scandal – all the accusations are untrue by the way – but I can't do much about that.

I am sure you have lots of questions, but wanted to explain everything in writing first to give you a chance to reflect. Once you have done that, I will be happy to do what I can to help you understand.

Please don't think too harshly about my deception.

All my love,

Julie

I read the letter carefully three times before folding it again and walking over to Nicki.

'Now, do you understand?' she said, on the verge of tears. 'I promised her I wouldn't say anything.'

My anger at Nicki had faded away like ripples in a well, only to be replaced by something else, a cold adrenalin-fuelled passion to protect and defend my sister.

'I understand perfectly,' I said. 'This explains everything very neatly.'

Nicki smiled. 'Oh. Thank God,' she said. 'I was so worried.'

Her smile faded as she saw the expression on my face. 'Come on, Nicki,' I said. 'You don't seriously believe any of this, do you?' I threw the letter onto the bed. 'Every word in here is total bullshit. Every word.'

Unravelling

Nicki must have been in Italy for twenty-four hours and I'd heard nothing. The phone I'd left her had moved from the airport to a car park in Bari and stopped moving. Something wasn't right. She should have been in touch.

I was on the point of of sending Signor Russo to go and check on them when she called.

'Sorry, Julie,' she blurted out. 'I know I should have rung before, but things got a bit … complicated.'

'Complicated?'

'Yes,' she said. 'I showed Sam the email you sent me. The one that explained everything.'

'You did what? I thought we'd agreed you wouldn't.'

'I had to. He found out I'd visited you in prison. I needed to do something.'

'Bloody hell. How did he find that out?'

'Apparently Daz asked the private investigator to do more digging.'

I held the phone away from my mouth as I struggled to swallow my involuntary screams of anger. Fucking Daz. I should have dealt with him first of all. What was wrong with him? Why couldn't he leave me alone? I took a deep breath.

'I see,' I said. 'Daz really is obsessed, isn't he?'

'Definitely,' said Nicki. 'But, to be fair, he was right to be suspicious.'

'I suppose so,' I said, fighting to keep my voice calm and relaxed despite the incandescent fury raging like a magnesium flare inside me. I looked down at my right hand where my fingernails had carved a neat row of crimson-oozing, new-moon crescents into my pale convict's skin. This was not going to plan. 'What did Sam say?' I continued.

'He said it was all bullshit, and that I was a naïve idiot if I believed any of it. I told him he was a paranoid child and left ...' The phone went silent for a few heartbeats. '... And here I am. Standing alone in a bloody carpark in Puglia.'

'Have you told him about Odell and Damocles?'

'Not yet, but I think I'm going to have to, don't you?'

'I think it would be a disaster.'

'So what should I do?'

'Stick with the plan. Bring him here and we'll fix everything together.'

'I don't think I can. I think he'll go straight home now.'

'Find a way,' I said, consciously willing my words to sink in and take root. 'Use your charm. Once he's here, I'll explain everything. I know he'll understand.'

Nicki didn't reply for a long time and I could picture the conflict raging in her mind – two halves of her personality sparring with each other like Judo fighters or Sumo wrestlers. One was a true warrior, strong and determined and the other was feeble and indecisive, but somehow the weakling was managing to hold on and avoid defeat.

We all started with those two personalities inside us, locked in a never-ending tussle. It was what made most people weak – they couldn't ignore the side which wanted to do "the right thing", which was afraid of taking risks, which didn't dare to go against the crowd. Growing up I'd been the same. Even when my father was at his worst, a part of me had always tried to understand him, wondering if it was all my fault or worrying about making things worse. The day I left that bastard bleeding on the kitchen floor, the weak, whining half of me stayed with him and I never looked back.

Nicki didn't know it, but she was close to her own moment of truth. She just needed to hold her nerve a little longer.

243

Old Friends

After Nicki stormed out of the hotel room, I was left standing alone like a rejected teenager at a school disco. Even though no-one was there to stare at me, I still felt awkward and self-conscious.

I sat down on the end of the bed, trying to make sense of what I'd just read. On the plus side, I could forgive Nicki for hiding so much from me. I'd watched her face while I was reading the email and it was clear she believed every word.

The minus side was much more disturbing and sinister, even by Julie's standards. I knew Julie well enough to know that the idea of her stepping in to help Joe was rubbish. Out of the goodness of her heart? I doubted Julie had ever helped anyone with anything. She only ever thought about herself and an apparent favour like that, even mixed with self interest, didn't make any sense. There were other secrets lurking behind the story of Nicki and Julie and the more I thought about it, the creepier it seemed.

Although I knew in my bones I was right, the revisionist history as painted by Julie was clever. All the questions and concerns that we'd had about Nicki's background were neatly answered – challenging any one of those explanations sounded paranoid and ridiculous even to me.

It didn't matter. I wasn't wrong. I'd seen the look in Julie's eyes when she'd pointed the gun at me in London. I'd heard her admit that she'd deliberately driven my mother to suicide and I believed she'd killed both her father and that policeman. Julie was a cold-hearted vengeful psychopath and would stop at nothing to achieve her warped goals. I'd always known that I was a target, but now

Nicki was in danger as well. I had to find a way to convince her of the truth.

'Sam?'

I turned to see Nicki standing in the doorway.

'I'm sorry I ran out,' she said. 'I just stupidly thought everything was going to be OK after you'd seen the letter ... and then ...'

'That's OK,' I said. 'I'm not angry with you. Quite the opposite, in fact.'

I saw the look of relief on Nicki's face and she stepped into the room pulling the door closed behind her.

'But,' I continued. 'We do need to talk. This is serious. When was the last time you were in touch with Julie?'

'I went to see her about a month ago, just after she'd been moved to Downview. She asked me to come. Said she didn't have anyone else.'

'And you never suspected she was lying to you?'

Nicki's nostrils flared. 'No. Why would I?' she said. 'I know that you and Daz and your father believe all sorts of terrible things about her, but she's only ever been good to me. She helped me as a child, she supported my dad financially and she kick-started my career. Let's face it, I'd have been stuck in the care system if it hadn't been for Julie.'

'According to her version of the truth. Julie's twisted everything in your mind. It's what she does. You need to ...'

'I don't need to bloody do anything.' Nicky smashed her hand onto the desk. 'You weren't ever in a care home. You've no clue what it was like. I never knew it was her who helped me get out, but when I found out ...' She glared at me, her eyes red raw and mascara-smudged. '... I owe her ... surely you understand that?'

I turned away and walked over to the window. Seeing Nicki so open and exposed felt almost indecent.

'Sam,' she said. 'I know you feel strongly about this, but so do I and I'm fed up with being told what I should or shouldn't think. You're almost ten years younger than me and it seems pretty arrogant for you to decide you're a hundred per cent right about everything, and imply that I'm just naïve and stupid.'

I didn't know what else to say. Trying to convince her that Julie was a dangerous psychopath was getting me nowhere. On the face of it, she had a point. The dilemma was real, as were the two truths. The only difference was that my truth came with a tangible physical danger and I'd actually seen both sides of Julie. Unfortunately, I could see that Nicki wasn't in any mood to be convinced.

'I'm sorry,' I said. 'I need to find a way to make you believe me, but now obviously isn't the time. Why don't we get something to eat and sleep on it? Then, in the morning, we can go and see Roberto as planned. Once that's out of the way, we'll sit down and have a proper talk. How does that sound?'

The relieved smile on Nicki's face seemed a little excessive in the circumstances. She must have been expecting a huge fight.

'Thank you,' she said. 'That sounds like a good plan … and I promise I'll do my best to keep an open mind.'

We took the coast road from Bari. I was navigating, and we had plenty of time. The first hour took us along the side of the beach and, although the place must have been wild and beautiful once upon a time, mass tourism had left its mark. The Italians colonised beaches like ants and we drove past mile after mile of regimented umbrellas set back from the sea in precise rows, dozens deep. Beneath and around the umbrellas, the dark slowly roasting bodies were lined up, almost touching, but not quite. It wasn't my idea of a holiday and from the occasional snort coming from Nicki, not hers either.

It wasn't until Manfredonia that the scenery changed. We turned up into the hills above the sea on a narrow road which wound its way between olive groves and then, as we entered the national park itself, Aleppo pines – their twisted trunks and the green haze of their needles stretching up the mountainside and down to the sea below.

This was what I'd been hoping for and the next half hour was more of the same. Nicki had been unusually quiet – I suspected she was nervous, both about meeting Roberto, and about the Julie conversation which we had planned for later.

A few kilometres after Vieste, right at the end of the Gargano peninsula, we were supposed to take a right turn, but there was no road and we drove straight past, before turning and driving back slowly.

'Here,' I said, pointing into the trees. 'It must be this one.'

There wasn't a proper road although the satnav insisted this was the right route. Nicki turned down the gravel track and into the forest. It was narrow, but well-surfaced and we wound back and forth between the trees for over a kilometre before the track opened up into a large clearing. Facing us was a high stone wall and a pair of ornate wrought-iron gates.

'Bloody hell,' I said. 'Where did Roberto get the money for a place like this?'

'I think he inherited it,' said Nicki. 'It looks huge.'

We drove towards the gates, which opened automatically, leading us down a formal drive flanked by matched cypresses and towards a huge ornamental fountain in front of the house. I caught a flicker of movement in the wing mirror as the gates swung silently closed behind us.

'Even if he did inherit it,' I said, 'it must cost a fortune to keep up.'

We parked in front of a row of stone-built garages, got out of the car and stared up at the villa. Even during my time with Julie, I would have been impressed by this place. We were approaching from the land and couldn't see the sea from where we were standing, but I could just hear the sound of the waves and smell the salt air. It didn't take much imagination to guess what the coast-facing side would be like.

'Wow,' said Nicki. 'What an incredible place.'

'I like Uncle Roberto already,' I said, walking towards the front door. 'Come on. We might as well say hello.'

As we walked up the marble steps, the door opened to reveal a small, pretty woman, dressed in black. She launched into a babble of Italian which was met by blank looks from both of us. She smiled. 'Please,' she said, and gestured for us to follow her through the house and out onto the terrace.

The coast-facing side of the house was even more spectacular than I'd imagined. Completely isolated and alone at the end of a long promontory, there were views to the sea on all sides. It must have been worth millions.

The woman – I assumed she was Roberto's housekeeper – gestured to a table which was already laid with a selection of drinks and a bucket of ice. 'Please,' she said again, before turning and disappearing into the house.

'Some wine?' I said to Nicki and lifted the bottle from the ice bucket.

'Why not?' she said.

I saw that she was avoiding looking at me and, as she reached out to take the glass, her fingers were trembling.

'Nicki? Is everything OK? Are you all right?'

'I'm fine,' she said, taking a sip of her wine and turning away to face the sea.

She wasn't fine. I was certain of it. Something was worrying her, and she didn't want to say what it was. I leaned over and rested a hand on her shoulder. 'You can tell me,' I said. 'I'm your brother. Whatever it is. You can tell me.'

Nicki turned towards me, tears streaming down her cheeks. 'I've not been totally honest with you,' she said. 'I should have told you about ...'

'It's OK,' I said. 'We agreed we'd talk later.'

'No I'm not talking about that. This is different. I ...' Nicki's eyes snapped wide open as she stared over my shoulder.

I span around to see a slim figure step out of the house and into the sunshine.

'Hello Sam,' said Julie.

Secrets and Lies

I wasn't used to uncertainty. Although people were erratic and unpredictable by nature, I'd always found it easy to keep them moving in the right direction, especially in groups. The herd mind was easier to manage; it didn't take much – a little nudge here or there, or a promised reward – to drag them onwards. Combined, or course, with the willingness to remove the odd rogue element if necessary.

Driving people to do what was required had become second nature to me; I never needed to think about it. As I stood alone in my bedroom that morning, I realised that I'd become complacent in my certainty that there would be no more major surprises in my life.

Events of the previous year had shaken that complacency, and I'd been genuinely nervous all morning. Would Nicki succeed in persuading Sam to keep the meeting with dear old Uncle Roberto? Or would she betray me and tell him about everything – Damocles, Odell, the lot? I had other options, of course, but I wanted this saga, this piece of Grand Guignol, to follow my new script until the end.

Much as uncertainty and nervousness felt unfamiliar, the euphoric joy I felt when I watched Sam and Nicki step out of the car was more intense than anything I could remember. It was an almost-sexual thrill, but without the fleeting, ephemeral nature of an orgasm.

The pleasure and excitement continued to build as I walked down the stairs reaching a crescendo when I stepped out onto the terrace. Looking at the look of surprise and terror on Sam's face, I almost blacked out.

Sam and Nicki were frozen in a rigid tableau, his head and shoulders twisted towards me, one hand still on her shoulder and fat tears were frozen on her cheeks.

I walked towards them, smiling and relaxed. 'I see you've found the wine,' I said. 'Would you mind pouring me a glass, Sam?'

The tableau fell apart. Sam turned back to Nicki, arms raised almost as though he might hit her.

'You knew about this?' he shouted.

Nicki nodded her head, looking at me to say or do something to help.

Sam's hands dropped helplessly to his sides. 'Bloody hell, Nicki,' he said. 'You've got no idea what you've done.' He looked back at me before running down the steps and out into the garden.

Nicki stood alone, watching him disappear into the orange groves at the side of the villa. He wouldn't get far. The cliffs, high fences and Signor Russo would see to that.

Sam was, of course, right – Nicki had no idea what she'd done. I walked up to her and wrapped her in my best attempt at a Godmotherly hug.

'Don't worry,' I said. 'He'll be back soon enough. Come and sit down with me.' I handed her a white linen napkin from the table. 'Here. Wipe your eyes.'

By the time Nicki had wiped the mascara off her face and calmed down, I was ready for a second glass of wine.

'I told you how he'd react,' I said. 'It doesn't matter. When he comes back, he and I will have a talk and straighten things out.'

'It was the way he looked at me,' she said, still shivering. 'He thinks I've betrayed him and I'm not sure he'll ever forgive me.'

It was long past time for some home truths. 'Nicki,' I said. 'Listen to me. I understand that you've been excited and confused to have a new brother, but you're forgetting a few things. Important things.'

'What?' she said, eyes on fire. 'All the terrible things he's supposed to have done to you? The idea that he and Dave destroyed Pulsar to get rich themselves? I've got to know him much better over the past few days and that really doesn't sound like him.' She leant back in her chair and glared at me. 'I'm sorry, Julie. I know how much you've done for me, and I am grateful, but I really don't know who or what to believe any more.'

Letting the two of them meet had always been a risk. Unfortunately Sam was one of those genuinely decent people who wore their integrity like a second skin. Just like his mother.

'That's a shame,' I said. 'You may want to take a moment to think how that makes me feel.' Playing hurt and hard-done-by wasn't my strongest act, but I did my best. 'Leaving that aside,' I continued. 'You have to remember Damocles. The virus you built, the virus you set loose on the two of them, and the virus which is set to destroy their lives over the coming weeks and months.'

I topped up both our wine glasses and smiled. 'Let's face it,' I said. 'You've already chosen sides and there's no way back.'

I expected Nicki to crumble as she was forced to face the hard truth. Telling Sam about Damocles would only make things worse. She'd have to admit that she couldn't call it back and watch as the virus did its worst. I'd seen her detailed specifications and there would be no defence.

In any event, Sam could never be allowed to leave the villa, but that was a detail she didn't need to know and it only affected the timing of his fall.

Nicki didn't crumble. I didn't see defeat dull the gleam in her eyes. All I could see was guilt and shiftiness. I was missing something, but what?

'There's something I haven't told you,' she said. 'I've been meaning to, but the opportunity never came up.'

'Go on,' I said, gripping the edge of the table as the blood started to pulse in my neck.

'We weren't able to find a way to stop Damocles once it was released.'

'I know. You told me.'

'In fact I don't think it's even possible,' she said. 'The innate survival instinct is too strong, just like a real virus.'

I looked at her, trying to work out what she was leading up to.

'So we found a work-around,' she said. 'Quite an elegant one, in fact.' She was gripping her wine glass in both hands, knuckles white with tension. 'We developed a milder version, a Damocles Lite, as it were. All we needed to do was to change the fundamental parameters of the mission. Damocles Lite is designed to be very invasive and annoying, but not totally destructive. If the target doesn't give in, we still have the option to release the full Damocles.'

'And Sam and Dave are experiencing Damocles Lite?'

Nicki nodded. 'I couldn't bring myself to use the full version,' she said. 'Not until I'd had a chance to meet him.'

And there it was. That feeble, indecisive weakling whispering in Nicki's ear and holding her back. I felt the anger building inside me, a white-hot furnace of rage. Nearly forty years to reach this point and she was putting everything at risk.

I wanted to scream at her. I wanted to slap her like the stupid little child she was.

She was still clutching her wine glass like a talisman – her eyes seemed mesmerised by the sunlight flashing sparks through the crystal – so she didn't see the fury and frustration which threatened to overwhelm me.

I couldn't bellow at her and tell her what an idiot she'd been. That would only make things worse. I felt as though I was standing alone in front of a crumbling dam, desperately trying to fill up holes only for more to appear. Why couldn't people just do what they were told?

I needed time to think.

'That is a disappointment,' I said, eventually. 'But it's been a long day. You must be tired. Let's continue this over dinner.' I clapped my hands together twice. 'Signora Russo will show you to your room.'

'My room? We can't stay. I need to get back. I didn't bring …'

'Don't worry,' I said, as I stood up. 'There are toiletries and some suitable clothes on your bed. We'll talk over dinner.' I turned my back on her and walked into the house.

Not Again

When Julie walked out onto the balcony, I knew I was dreaming. My nightmares often ended with her appearing, as if by magic, smiling, and saying 'Hello, Sam' in that sultry voice.

I ran, as I always did in my dreams, feeling the familiar balloon of panic rising from my stomach and filling my throat. As I scrabbled and pushed my way into a grove of tightly planted orange trees, the heady scent of ripe fruit wrapped around me like a blanket, making it ever more difficult to breathe. Time to wake up.

Time to wake up, but it was no dream. I felt a sharp pain in my arms and saw how the freshly pruned stems had gouged deep scratches in my skin. Crimson droplets materialised like tiny rubies in front of my eyes. There was never any blood in my nightmares. It was no dream.

I stopped and listened, desperately trying to control my gasping lungs. There were no sounds of pursuit and I moved forward more slowly, doing my best to slip carefully and silently between the citrus-heavy branches. I had to try to find a way out even though I knew I would be wasting my time. Julie would never have let me see this place if there was any chance of me leaving in one piece.

I tried my phone with the same sense of futile obligation. There would definitely be some sort of jamming system in place. It was the first lesson I'd learnt when travelling with Julie – no unauthorised phone or wireless network ever worked within five hundred metres of her. On the few occasions when I'd been responsible for paying our hotel bill, we'd been charged thousands of dollars extra to compensate other guests for the inconvenience. Julie hadn't blinked;

she was the most wanted target for every serious hacker cooperative worldwide and had no intention of letting them in on the ground floor.

Nothing had changed. There wasn't even a glimmer of a phone signal and I walked on, stopping every few paces to listen for pursuit. I can't have gone more than a couple of hundred metres before the orchard came to an abrupt end at the edge of a cliff – a seventy-five metre drop of vertical, crumbling limestone karst. At its base was a narrow, raised strip of fallen rocks, maybe five metres wide, maybe ten. It was impossible to judge from the top, nor to guess the depth of the sea beyond the beach. The breeze was coming from behind me, but it wasn't strong and I doubted I'd survive the fall even if I managed to jump past the boulders.

I couldn't stop myself smiling as I realised that I really was caught between a rock and a hard place. I looked over the edge one more time and drew the same conclusions –trying to climb down or jump off the cliffs meant almost certain death. I would have to try my luck with the hard place.

I should have jumped.

I was in no hurry to get back to whatever was waiting for me at the house and Nicki had the car keys, so I followed the narrow tractor track around the edge of the cliff, stopping from time to time to look for an easier descent. Hope seemed reluctant to die despite everything I knew about Julie. After a final fruitless check, I turned back to find a man standing on the path in front of me. He was about my age and looked Italian. A black cap was pulled down over his eyes, but my attention was drawn magnetically to the small pistol in his right hand.

I had no more luck with language than we'd had with the housekeeper – his wife I suspected – and he seemed happy to leave the pistol to do the talking. My mind was still racing, fuelled by adrenalin, but each time I ran through my options, they would end with a bullet in the leg at best. I could only hope that Julie had become a different person or that Nicki might be able to persuade her to let me go. At the very least, Julie would want to gloat and there might be a slightly better opportunity when she did.

Once we were close to the house, he motioned me towards a small stone building set against the walls of the garage. There was a blue wooden door which he clearly wanted me to open. I looked at the door and knew beyond any doubt that, if I went inside, I would never come out. So I turned and made a clumsy grab for the gun while swinging a punch at his jaw.

Neither came close to connecting as he stepped lightly to the side and, before I could re-balance myself, a black object blurred at the edge of my vision. I fell heavily, a searing pain shooting through my head. My captor, who was now standing slightly further back, looked at me with cold, black eyes, his twisted smile full of contempt. He flicked up the barrel of the pistol once more – it was time for me to go inside.

I tried to stand up, feeling my head spin and the sting of blood seeping into my left eye. I rolled over carefully and, as I pushed myself up onto my hands and knees, I managed to slip my phone from my pocket and drop it behind a rock. It seemed like a futile gesture. I was on holiday in Italy; why would anyone try to trace my phone? A futile, desperate waste of time, but I wasn't ready to give up hope.

The blue door sat at the top of a spiral stone stairway which wound down into the bedrock. The steps were worn smooth and must have been there for centuries. At the bottom, a short passageway led to a green-painted metal door. The door was open and, as I reached the threshold, I felt a firm push in the small of my back and stumbled forwards into a larger room. Before I could turn around the metal door slammed behind me and I heard the grating of a turning lock. I wasn't going anywhere in a hurry and there was clearly no point in shouting for help.

Having double-checked that the door was actually locked, I looked around. I was in a wine cellar, the size of a small hotel room, which appeared to have been carved into the limestone of the cliffs. A single bulb dangled from the stone roof and the walls were covered by floor-to-ceiling wine racks. The grille in the door let in enough air to keep my claustrophobia at bay and at least there was light. If push came to shove, I could drink myself into oblivion.

I felt a strange calmness settle over me – I had no idea what Julie had planned for me and there seemed little point in upsetting myself further by letting my imagination run riot. There was nothing I could do until she decided to make her next move and so I sat down on a wooden crate, stretched out my legs and settled in to wait.

Control

I waited until I heard Nicki having a shower before going downstairs.

The Russos were standing in the corner of the kitchen dressed in their everyday clothes and ready to leave. They were competent and discreet, but they were Sicilian and the standard agency contract always included taking Sunday off. Besides, I wanted the place to myself.

Signor Russo wasn't exactly a garrulous man – he used no more than two sentences and a grunt to describe his recent encounter. I wasn't surprised to learn that Sam had found his way to the wine cellar without problems. Signor Russo came very highly recommended, and I knew Sam didn't have the guts to jump from the cliffs. A smart move as it turned out – the water beyond the rocky beach was no more than a metre deep in most places.

His wife was much chattier and spent five minutes talking me through the food and wine she'd prepared for me, opening the fridge and pulling out each dish with obvious pride. I made the effort to tell her how beautiful everything looked and she smiled and touched me briefly on the arm before grabbing her husband and leading him outside. I watched them walk to their car, laughing and holding hands like any other young couple on their way out on a Saturday night.

I thought ahead to my dinner with Nicki. I'd hoped for a little more time, but circumstances had moved faster than expected. She'd been influenced too much by whispers in her ear and I couldn't wait to formalise her inheritance. That would bring her back to me.

First, I wanted to pay a visit to Sam. Over the past year I'd allowed myself to imagine many different futures for him. He was just a foolish boy; he was still Fabiola's son; he'd only been a two-year-old-when she killed herself; none of it was his fault; Dave, Rupert, Virginia and Daz were the real villains; Sam couldn't hurt me … maybe I could simply leave him alone to live his dull life? Idle thoughts and fantasies which had helped to pass the time staring at prison walls but, as I walked across the car park, white gravel crunching under my heels, I realised that I'd always known how our story would end.

The moment he'd seen that old phone with the screenshot of me and Fabiola, the moment he'd realised who I was, the moment he'd drawn his conclusions, that was the moment when our lover's affection turned to eternal enmity. I was the lover scorned, and he was the vengeful son – there was never going to be a fairytale conclusion.

I wasn't in a hurry. The final page of our story wasn't yet written and a lot would depend on Nicki. If it turned out that Sam had succeeded in turning her against me, if he'd corrupted the fruits of a lifetime's nurturing, if that, then … my knees buckled and I leant against the door frame while the anger flowed through me and away. That wasn't going to happen. Nicki was mine. She would understand everything. I knew it.

I opened the upper door quietly and looked down the staircase which spiralled down like an ammonite fossil in the evening sun. There was no sound – he must have realised that banging on the door and shouting would get him nowhere.

He didn't hear me walk down the steps and up to the door. I peered through the metal grille and saw him sitting in front of me, hunched forward with his head in his hands.

'Haven't we been here once before?' I said, softly.

His head jerked up, and he jumped to his feet. 'Julie!' He walked towards me, clearly terrified. 'Let me go … please.'

'I'm not sure I can do that,' I said. 'Apart from anything else, I love this house and I want to stay here.'

'I won't tell anyone where you are,' Sam said. 'I swear it. You can stay here. I'll go home.'

'And what about Nicki?' I said.

'What about her? She doesn't need to have anything to do with it.'

'Oh, but she does,' I said. 'She's the key to it all.' I tapped my fingernails on the metal door. 'Come closer, lovely boy.'

He walked up to the door and stood facing me, our noses no more than three inches apart.

'I'll be back later, but first I want to tell you something,' I whispered. 'You'll be the only one who knows. Don't breathe a word.'

Sam leant forward as I pressed my lips to the rusty wire and told him my secret.

He jumped back from the door, lips flopping up and down silently like a freshly landed fish. I couldn't have hoped for more.

Not wanting to ruin the moment, I skipped up the steps before he had a chance to say anything. I smiled and hummed to myself as I double-locked the outside door and turned off the cellar lights. There was no point in wasting electricity after all.

When Nicki came downstairs, I was already out on the balcony, sipping a glass of very special prosecco and nibbling at a delicious morsel of sea urchin bruschetta. I was pleased to see that she'd changed into one of the outfits I'd laid out, a knee length summer dress with a floral print. She looked poised and calm – a lot better than she had earlier.

'Hi Julie,' she said, sitting down opposite me. 'Sam not back yet?'

'He left,' I said. 'I was wrong. He refused to listen to me, wouldn't even look at me. He just asked for a lift to Peschici and I told my gardener to take him. I'm sorry. This whole trip's been a waste of time.'

'Oh, bloody hell,' she said. 'He must be unbelievably pissed off with me.'

'You think?' I said, laughing.

It took Nicki a few moments to see the funny side. 'I guess he'll come round eventually,' she said. 'He's a man. They don't know how to hold grudges.' She looked at me, as if for affirmation, before grabbing the prosecco bottle from the ice bucket and pouring herself a full glass. 'I need a drink,' she said. 'It's been a hell of a day.'

'That it has,' I said, raising my glass. 'Cheers.'

We sat in silence for a few minutes, watching the swallows dipping and diving over the cliff edge. I loved this place and no-one was going to take it away from me. Never.

'Julie …?' she said, in a quiet voice.

'Yes.'

'I'm sorry about the Damocles Lite thing. I should have told you. I know that.'

'The thing is, Nicki,' I said, eventually. 'Men don't know how to hold grudges, but I do. And I still want Sam and Dave punished for what they did to us. I built Pulsar for you and they took it away.'

'I know that,' said Nicki. 'But can't we just forget about it? I already have so much more than I need, anyway. Wouldn't it be better to leave things alone and get on with life? Damocles Lite will be a thorn in their sides for ever. Even though it won't destroy them completely, it will definitely punish them. Isn't that enough?'

'No,' I said. 'It's not enough for me.' I reached over the table and took her hands in mine. 'I need you to send out the proper virus. To complete the mission we agreed on.'

I watched the inner battle dancing across her eyes as we sat facing each other until, with a sudden jerk, she pulled her hands away, stood up and turned to face away.

'I'm sorry. I can't do it,' she said. 'I know what you've done for me, Julie. I realise what I owe you, and I'm truly grateful. But Sam's my brother. He's the only family I've got and I can't do that to him. Anything else, but not that. Surely you can understand?'

I pictured her beautiful face, now made ugly and twisted by the fight between conflicting loyalties, and realised that it was time. I was left with a single choice. I was going to have to tell her the truth.

I walked up to Nicki and turned her around to face me. Her face was red and blotched and her mouth set in a determined sliver.

'I thought you might say that,' I said. 'I hoped you wouldn't, even when I thought you might.'

'I'm sorry,' she said. 'You do understand, though? Don't you?'

'I do,' I said, 'But it's not that simple. Things rarely are. You see, I've been keeping secrets from you too.'

She pulled away. 'Oh? What secrets?'

I couldn't find the words.

'What secrets?' she asked again.

'I'll tell you,' I said, 'but give me ten minutes. It's hard.'

I left her alone on the terrace and walked down to the cliff edge. I was close to tears as I sat on the low wall and looked out over the Adriatic. My whole adult life had been leading up to this point, and I was afraid for the first time in a very long time.

Before I could tell Nicki the truth, I needed to go back, go back to that hidden place inside of me which I'd kept locked away for forty years. A different person, a different time, but I couldn't hide from those memories any longer.

Dark Memories

After I left my pathetic dad stretched out on the floor of our cold Norfolk cottage, I grabbed the bag of cash and left. No point in running. He wasn't coming after me in a hurry. I was taking control for the first time in my life, and no-one was ever, ever going to mess with me again – not with my body and not with my mind.

I had to disappear though, and London seemed like the best bet for that. First, I needed to find a place to stash the money, followed by a roof over my head, something to eat and a few days to think. I got a safe deposit box at King's Cross and found a room round the corner for eighty quid a week, no questions asked.

For the first few days I spent hour after hour sitting on the sagging sofa, staring at the yellowing wallpaper and jumping out of my skin every time I heard footsteps in the hall outside. But no-one was coming for me; I'd made a clean break, and it was time to turn my dreams into reality.

It wasn't too late. I could do my A-levels online – Maths, Further Maths, Business Studies and Physics – and I'd get a place on a Computer Science degree course somewhere good, and a long way from Norfolk.

Before I could do any of that, I needed to find out how to get a new identity. I'd read a few days earlier that my dad had actually bled out on the floor – that would teach him to be too mean to pay for a phone – which meant they'd be putting a lot of effort into looking for Janice Cargill. I wasn't worried short term – I'd already cut off all my long hair and dyed it blonde. I didn't even recognise myself, and why would they look for me here? In the longer term though, I had to become somebody else.

And then I missed my period. I couldn't believe it. That bastard was even managing to mess with my life from beyond the grave. The decision was clear. Get rid of it and move on. Clear, but not easy. I didn't know anyone and the idea of asking about for some back alley abortion filled my thoughts with graphic memories of my father lying in a slowly spreading pool of black blood.

With no paperwork, I didn't have the option to go to a GP or Marie Stopes. The walls were closing in again and I tasted the metallic tang of panic on my tongue. I couldn't allow it. Not again.

It wasn't easy for a fifteen-year-old girl in a strange city and it took months and several disgusting blowjobs before I found someone who could help me. Frank wasn't the worst of them – although he was a sleazy lowlife at best – and he put me in touch with a real identity specialist.

I probably learnt more from Ernst Bauer than from anyone after. He found me Jacqueline Daniels, helped me sort out my social security number and I became Jax. But it was too late. No-one was going to give me an abortion so late in my pregnancy – maybe I could have found a way, but I didn't want to do anything to make myself noticed.

I was also finding it too easy to come up with excuses. Although I hated the thing growing inside me, it seemed to have a voice of its own and it wanted to be born. Luckily Frank was a weak-minded loser, and it wasn't hard to persuade him to stay with me. By that time, he would do anything I asked; it hadn't taken me long to realise how pathetic and feeble most people were.

We moved out to Uxbridge where he helped me give birth in our damp and grubby flat. There were no complications and no-one was any the wiser. The child – it was a girl – was perfect, with the right number of fingers and toes and everything else in the proper place. No webbed feet or Chinese eyes which was fortunate considering her parentage. Frank was besotted with her; I think he genuinely believed we were going to play happy families for ever after.

That wasn't my plan. I'd made a promise as I stood over my father's dying body and I intended to keep it. I was going to control my life. I was going to decide what happened. I was going to be in charge.

The baby didn't fit with that plan, but as she looked up at me with those demanding eyes, I couldn't bear the thought of leaving her with Frank. What sort of life would that be?

So one morning, when Frank was out, I took her and all my stuff and left. No note, no trace.

I chose the Royal Free Hospital because Hampstead was full of rich people. It was before security cameras were everywhere and I simply strolled in the front door carrying her Moses basket, followed the signs to the maternity wing, put the basket down on a chair and left.

As I walked away, the child was still attached to me by an invisible cord, trying to hold me back, but I kept on walking. The invisible cord didn't break until I was out on the street and then, when it finally snapped, I felt a sharp pain followed by an aching emptiness which left me doubled up and gasping as I stood alone at the bus stop.

More Secrets

I hadn't cried back then. I hadn't dared.

Finally, as I sat on the low wall overlooking the cliff, I found myself sobbing uncontrollably. Crying for my lost childhood, crying for what I'd left behind and crying because, at long last, I could.

I heard Nicki's footsteps crunching on the gravel behind me.

'Are you all right?'

'Not really,' I said. 'I've not cried since I was a child.'

'Oh,' she said, sitting on the wall next to me. 'I'm sorry if it's my fault. I didn't mean …'

'Stop! Never say that. It could never be your fault.'

'So, what's going on? I'm totally confused.'

I turned towards her and, all in a rush, the words came.

'Nicki. I'm your mother.'

'What? What? No. I don't understand.' Shock and confusion filled Nicki's face.

'You're not Fabiola's daughter. That was a story I invented. The part about the young girl going into Hampstead Free Hospital with a baby is true enough, but it wasn't Fabiola. It was me.'

'No!' she said. 'You're saying you're my real mother? Now. After all this time. I don't believe it. Why wouldn't you tell me before?'

'I wanted to, but I couldn't … I'm sorry.'

'I don't believe you. It doesn't make any sense. There were DNA tests and everything.'

'Easy enough to fake. You know that.'

'So, Dad wasn't my real father?'

'No. Although he thought he was. That was why I couldn't say anything.' I grabbed her by the shoulders and half-shouted, half-screamed at her. 'My father raped me when I was fifteen. How could I tell you that?'

'Jesus Christ,' said Nicki. 'This just gets worse. Why didn't you get a bloody abortion?'

'It's complicated. I was hiding from the police and I was afraid. That's the only rumour about me that's true. I did kill my father. He was a sick, vicious man, and he got what he deserved.'

I saw Nicki's expression change when I told her about my father. Her semi-hysterical shock was replaced by something more calculating and analytical. I felt my heart doing somersaults in my chest – maybe she was experiencing her moment of truth at last. Maybe everything would work out.

'OK,' she said, face set in a mask. 'I want to know everything. Start at the beginning.'

We sat on the edge of the cliff watching the darkness spread over the sea. I talked and Nicki listened. There was no-one to switch on the outside lights and, after a while, I couldn't see her face.

'Shall we go inside?' I said, once I'd finished.

'I'm fine here,' she said. 'I just need a moment to try to process everything.'

I didn't expect forgiveness from her. That ship had foundered long ago, broken apart on rocky reefs of deception. All I was hoping for was an acceptance of who and what she was.

'How old was I when you first tracked me down?' she asked.

'Four,' I said. 'It took me a long time to work out how.'

'And you've watched over me since then?' she said. 'Spying on me from a distance.'

'I wouldn't call it spying,' I said.

'I would,' said Nicki. 'And the fact that I chose to study what I did and became a Pulsar Scholar? Was that all coincidence?'

Nicki was a trained statistician. She understood probability better than most. 'No,' I said. 'Of course it wasn't. You had the raw talent, but I gave you a few nudges here and there.'

'And you didn't think that I might want a say in my own life?'

'Everything I did was for you, Nicki.'

She didn't reply. It was dark, and she had become no more than a shape in the shadows.

'Nicki…?'

'Wait. I'm thinking.'

I could hear her breathing, short, angry snorts through her nose. It was understandable that she was upset, but that would pass.

'Damian and Akiko,' she said, after a long time. 'Did you plant that pornography? Was that all you?'

I didn't know what to say. I'd been prepared for the conversation about Sam and Damocles, but why was she so fixated on the past and her childhood?

'Was it?' she shouted.

'Yes,' I said. 'Yes. They weren't right for you.'

'Weren't right for me?' She stood up. 'Weren't right for me? I was happy with them, Julie. They were good to me.'

'I genuinely believed it was for the best,' I said.

'And I've been defending you to everyone,' she said. 'Blindly taking your side out of loyalty.' She spat out the words. 'Loyalty. Because you rescued me from that horrible care home.'

This was not going to plan. Why couldn't she see how difficult it had been for me?

'I can't believe how fucking stupid I've been,' she said, hands now curled into rigid claws. 'Rescued me? You fucking put me there in the first place.'

She started stomping back up the path towards the house and I followed, half running to keep up. I grabbed her arm and she span round to face me, eyes glinting in the starlight.

'Don't … you … touch … me,' she said, pushing me roughly away.

I stumbled and fell hard against the edge of the steps, cracking my head. For a moment, I saw Nicki's shape silhouetted against the night sky. She leant down over me, mumbling words I couldn't make out, and then …

Nine Lives

I should have known Julie would switch the lights off after telling me her dirty little secret. At least there was still fresh air. I actually didn't mind the dark so much, although it would start to get to me soon enough.

Nicki was Julie's daughter. That made so much sense. I couldn't believe I hadn't thought of it before. We'd all been so happy to believe in the idea of a Fabiola-centric universe. Keeping my mother's mythology alive had felt good.

But Nicki didn't know. I was sure of that. What would she do when she found out? However much Julie might have wished for it, Nicki wasn't a psychopath. She was a normal kind person and I couldn't see her fitting in with Julie's warped vision of the world.

As I sat in the darkness, I realised that none of that mattered. Whatever Nicki's response, it would be too late for me. Julie was going to win, just as she always did.

I closed my eyes and settled down to wait.

Was that screaming? It sounded like a woman screaming. It sounded like Nicki. What was happening?

I stood up and walked towards the door, smashing my head and elbows against several protruding wine bottles on the way. The screaming was slightly louder close to the entrance and I added my own shouts, banging and kicking on the metal door, throwing wine bottles against the wall, anything to be heard.

The screaming stopped and I redoubled my efforts. Surely she'd be able to hear me? I stopped shouting and listened. Nothing.

All of a sudden the lights flicked on and I froze, realising this was probably just Julie playing mind games with me.

'Sam?' It was Nicki's voice. No doubt about it.

'Nicki. I'm down here.'

Thirty seconds later I saw her wonderful face on the other side of the grill. I watched her fumbling with a set of keys, nervous fingers struggling to find the right one.

'Thank God you're here,' I said, pushing the door open and wrapping my arms around her. 'Thank you.'

I didn't look at Nicki properly until we were outside in the fresh air.

'What happened to you?' I said. 'You look even more terrified than me?'

Nicki's fingers danced around like things possessed and she kept looking over her shoulder. 'I had a fight with Julie,' she said. 'I pushed her and she banged her head. She's unconscious and there's blood … so much blood.'

'Calm down, Nicki,' I said. 'Give me a sec to clear my head and we'll go and check on her.'

And then my own heart stopped beating for an instant – memories of dark eyes and a black pistol filling my mind. 'Oh shit,' I said. 'Where's the housekeeper? And her husband?'

'They've gone until Monday,' said Nicki. 'It's just us.' She stopped twitching and looked at me. 'Did you know Julie's my real mother?'

'She told me a few hours ago. Part of her sadistic little game.'

'I don't understand. What game? What were you even doing locked down there? Julie told me you'd gone home.'

'Her gardener forced me there at gunpoint. I tried to tell you about Julie, but you didn't want to hear. She would never have let me leave this place alive. Can you still not see that?'

Nicki sank down to her knees in front of me. 'Oh, God. I'm so sorry,' she said. 'I've been such an idiot. I should have listened to you.' She looked up at me, tears running down her cheeks. 'She admitted everything, Sam. She's been controlling me my whole fucking life. I even think she might have killed my step-father.' She was crying properly now, struggling to draw breath and she had her

269

arms crossed in front of her, fingernails gouging into her shoulders. 'Oh God. I can't believe it's true. It's like I've got spiders hatching under my skin.'

'It's all right,' I said, bending down and hugging her close while I waited for her breathing to calm down. 'You'll be OK. Trust me. I'm probably the only other person in the world who can understand what you're feeling right now.' I took her face in both hands and looked at her. 'I can't believe you managed to find me. Thank you so much. I thought I was going to die down there.'

She managed a forced laugh. 'I'm pretty glad I found you too,' she said. 'I thought you'd gone for good.'

'So. How did you know where to look?'

'Pure luck,' she said. 'After Julie fell, I panicked for a bit. I switched all the lights on and went to look at her. She wasn't moving and there was blood everywhere. I decided to call you, but my phone hasn't worked since we got here. Then I checked Julie's phone; it had a signal, but you didn't reply. I tried a couple of times and then came out to get the car. I don't know quite what my plan was but, when I got here, I thought I'd try your number one last time … and that's when I heard the ringtone.' She laughed nervously. 'When I found your phone on the ground, I finally lost it and started screaming my head off. It was lucky I ran out of breath or I'd never have heard you shouting back.'

I stood up, pulling her with me. 'Come on,' I said. 'Let's go and see what's happened to Julie.'

Nicki wasn't joking when she'd talked about putting all the lights on. Every security lamp was blazing white and the terrace had turned into a modern art masterpiece of stark criss-crossing shadows.

We walked down the steps to where Nicki had left Julie. There was a huge pool of blood on the stone, but no body.

'She can't have gone far,' I said. 'Look at all that blood.'

Nicki's face was chalk-white and I suspected she was about to either pass out or throw up. I took her arm and guided her to a wrought-iron chair at the side of the steps.

'Sit here,' I said. 'I'll go and find her.'

'But she m-m-might have a gun,' she said.

I looked at the size of the black stain spreading in front of me. 'I'll be careful,' I said. 'You wait here.'

It wasn't hard to follow Julie. She'd left a trail of sticky blood like snail slime as she'd dragged herself out towards the cliffs.

And there she lay, perfectly floodlit in the centre of an ornate stone circle.

Was she moving? Was I imagining it?

The first fingers of dawn were creeping over the horizon as I walked over to the body. Julie wasn't dead; I could see the gentle rise and fall of her chest and the mist of her breath ebbing and flowing on the pool of blood. Amazing how she could still be stubbornly holding onto life.

I felt, rather than heard, Nicki walking up from behind. She stood next to me and whispered as though afraid of disturbing the prone form in front of us.

'Is she...? Is she ... still alive?'

'I think so,' I said. 'I can see her breathing. Have you still got her phone? We should call an ambulance.'

Nicki handed me the phone without speaking, her eyes still locked onto Julie's body.

I turned towards the light and dialled 112. Then, just as I lifted the phone to my ear, a hand reached out and grabbed hold of my wrist, knocking the phone clattering to the ground.

'No,' said Nicki, her whole body shaking. 'Don't!'

The phone lay on the stone flagstones at Nicki's feet, a jagged black crack stretching across the flickering screen. A disembodied voice was calling up to us. '... *pronto, carabinieri ... pronto ...* '

'Are you sure?' I said.

She looked deep into my eyes before reaching down, picking up the phone and ending the call.

Nicki then turned away from me and walked past Julie's body to the low wall at the edge of the cliffs, where she sat down facing out over the sea, her lonely shape back-lit by the hazy pink of the morning sky.

Epilogue

I'd invited everyone around to my flat to watch the coronation on my PixelWall. Even though the special effects had become a bit lame, it still delivered the best TV experience I'd ever seen.

Daz was sitting by the window, pretending not to watch and mumbling about the pointlessness of still having a monarchy. Liz was on the sofa next to my dad and Nicki, leaning forward and glued to the screen. Looking at her, I couldn't help wondering if she and Daz had any interests in common at all

'No-one thought Charles would ever become king,' she said, continuing her seemingly inexhaustible running commentary of useful facts about the Royal Family. 'We all thought he was too old … and a bit strange as well.'

'I always liked him,' said Nicki. 'Apart from the ears, of course.'

'As it turned out, he did a pretty good job,' said my dad. 'Twenty decent years … and in quite tricky times.'

I was more agnostic than Daz when it came down to the royals, but it was embarrassing to hear the three sofa pundits spouting all these facts and opinions. Why were they so interested in all that archaic, irrelevant pomp? I could cope with a small amount every now and then, but this had been going on for hours and I was beginning to lose the will to live.

I was pulled out of my half-doze to see the screen filled by a row of impossibly long, flag-dangling trumpets raised high and blasting out a regal fanfare. The presenter's voice dimmed to a respectful, bass rumble ….

'They're coming out,' said Liz, jumping to her feet. Either out of respect or from pure excitement – I wasn't sure.

'Oh, for Christ's sake,' said Daz, stalking out to the balcony and pulling the door closed behind him.

I didn't blame him. Enough was enough. I went to the kitchen in search of more beers, followed by the roars of the crowd and the presenter's voice, now almost screaming in barely suppressed ecstasy '... *Listen to the people cheer as they welcome their new king. What joy! Such a moment. Such a special day. Long live King William! Long live the king ...*'

I opened the bottles and looked at my watch. There was still another hour to go. Maybe Daz and I could go to the pub?

Back in the living room, Dad, Nicki and Liz were now all standing up, eyes bright with joy. They didn't even notice when I put fresh drinks in front of them. At least they were happy.

I was half way back out to the kitchen when the balcony doors burst open and Daz came running in. 'Put the news on,' he shouted, waving his phone and grinning like a man possessed.

'Why? What's going on?' I said. I pointed at the TV. 'They'll kill me if I switch this off.'

'They can watch it in a minute,' he said. 'Switch over. You've got to see this.'

I punched the remote, and the screen was filled with the perfect, smiling face of Serena Walsh, the new darling of the BBC news team. Behind her was a backdrop of a bright sunlit Mediterranean scene where dizzying drone images circled around a tree-lined promontory before zooming in on a white stucco building capped with red tiles. Black uniforms, cars and flashing lights were everywhere and, in the bottom right-hand corner was another perfect face – one that I knew all too well.

The images, the sound of Serena's voice and the rolling red-on-white banner text all blurred into one '... *fugitive ... Italian villa ... found dead ... tragic figure ... fall ... accident ... alone ... Peschici ... sorry end ... no suspects.*'

'She's dead,' shouted Daz. 'I was beginning to believe that bitch was immortal, but she's dead.' He bounced around like a teenager, kissing and hugging every one – even Nicki.

My father didn't speak. He stood like a statue, staring at the screen as though waiting for more proof. Some sort of final confirmation, perhaps. The words rolled past for maybe the tenth time … *Julie Martin, founder of Pulsar, has been found dead in an Italian villa …*' and then I saw his ramrod shoulders slump forward and the glint of a tear rolling down his cheek.

'You OK, Dad?' I said, wrapping my arms around him.

'Yup,' he said. 'I'll be fine.' He wiped away the tears with the back of his hand. 'I just can't believe it's finally over. I've been so worried about you this past year. That woman took Fabiola from me and she would have come for you sooner or later. I don't know what I would have done if anything had happened to you.'

Daz bounced over to us.

'Come on, Sam,' he said. 'You must have some champagne in this posh pad of yours. We need to celebrate.'

'All right,' I said. 'Keep your hair on. Let's hear the rest of the story.'

It was breaking news and, as the Italian police hadn't released much actual information, the news team were recycling the same limited facts and padding it out with old reports from the court case, Julie's escape and the few interviews she'd given over the years.

'Peschici?' said Liz. 'Isn't that where you and Nicki went last weekend?'

'Yes,' said Nicki. 'It's where Fabiola's family came from.'

'Not such a surprise that Jax chose to hide there,' said Daz.

'I guess not,' I said.

'… But you never got to see your uncle?' said Liz.

'No,' I said. 'He's very ill, apparently. Wasn't allowed visitors.' I looked at Nicki and smiled. 'It was good to spend time with Nicki, but the rest of the trip was a waste of time.'

She looked back at me and I knew our shared secret would be safe. 'Great scenery, great food, great wine and great company,' she said, before shrugging her shoulders. 'Otherwise a complete washout.'

We did manage to share a glass of champagne together, but it soon became clear that none of us felt much like talking. By six-thirty, I found myself alone with the BBC news, which was flick-flacking between the coronation and Julie's death. I'd had my fill of both stories and switched it off.

I took my half-glass of warm champagne and walked into the bedroom. I'd always kept my favourite picture of Mum by the side of my bed. It was taken when she was pregnant with me and she was laughing, happy, totally radiant. I lifted my glass and took a sip before putting it down next to the photo.

In the drawer below were two antique mobiles laying next to each other – my mother's old phone and Jax's matching model, the one I'd discovered in Julie's Knightsbridge apartment. Each, in its own way, had played a pivotal role in the story which had so recently come to an end.

I reached into my pocket and pulled out a modern state-of-the-art phone – 3-D display, featherlight construction and made entirely of gleaming glass. A jagged crack stretched diagonally across the main screen like a black lightning bolt. I knew it was probably crammed full of secrets, maybe even access to billions in hidden cash reserves, but I didn't care. I didn't want to forget, but I did want to move on.

I placed the third phone next to the first two and closed the drawer.

The Old Orchard

by Tony Salter

The family thriller that will grip you until the last page.

Finance Director, Alastair Johnson, is in trouble. He needs a lot of money, and he needs it very soon.

Alastair's solution is unorthodox and completely out of character – the fallout leaves his family torn apart.

But everything is not what it seems ...

"What a cracking story! Loved the way it all unfolded at the end. Really clever and credible and I didn't see the twists coming."

"FLIPPIN' BRILLIANT!"

"The Old Orchard is a pacy, tense, domestic thriller which builds an original and satisfying plot around real characters we can believe in. The prose is light and evocative with vivid descriptions and many moments of real insight and human wisdom."

The Old Orchard is AVAILABLE NOW in paperback or eBook format from Amazon and most booksellers.

Best Eaten Cold

by Tony Salter

The Bestselling Psychological Thriller you can't put down.

Imagine that someone wants to do you harm. Someone you once knew, but have almost forgotten.

Now, imagine that they are clever, patient and will not stop. They'll get inside your head and make you doubt yourself.

They'll make you question who you are, and ensure that everyone you care for starts to doubt you too.

***** "Fast-paced, terrifyingly believable, chilling at times... the kind of book that's hard to put down"

***** "I admire any author who can hold my attention so thrillingly from beginning to end"

***** "Much superior to Girl on the Train."

Best Eaten Cold is AVAILABLE NOW in paperback or eBook format from Amazon and most booksellers.

Acknowledgements

Writing novels is a solitary task but I don't think I could enjoy it without some company along the way. Feedback, encouragement and patient support are essential emotional props, but so are the sweeping blows of honest criticism which help to remind me that I am writing for readers and not only for myself.

I need to thank all of my friends and family for their help and, in particular, Sue Brown, Emma Newman, Annie Eccles, Dana Olearnikova and Kath Watson. Thanks also to Jamie Groves at Story Terrace.

Finally, I must thank my wife of twenty-nine years, Gro. Without her love, support, patience and tolerance, none of this would have been possible.